America Has Gone to Hell

"It's almost cheaper than shoplifting," raves about his system for deep-discount shopping. century', Charles Rochambeau despises te and internet shopping. He was cursed with 'bad timing' as his father squandered the family fortune on Wall Street. As a scion of the legendary French general who helped Washington defeat the British in The Revolutionary War, he has become a 'Certified Professional Shopper' in the service of an aristocratic divorcee, Beatrice Wolcott, whom like Charles, has endured a life of bad luck and tragedies.

As Major Domo for her estate in Westchester County, Charles witnesses her close relationship with Ryan Keneally, the longtime family plumber, whose son, Trey reveals several shocking Wolcott family secrets. Charles suspects her friendship with Ryan seems much too close be platonic.

Yet, Charles maintains his belief in 'The American Dream' and holds his ground as 'A Soldier of Truth' despite privation and adversity. He is dedicated to 'The Madame' and hopes to rectify the past, so they can both recover their lost dreams and proud family legacies.

The Great Pandemic arrives and shuts down most of the shopping malls. God is dead. Like Ignatius Reilly in *A Confederacy of Dunces*, Charles realizes he is trapped in a corrupt modern world, over-run by duplicities, politics and lies. Has The American Dream become Paradise Lost? Is Charles crazy or has *Le Monde* simply gone mad?

Like Dante's *Inferno*, *The Bargain Shopper* is an unexpurgated account of a Pilgrim's journey to Hell and back.

MORE RAVING REVIEWS FOR
THE BARGAIN SHOPPER

*There are no words in the English language to describe my
revulsion to this embittered, pretentious, amoral and utterly
pornographic screed. Try a few of these words for size:
Disgusting, sickening, filthy, ghastly, sordid, horrible, nauseating,
repugnant, abhorrent, vile, decadent, vulgar, profane, foul, loathsome,
nasty, prurient, detestable, horrifying, hateful, nauseating,
despicable, odious, depraved, debauched, reprobate, revolting, debased,
blasphemous, fecal, immoral, iniquitous, obscene, stercoraceous,
foul, smutty, crude, rude, lewd and hopelessly misogynist.*

*Please remit my ten-dollar Starbucks gift
certificate ASAP. Have a lovely day.*

—Alicia Dykeman, Executive Director,
The Beulah Mukluk Women's Resource Center
Northern Minnesota State University

✤ ✤ ✤

*A **tour de force** on reality as a social construct. I read this novel
constructively, which, I believe is far more efficient than turning
the actual pages. Highly recommended for actual readers.*

—Headley Smithers, Dean of Supine Conformity
East Epicene State University

✤ ✤ ✤

The

BARGAIN SHOPPER

The Confessions of A Soldier of Truth In the Age of Pandemic

A Novel
WC LATOUR

Bridlegoose Books

NEW YORK

Bridlegoose Books

The Bargain Shopper is a work of fiction. References to real people, dead or alive, events, establishments, organizations, or locales are only intended to provide a sense of authenticity and are used fictitiously.

All other characters and all incidents and dialogue are drawn from the author's imagination and are not to be construed as real. No lepers were abused during the writing or publication of this book.

First Edition

Cover Design by Roberta Fox.

Paperback ISBN: 978-1-7365347-0-0
eBook ISBN: 978-1-7365347-1-7

To: Lloyd Buchanan

Qui non laborat non manducat

"*What is commonest and cheapest and nearest and easiest is Me*".

— WALT WHITMAN
SONG OF MYSELF

CHAPTER ONE

"The gods had given me almost everything," wrote Oscar Wilde in *De Profundis*, his infamous letter to Lord Alfred Douglas. "*I had genius, a distinguished name, high social position, brilliancy, intellectual daring: I made art a philosophy, and philosophy an art……*"

My name is Toulouse Charles Rochambeau. I was born feet-first and ass-backward into this tormented civilization that originated with Genesis. I pray it will end mercifully with The Second Coming of Jesus Christ. As a Man of Faith, I am awaiting my salvation in The Age of Pandemic.

I never looked upon "*Art as the supreme reality*" as Wilde did or awakened "*the imagination of my century so that it created myth and legend around me,*" yet my sympathies align with Mr. Oscar.

We all leave our marks on society, mostly tiny blots or smears. My Lilliputian niche was carved out of necessity. Yet, I transformed The Art of Bargain Shopping into a Science, which might certify me as legendary— if only in my own mind. Foremost, I remain a Man of Science.

My fellow Pilgrims, I started writing these confessions, fast and furious, only four months ago, on the Fourth of July, as a testament to Jean Baptiste Donatie de Vimeur Compte de Rochambeau, my ancestor, famed as *Le Marechal* who served as Marshall of France, until his death in 1807. He left behind a footprint as Gargantuan as his name. The general had been commissioned by King Louis XVI to lead the French Auxiliary Forces during the American Revolution and marched beside Washington, right up to the

victorious Siege of Yorktown. Tragically, the king was doomed to be guillotined by the revolutionaries.

Many historians consider Rochambeau a 'Founding Father,' as red-blooded
as any American patriot. But he was shortchanged out of well-deserved glory
by his French compatriot, the youthful Marquis de Lafayette, whom Louis had
passed over to command this army. Many historians agree that without the
strategic advice of *Le Marechal*, victory by the Continentals might have been
delayed for many years. Or the British might have even won the war.

I heartily concur. His biographer concluded that the general was more
Republican in spirit than Lafayette. With the experience gained during The
Seven Years War, Rochambeau deferred Washington's plan to invade New
York, which might have been a military blunder. Ron Chernow stated in his
biography of Washington, "*With the benefit of hindsight, Washington's preoc-
cupation with New York seems a colossal mistake, just as Rochambeau's empha-
sis on Cornwallis and Virginia seems prescient.*"

Washington admired *Le Marechal* for his military brevity and modesty. It
was said, "He took no pains to carve his own statue." His first statue was un-
veiled in Washington D.C. in 1902 by President Roosevelt, long before the advent of 'Cancel Culture'. But Rochambeau was eclipsed by the Marquis once
again, as the ceremony was held in Lafayette Park. As a scholar of military
history, I first read *Commentarii de Bello Gallico* in high school. I confess to
my bias regarding *Le Marechal* and admit that I'm not an accredited historian.
But facts are facts, and truth is truth. Whatever.

Don't get me wrong. Lafayette, like Rochambeau, was a 'Man of Two
Countries.' But more a diplomat than a soldier. Both men were imprisoned by
the Jacobins during the French Revolution.

Rochambeau never played second fiddle to the Marquis. Or anybody else,
even to Washington. He earned his true Gloire on the battlefield using his
brains and testosterone, as he marched his army across our colonies. Risking
his life each day in mortal combat against the marauding British Redcoats. And
he helped The Revolutionary Army build an American nation. And that is
the *honest* truth.

⚜ ⚜ ⚜

I AWAIT THE RETURN OF OUR SAVIOR, while I get impatient
with the dreads. Once a 'Soldier of Christ', I'm not even sure I believe in

Jesus, anymore. Call me 'post-Christian' like Kierkegaard, or an existentialist like Sartre or Camus. The Zoroastrians abandoned their old gods. But I'm not going out on a limb just to spit on the crucifix, either. Petty arguments give me attacks of the natty dreads, like this one

I am a pantheist like Spinoza. Yet, I dabbled in studying polytheistic religions, like those of the Hittites. I have propitiated several demigods for my own personal use, conferring them certain obligations.

Emerson said, "As man's prayers are a disease of the will, so are his creeds a disease of the intellect."

I can assure you I am not an atheist. Especially during a pandemic.

The main problem with Christianity is that anyone can get away with murder. As long, as they repent for their mortal sins, no matter how God awful. Until Jesus returns to save our planet, I will continue to sanctify the blessings of any competent deity I can get my hands on. And hedge my bets to live and fight another day. Pascal's Wager serves me well as a perfect safety net, so regardless of any dubious spiritual devotions, I can weaponize my prayers.

Allow me to confess. There is a good reason I pound the bongos of despair in our modern primordial abyss. Bad timing. I was born into the wrong century— long-after my family lost their titles and estates, castles and jewels. Even our loyal serfs, but mainly the money. Like an obedient monk, I have accepted the challenges of a world deprived of many basic material comforts.

In my seventh decade on this cosmic sphere, all I possess are the ataxic lapses of my body, mind and soul. Yet, I await the clarion call from choirs of avenging angels, flying through darkening clouds.

I spent a decade of my life— don't ask me why— in Santa Monica, performing panegyric rhumbas. Chanting dithyrambic verses updated from ancient Dionysian rites. I ran naked around wild bonfires, burning on the beach, all night long, while screaming vulgarities, along with my fellow cabbalists.

When Christ returns on Judgement Day, our savior will be mired in a wasteland of greed and folly. Subjugated by intransigent dogmas, the crassitude of fossil-fool politicians and rank stupidities of the Woke media, along with fabulist delusions of the vox populi. My Sweet Lord will breathe in the putrescence of the vast ruck of humanity. But find himself trapped inside the gates of a resurgent Gomorrah— direly in need of a severe douching by the Almighty.

Nothing has changed in the 'old neighborhood' since his ascension into Heaven. We remain savages with the fractured souls and minds of primal beasts, barely emergent from Paleolithic caves.

Space and Time are relativities on a continuum, as Einstein once reckoned. If I seem erudite, you are correct. But if I appear pedagogical or pretentious, you can blame it on opioids, or the sublime medication of an Ivy league education. "*It is basically useless*," Oscar Wilde decried of Art. A criticism that applies to the current value of a college education.

I am growing old. Last year, I underwent ventral hernia surgery in Sleepy Hollow. My stomach was bulging out like a monster. I had ruptured my groin during a Frog Bowling Tournament. The surgeons who performed the operation were the good doctors, Lo Mein and Ravioli. If this seems ridiculous, check it out at Sleepy Hollow Hospital. They amputated my entire belly button. I was criticized for going Frog Bowling in my loafers and ordered to limit myself to either Disc Golf or Kitty Croquet. Neither of these games are recognized as Olympic sports. Whatever. Play Lotto.

In the *Upanishads*, the Hindu God, Vishnu sleeps in the cosmic ocean, and the lotus of the universe grows out of the naval. I sleep in the tenement bed by a scummy pond. My stomach is The Gates of Hell, where nothing edible grows.

Let me warn you, before I wax atavistic. I prefer not to alienate myself from any polite company, including my own. I only confess the *Truth*— horrific as it is. I grow old and remain 'Old School', but don't want to be tweeted by pukey, new emojis. I don't do selfies or podcasts, Twitter or Facebook. I am exactly who you think I am, The Bargain Shopper.

This morning an eructation attacked my sphincter. I jerk-thumped my bum-gut, until a dung serpent slithered its way into my toilet bowl. A typical start to a fruitlessly prolific day during The Great Pandemic. An age I was born into by accident. Most likely by an unfortunate divine mistake. As promised, I have warned you.

⚜ ⚜ ⚜

I AM NOT A MODERN MAN. Bloggers are what I blow out of my nose using Kleenex. I will never submit to the invasions of privacy, the harvesting of my personal data or mind controls of the Thought Police or their media arsonists. Or the diabolical coven of tech oligarchs and jack-booted *shutzstaffel* who shill for these Marxist millennial crybabies.

King Solomon warned of this menace long ago: "*Wisdom entereth not into a malicious soul, and science without conscience spells but destruction of the spirit.*"

Like Washington, I proclaimed my independence. From the tyranny of modern technology. Freedom from the clickbait junkies and mindless minions of techno-charlatans who prevaricate in the free space surrounding my personage. A province where they can openly brag about their latest 'disruptions.'

I am *not* impressed. They are chattels for an antisocial social media run amuck. Their craniums are plugged into microchips like umbilical cords, processing endless reams of data without a blip of legitimate context. Human capacitors, lost in cyberspace, using their eyes and ears as anodes for sending electronic signals into robotized organs.

Organs they insist on calling human brains. Neurotic minds lose the capacity to think. As Yoda said in *Star Wars*, "*Turn off the computer and trust your feelings.*" Try adding a new chip to your head and trust in your own *common sense*.

Mormons prophesied the period before Judgement Day will feature war and pestilence. Before the coming enlightenment and a new creation. I will not quibble. But we are mucked in a world of plague without any proven therapeutics, vaccines, or decent testing. As a Man of Faith, I will search the earth for any sign of our savior's return. The sacred body and blood of our lord, Jesus Christ.

In my morning *toilette*, the only blood I found was in my stool. So, I flushed twice.

Forgive my coarse language and demonic rants. Screams from the soul of my *contemptua mundi*. I am a Soldier of Faith and Science. I was hammered hard as a steel sword, chained upon an anvil and even to the yardarm, since the traumatic day of my unhallowed birth. Follow the Science: I was conceived by a sperm cell who swam fastest in a protozoan race on a vast mucous river inside my mother's amniotic sac. One in sextillion of all the genomic possibilities of our species. Finally, these two great gametes conjoined.

Then the egg— an egg consisting of me, was fertilized. The zygote split into two parts. You may refer to them as either 'good' or 'bad,' without imposing prejudice upon either. My brother and I entered this kingdom as fraternal twins. But Jean Baptiste II was born to die. Then buried beside our great-grandfather in Valhalla, only a few days later.

Like Nietzsche, I am a modern Orpheus. An elegist for 'The Real Me.' A disciple of William Blake with the music and fervent visions of the *Spectre of Urthona*. Infused with signs of revelation, befitting an outcast prophet.

I get the dreads— the *natty dreads*. I am The Bargain Shopper and a proponent of his decretals. Like Alan Ginsberg proclaimed in *Howl*, I have seen 'the best minds of my generation destroyed by madness'.

They will never be forgotten. I am a true Bohemian.

Please forgive me. I must warn you, as nature calls. I need to urinate copiously into my toilet. A full bladdered hot piddle utilizing *Limber Dingus*, my shrunken middle leg. An obedient organ, unless summoned by the great God, *Priapus*. Then, my monster, *Dingle Screw* appears, aroused from his lair by sheer goad of the flesh. So hot for the larruping of an entire *hetaeras* of lascivious strumpets. As promised, I have warned you.

⚜ ⚜ ⚜

I AM MYSELF. AND YET ALL THINGS TOGETHER. I welcome you as my coreligionist. Walt Whitman asks: "*Do I contradict myself? Very well, then I contradict myself. I am large. I contain multitudes.*"

Like Adam, I am primal man. One spawned from half a zygote. Eager to till the soil for a new Garden of Eden. God, give me a Mulligan, like in golf. Another shot to restore mankind to its pristine state. A perfect garden as before The Fall and advent of Original Sin. Let me grow fruits on the Tree of Knowledge. I promise to feed 'The Five Thousand'.

Yet, I am fated to fall, damned for eternity, since the day I was born. Damned to burn in the Seventh Circle of Hell, where the Phlegathon drowns even the pious, in a red river of boiling blood.

I am The Bargain Shopper. Frugal with my ducats, but not my opinions. Do not blame me for my beliefs. I never Google anything. When I need information or settle argument, my mind crawls out of my quiescent brain and tells me exactly what to think. With a voice resounding from the Celestial *Mana*. *Stronger* than any ever sent to me by teleprompter direct from The Great Architect of the Universe.

I think about Jean Baptist II. I think about him again and again. If only he had lived, would my life be better, was he my better half? I await his wisdom. His untold secrets. I exorcised computers out of my life. As a proud Luddite, one step ahead of the Amish, but sometimes a furlong behind. I don't own anything with an I that precedes it: computer, pad, wristwatch or smartphone. My Jitterbug flip-phone with the generic ringtone I love, is eons smarter than I.

Laugh at me, if you dare. But be forewarned. I am learned in the fidelities of Archimedes, *The Six Enneads of Plotinus*, the *Antiquities of Athenaeus* and the precisions of Rhetoric and Geomancy.

I am also a regular guy. Overwhelmed by the dreads, I still joyously partake in the jollies of life. Do not be fooled. Contradiction is the essence of my wit and wisdom. Yet, I refuse to submit to the radical pieties of the prevailing Vatican of falsehoods. Let me be clear. We are *not* a progressive civilization. And I am deaf to the charlatans who insist our lives resemble any previous age of historical enlightenment.

Dunk your brain in a bell jar of formaldehyde, if you believe these lies. Play Lotto. Our age is neither of enlightenment nor reason. The Hittite Empire lasted half a millennium before King Tellepinnu II decreed the end of incest. Surely, they considered themselves blessed inhabitants of The Golden Age. But it was only The Bronze Age, already dissipating into the fine, black dust of an insurgent oblivion.

Coronavirus 19 might well be the finale of our vastly overrated civilization.

Time is real, but only a deception. According to the laws of relativity, we live in The Dark Ages. Primitives who have unwittingly degraded the Godhead, we are condemned to the Age of Pandemic, awaiting our Lord Jesus Christ. But I pledge to germinate the rhizomes of Promethean knowledge. The maps and compasses for our future. I will arm myself with the synergistic tropes and inventions to save our goddamned civilization.

Listen to my words. Like Baruch Spinoza, who was excommunicated by the authorities, I live abandoned and alone, denied of my rightful patrimonies. Yet, I will dedicate myself to refine the philosophies and build a firm foundation for a New Enlightenment. And I promise to prove the null hypothesis before the coming Apocalypse.

On the scales of Time Eternal—the metrics of Infinity, our civilization currently resides in the danger zone. It gravely registers near zero. Without the help from the *corpus* of 'modern' medicine, our sickly planet may be well beyond the point of its preternatural expiration date. Play Lotto.

I am awaiting the Second Coming of Christ.

CHAPTER TWO

My fellow Pilgrims, there are only a handful of farms, forests or fauna in Westchester County. I reside here, north of Manhattan. Far from our ancient civilizations, yet renowned as the wealthiest suburb in America.

Melville Corners is a poor town. Sharing frondiferous parks, beaches, empyrean skies and an aethereal firmament with over-consumers from rich towns. They crisscross the asphalt grid, riding inside luxurious horseless carriages.

Life is democratic in a way. We generally eat the same food – refrigerated, frozen, processed or canned. Ossining boasts of Sing-Sing prison. 'Corners' promotes cheap apartments and low property values with the help of an ebullient leper colony, recently re-located inside a stunning gated community.

A leprous leader confided to me our school system 'sucks.' He needed volunteers from both inside and outside the colony to canvass for reform candidates, running for school board. I am apolitical and have never registered to vote. If I had voted last time, it would have been for a Royalist party candidate. I might have voted for Bernie— far less of a liar than Trump or Hillary. Without children, I don't have any 'skin in the game.' Especially when it comes to roiling political controversies. The last thing I need is any more hassles.

I signed up anyway. Lepers are vocal in electoral affairs. They vote in a bloc on certain issues— just like Hasidim. I consider lepers both friends and allies, but I admit they epitomize 'Group Think' at its worst. Schools are a major topic of conversation for many Westchester County residents. Competitive bragging rights are always on the line. But I always try to reciprocate favors with my friends.

It always helps to make friends. When the stores ran out of facemasks, many months ago, I was able to borrow some from the colony. They usually stockpile them anyway, even since long before The Pandemic. I was forced to pacify the belligerent, but 'essential' mask-o-maniacal fascists working the dirty aisles and virus-ridden checkout counters of our formerly friendly, Gulag Shoprite.

Melville Corners sharecroppers, besides itinerant herds of activist lepers, are mostly kulak tradesmen and churls. The kind my grandfather snobbishly referred to as *San's Culottes*, like many of my hog gelder, hod carrier and dung farmer neighbors. Yet, I am only a Frisbee throw away from the Clinton's in Chappaqua, one of several nearby rich towns.

I live amongst blocks of concrete and steel. Where roaring engines spume clouds of black-carbon geysers. Yet, I imagine myself strolling in the *Garden of Jetavana*, through lovely rose paths, fig gardens and mango groves. I delight in the sweet songs of the hermit thrush. And to the fresh scents of honeysuckle and sprigs of lilac. At least, in the solitude of my own mind's eye, ears, and nose. Life is but a dream. An American Dream.

And I dream of being born again with Jean-Baptiste. To sing with him majestic verses, the music of our souls, joined again in eternity. With the veil of Maya lifted from the visible world, revealed as a deception. Siddhartha had it right from the beginning. Our material world is every bit as bogus as my dime-store plastic Jesus—hanging on a lanyard and waiting for Godot from a dirty, rearview mirror on my unwaxed, gray Corolla.

⚜ ⚜ ⚜

DO NOT CONFUSE 778 Fern Hill Road in Melville Corners with Fern Hill Avenue in Pleasantville. Otherwise, you will get lost. My studio, where I have flopped for thirteen years, was designed by Frank Lloyd Gauche as a tribute to *Gauchery*. An architectural concept widely disparaged in the progressive modern world. Also referred to as *Twentieth Century Flophouse*. It is cheap, yet so tiny.

Professor Gauche adapted the classic model of the swine habitat. So, where I *eat* and where I *shit* are but a few scant feet apart. Where I *live* is a short commute from where I *work* as *majordomo* of a tidy three-acre estate owned by Madame Beatrice Wolcott. Yet, I subsist happily on this arrangement.

Baruch Spinoza lived in sparse quarters, as did Professor Kant. I am satisfied to dwell like a Philosopher King— an aristocrat of ideas, rather than as a rich vulgarian. Wall Street is the Babylon that sustained my family. Ultimately it became the poisonous mammon that destroyed us. As it surely will to these others and has done to me. I was born a Rochambeau, a soldier with a warrior ethos. I am a survivor, now fully evolved into The Bargain Shopper.

My sparse hovel is owned by a close friend of Madame's contractor, Ryan Keneally. He maintains both manse and grounds on her estate in Briarcliff Manor. Dowagers with brocaded social ancestries can be extremely tight-fisted with money. So, they may never need to earn it themselves. Avaricious caterers, pettifogging lawyers and greedy tradesman, who think they've hit the jackpot with Madame Beatrice must learn this lesson the hard way.

She knew my low rent would mitigate my need for salary increases. Thrift is deeply ingrained in her Old Yankee pedigree and permanent membership amongst the First Families of our colonial cities. Her ancestors from Massachusetts had profiteered in the Triangle Trade. Bartering shiploads of rum, molasses and African slaves, while luxuriating in another popular Pilgrim pastime of Olde Salem, besides Thanksgiving. The art of flame-broiling dozens of screaming, innocent witches alive on burning stakes.

This is one of my privileged and slanderous bad jokes— not hers. Please, forgive me. Madame and I share a fine sense of the jollies. Together, we laugh out loud at my occasional blasphemies.

I met Beatrice working the bridal boutique at Macy's at Jefferson Valley Mall. She was sending out many gifts. Far too many. I offered to teach her how to maximize savings. Whenever I learned an item Madame desired was going on sale, I suggested she wait a few more days —or even weeks, before placing her order to insure the best price.

She ran all her purchases from Macy's through my register, until her long-time butler retired. Then she offered me his job. I taught her the Decretals of The Bargain Shopper. How to maximize *utils*, a concept from Microeconomics.

We all do this, either consciously or unconsciously, I explained. Her eyes shined bright as a full moon. She never took economics at Vassar but majored in English. I wish I had done the same. No matter. Bea has many *shopaholic* friends who boast of discounts scarfed from clearance sales that proliferated prior to The Pandemic.

These are *hobby shoppers*, I explained. An epithet coined by a wag of a re-tail executive referring to the female customers they use to pay the rent. Never confuse me with these amateurs, I scolded her. I am a Certified Professional Shopper (CPS)and her friends are merely the *fools* who subsidize my bargains.

My attitude is Spartan. I am a Soldier of Truth. Fanatical in treacher-ous times. My Decretals are as essential and sophisticated as any science in our curriculum. Not just a soft social art. I put my *Faith* in God, but my *Trust* in Science. Madame started calling me *Monsieur Bon Marche*, first as a joke. I consider this a compliment and true sign of respect. Saving money was the primary reason she hired me from Macy's. But I'm convinced that my penetrating intellect, vintage humor and ribald sensibility clinched the deal. Whatever. Play Lotto.

❖ ❖ ❖

SOMETIMES, I DESCRIBE MY ABODE as *Ancient Etruscan*. Whenever a friend of mine drops me home, I say, "Go up the hill and stop at the entrance on your right...See that eggshell-white *Macedonian Bauhaus* mansion?"

My gimlet-eyed slumlord, Clodhopper St. Ninny Poop prides himself as a man of many hats. He *claims* he can fix *anything*. He performed a miracle on my showerhead, but not to the permanent pinhole leak on my roof. I admit he wears many hats quite well, along with his cruppers and codpieces, in a unique pursuit of yeoman excellence. I must remind you again that I am *not* a modern man and vastly prefer divine wisdom from ancient scrolls.

Mister Clod is a peerless rodent warden. A cockroach whisperer *par ex-cellence*. Unfortunately, none of his hats covered broken toilet seats. At least, not the one adorning my porcelain crapper. He sent his varlet, Clod Jr., a rois-tering wompster of almost seventeen, who was flummoxed by this formidable task, until his first fully sober attempt.

Here is the precise architectural description of my residence: I have nev-er seen a trick-or-treater within a shotgun blast of my door during thirteen Halloweens I have brooded here alone, waiting for some brightly costumed young guests to appear and request their rewards. Sadly, I have saved myself a fortune on apples and candy.

Yet, it comforts me to live here. To reside fifteen minutes from the hospi-tal where I was born in Mt. Kisco. Even closer to our family plot at Kensico Cemetery. *Humans are the only animal species on earth that bury their dead. I* heed these words, as I harken to my own mortality. The Pandemic allows me to stare Death in the face, every day.

When I cough, I imagine shovelfuls of quicklime tossed over the shrouds of my lifeless body. I am reading *The Plague* again, by Albert Camus. I first read it in French as *La Peste*. In his sermon in the novel, Father Paneloux says: "*Yet this calamity was not willed by God. Too long this world of ours has connived at evil, too long it has counted on the divine mercy, on God's forgiveness. Repentance was enough, men thought..........God gazed down on this town with eyes of compassion; but He grew weary of waiting...*"

I will not make God wait. I will flail cruel leather thongs on my flesh. Splay them over my naked body, as I beckon the stigmata. I await the Second Coming of Christ and proffer repentance for my sins. I will beg for divine mercy.

Especially without any proven medical therapeutics in sight.

I am a Man of Science. Yet it might yet fail us. Sinners repent. Trillions of *Ave Marias* were issued during The Black Death in the fourteenth century. Zillions of prayers issued to battle 'The Spanish Flu' in 1918 or 'The Kansas Flu', if the truth is told of its real origins. Have our rosaries ever saved us from extinction? Perhaps, it was the onions in the onion soup, as many believed in 1919? Today, nobody has proven anything with any scientific conviction.

I know one true thing. Every day brings me closer to my death. With or without Covid-19.

I muse upon my fate. I live in a state of thanatopsis every day, like a prisoner on death row. Four generations are interred near me in Valhalla. Beginning with my great- great grandparents, who emigrated from France to Montreal, before the first shots were fired in the Civil War. I am ready and willing to join Jean Baptiste II. He will remain in my prayers. Until I am summoned by our hypothetically merciful God, who I hope will be, our Lord, Jesus Christ.

My older sister, Molly lives with her husband, Dr. Jeffrey Goldstein in Vermont. The eminent psychiatrist with three grownup sons. My mother resides in a nearby facility, almost ninety, but crazy as ever— crazier than a loon. You can easily see why my sister decided to major in Psychology at Bryn Mawr.

Mom will never agree to burial next to our father, Richard Delacroix. She prefers to be called by her maiden name and has never forgiven my father for his sins. Neither have I.

He *fucked* us all. Whether he meant to or not. And I suffered the brunt of it. I apologize for my language, but it haunts me to this day. I'm not talking about child abuse, either—at least, not technically. But I am still proud to be a Rochambeau, a soldier by trade. Born with a military mind, instead of an aesthetic one.

Maybe there is a God. Play Lotto.

I am ready to depart my encampment on our sickly planet to my eternal grave. I will it leave it cleaner than I found it. I was born into a life of scarcity, yet I have survived. And I still hope to save the world.

Or fulfill my manifest destiny as The Bargain Shopper.

I never took a chic, submissive oath of poverty, like Gautama had done. I did it out of bereavement and stupidity, four decades ago, after I joined The Archangels of Golgotha in California. A cult that gives me the dreads whenever I ponder my past life, as I am doing now— but only for your edification.

What caused my fall from grace? I never took a bite of the Forbidden Fruit.

Bad luck? Branch Rickey said it best: *Luck is the residual of design.* Should I blame myself?

My father never indicted himself for his innumerable fuckups or chronic *bad luck.* He blamed *bad timing.* Look at me. I am a perfect example of *bad timing.* I was even born into the wrong century.

Maybe, I could blame Providence. Not only was I born backassward, but I am destined to die in The Aquarian Age of Pandemic. I have been sentenced to burn forever in The Inferno.

You decide — anybody but me. As a Man of Truth, I must submit my confessions. But I reserve my natural right to decide on my ultimate judgement. Who knows, maybe I only abused myself?

⚜ ⚜ ⚜

IN *THE GREAT GATSBY*, Nick Carraway confides to the cultured classes of the American Jazz Age: *I am one of the few honest people that I have ever known.*

Holden Caufield, in *The Catcher in the Rye*, brags the opposite: *I'm the most terrific liar you ever saw in your life.*

I have heard: *If you eat too much of the truth— you will die of the truth.* If you are dying, as you read my confessions, please put Truth aside for a moment. Give your mind and soul a rest. Play Lotto.

Despite my agnostic stance on religion, I was inspired by the honesty of St. Augustine. I promise to uphold his ideals in my confessions. I am disgusted by lies. The bleating of politicians arguing irrelevancies. I have become bipartisan on this issue. I hope you will agree: Goddamn every *fucking* one of them.

Pontificating from media echo chambers. Full of doctrinaire deceits scraped from the buttocks of our polluted democracy. Far worse than eating the wontons of a mutant batshit scourge from China. Or direct from Hell. Whatever. Politics is the main disease infecting this country. The pandemic is a plague of lies that makes me sick enough to puke every day. Politicians are the fleas and rats, with contaminated brains, who had transmitted The Black Death to the gullible human populations in the fourteenth century. And here I am today, living in the wrong century.

Here we go again— *Deja Vue.* Although, I place my trust in Science, I pray to a merciful God to deliver us from evil. The Great Pandemic. I promise to tell only the Truth in my confessions—Orwellian as it may be.

My gold standard of honesty lies somewhere between decorous Nick Carraway and whimpering Holden Caufield. Remember— *If you eat too much of the truth you will die of the truth.* But if you eat too many carrots, your hair will grow orange, like the hair on the head of President Trump. He gives me the natty dreads. You need to put your trust in either Science or Faith. Remember to say your prayers. And roll the dice for your life. Play Lotto.

Socrates spoke the truth. *All I know is that I know nothing.* I don't know everything, but I don't know nothing, either. I *do* know I can no longer live my life like Socrates. Do you think I'm crazy? Certainly not in the throes of our current medical and political crises. I would rather quaff a fatal cup of hemlock than tell a single lie. I am sick of lies, lies and more lies. I drink only the tonic of *Veritas.* The absolute truth poured from the purest fountains of Nirvana— except for an occasional tarradiddle or two. Okay, make it three. Or possibly, even four. Whatever.

Truth is relative. Emerson informs us: *There is no history, only biography.* Now, you know who I am. Neither a cheapskate nor miser. Not a hermit or a misanthrope. I am The Bargain Shopper. Two plus two equals four squared. I will prove the math to you. And I can prove everything that I am about to confess to you.

CHAPTER THREE

Call me *Monsieur Bon Marche.*

I am The Bargain Shopper. I recall a fine, warm morning of Indian Summer on the start of my workweek at Kohl's in Bedford Hills. It was the first Monday of October, prior to the pandemic.

An eternity has passed.

Morning sunshine bathed the parking lot at nine. I marched across the pavement with my shopping list. Ready-to- wear men's clothes, gifts for friends of The Madame. An easy start to my week. Buying men's clothes is easy. Retail executives agree women's fashions are the major challenge for department stores. They make you or break you.

Store coupons tucked in my wallet. I inspected them at McDonalds, while enjoying my Maximum Value Restaurant (M.V.R) breakfast. A sausage bur-rito (no sauce) and a senior coffee.

I pushed through the front doors. Porcelain tiles glistened in liquid rect-angles, glowing from the fluorescence. Music blaring, as I passed displays of menswear: sweaters, long-sleeved flannel shirts and cotton chenille. Pairs of corduroy and winter-weight khaki pants on tables. Clothing suspended on hangers or dangling under the eaves of recessed racks.

I saw them all—but I was blind. This merchandise was invisible to me.

Price check — minimal discounts. No dice. None of the items were 'hashed out.' Which means marked down on the price tags, so I do not see them. I will find them in three to six months, following their rightful demotion to lesser

racks. 'Hard-marked' to fester under those garish red and white signs called
FINAL CLEARANCE.

I push to the back of the store. The valley of markdowns, sixty to eighty
percent off. Now, I see everything clearly in the promised land of maximum
discounts. I manage Beatrice's present list with a proprietary, low-tech system
for purchasing, cataloguing and gifting. A gunmetal strong box for receipts
and a card filer labeled *Petite Cadeaux.*

I buy 'little gifts' for friends and family. Apparel from clearance racks, a
year ahead of delivery. I store them in a dozen plastic bins, labeled by size and
gender. Stacked in double rows in the basement of her mansion in Briarcliff
Manor.

Ten bins are assigned to 'The Madame.' Two labeled for me, 'The Bargain
Shopper.' Let me assure you, Beatrice is thrifty. One of the core values we
share. Alas, she was born a *giftaholic* and there is no cure. There are no
clinical programs for this addiction as there are for druggies, gamblers and
drunks.

Madame gives presents to everybody. Except incarcerated murderers,
even for trifling reasons. Her Vassar roommate's grandson is toileted-trained.
Celebrated with presents for Grandma, Mommy and *le petite garcon.*

You dare laugh at the *sine qua non* for Madame. Or *de rigueur,* as we say
in French.

Follow the Science. The discipline of removing red or yellow clearance
stickers off tricky- sticky price tags. They wad up. You must be meticulous.
Pinch the edges and pull off each sliver. Never rip it off fast, like a band aid.
Tags must remain intact to display the original prices. Remove the glue build-
up by gently rubbing with your forefinger. It will sliver into a black strip which
you peel off gently. Remain patient. *Voila!* The price tag looks new again.

I suggested to retain original price tags on inventories slated for gifting. Madame was horrified. This idea was so foreign to her upbringing it
reeked of subterfuge. Or criminality. To her patrician sensibility, it seemed
barbaric. I changed her *mindset.* I'm not screaming *braggadocio,* but I only
remove price tags on merchandise NOT overpriced. *It's the thought that
counts.* Remember that classic line? I often remind Madame of this time-
honored platitude.

Think about it. What is the shame in high prices? If the giver pays a low
price, then both parties' benefit. Shame, like guilt is the curse of the *haute
bourgeoise,* the lost province of *nouveaux riches.* I can only serve nobility. I

could not deter the profligate gifting by Beatrice. Yet, I slashed her costs by a fortune. And I managed to keep her in good conscience. Never an easy task, to maintain the pleasures of Madame Beatrice Wolcott.

⚜ ⚜ ⚜

LORD ALMIGHTY. THE HORROR. My beautiful clearance racks have been invaded. By a troglodyte with a mullet, in a garish red t-shirt. Chancre sore on the upper lip, sweaty armpits, mandibles inside grimy pockets. The horror. Squeezing past my aisle. Flaunting in close quarters. Obliviously grazing my pastures. Slouching back and forth, yanking hangars, be-mucking itself insidiously, sniffing snot bubbles on every garment in sight. Including the virgin underwear.

Hark! I will pray to Zephyrus. Once implored by Achilles to blow mighty winds upon the funeral pyre of his beloved Patrocles. Protect me, great gaseous one. Summon my demigod, Fartida. Beseech him to unleash his fiercest excremental breeze upon this abject mendicant.

The gods have answered. A tart emission is released— so profound, a tiny turdlet is loosed upon my perineum. Culminating with a sibilant hind blast. The varmint poacher winces, snarls at me walleyed, before retreating to a far-away clearance territory. Not everyone is as fortunate. *Willing and able* to harness personal demigods in times of crisis. I have contemplated solutions to this existential challenge, long and hard. I envision a rubber bladder emanating with the sounds of flatulence. Attached to an aerosol can with profound stenches. For fumigating troglodytes, fools, proletarians or breeds of undesirables in retail stores, movie theatres and public places.

I will patent my invention with an iron- clad trademark. Market it as *The Fartidalator.* I am a juggernaut for ideas but short on investment capital. The tragic story of my life. Do not dare to laugh. Or I will call you a fool, a knave, or a booby. Emerson advised us in *Self Reliance: In every work of genius, we recognize our own rejected thoughts.* He warns us not to dismiss our original creations, however ludicrous they may seem. Whatever.

My fellow Pilgrims, please do not dare to question the radiant Concord wisdom of Mr. Ralph. Remember Chia pets and the Pet Rock? I envision another billion-dollar baby. A chain of grilled-cheese restaurants. Please keep mum. I must be ever vigilant to protect the legal rights of my valuable intellectual properties.

✢ ✢ ✢

BACK TO THE BUSINESS OF SHOPPING. Menswear. Summer leftovers. Polo shirts, traditional golf shirts, lightweight sweater vests. I hit on
double rows of racks. My hands move like lightning, yanking and pulling
hangars, glancing at price tags, culling losers from keepers. I pile winners into
my shopping cart. I keep on hitting. Hitting and hitting, as I've explained to
Beatrice: Bargain shopping is like tennis. Madame started playing at five. She
played varsity tennis and squash at Masters in Dobbs Ferry and at Vassar.
Except for her elbow, she could play like a champion today. Her favorite
writer is Vladimir Nabokov because he was an avid tennis player, who once
taught at Wellesley. *Lolita* was her favorite novel. Go figure. Her favorite
professional tennis player has always been John McEnroe.

I do my hitting in the stores. Like McEnroe hits tennis balls. Or Nabokov
wrote his stories. This morning, I hit on Van Heusen, Croft and Barrow, a
Kohl's store brand, or Chaps, owned discreetly by Ralph Lauren. I found two
Izod sports shirts. 'Just keep hitting,' I always remind her.

I am finished. I do not linger. I stride to the register and wait. I am subsidized by the shopping universe of hapless full-price shoppers and bargain
pretenders. Like you and countless status vultures in a landscape infected by
lethal viruses and contemporary malaise. My lips curl into a grin. You flump
down plum petticoats and doublets. Dung colored buskins, shalloon-lined tu-
nics, farthingales and pink velveteen knickerbockers for your latest *rentier*
boy along with several bright codpieces to adorn his pendulous swag dangle.

The cashier smiles, obsequiously. While praising your ghastly pile of can-
kered muckworms.

I drop my clothes on the counter. Paid for by the aggregate of all the boo-
bies who shop in our national bourgeoise: seven polo shirts, a three pack of
men's socks and a sweater vest.

The tale of the tape: original list price $309. 60 My total cost was only
$34.20. The net price of seven items under three dollars. Only the pair of Izod
polo shirts exceeded five dollars.

Try doing this on Amazon. No way. Easier to find a four-leaf clover in a
dumpster. My savings totaled $275. 40 off the Total Retail Value, known as
the TRV. I never buy online. If that day ever comes, then I am worshipping
Beezlebub. Most department stores closed last March, and I received a stark

vision of our coming Apocalypse. I departed on a journey to Hell and back. And this was no nightmare.

The first decretal of The Bargain Shopper. A discount averaging over 75% off T.R.V. Remember: Two plus two equals four squared— or 16. The difference is 12. My savings on this purchase was greater than 75%. I have proven my theorem, as you would expect from a Man of Science. I am not a mathematician or a C.P.A. I am a qualified C.P.S. The savings rate of a Certified Professional Shopper averages over 87.5% in discounts during a shopping year. Dust off your abacus. Compare the difference between 87.5% versus 75%. You will receive *double* the merchandise for the same dollar amount. Trust me, first. Then do the math. I will prove everything in my *Confessions*.

⚜ ⚜ ⚜

DONNA, A MIDDLE-AGED ITALIAN "ASSOCIATE" with cobalt- blue mascaraed eyes, fawns over me with more than the usual piffle, complimenting my deals as she rings me up. But I am obliged to tell the truth. And 'Follow the Science.' Shopping, especially bargain shopping promotes an overflow of pheromones into the hidden rivers flowing inside the human body. And these impulses are acutely *sexual* in nature.

Many people fail to realize that shopping is a sex act. And bargain shopping is orgasmic. To help you grasp this concept, I describe a conundrum that I have observed over many decades as The Bargain Shopper.

To put it bluntly, my *vendeur*, Donna has been transmogrified into a horny wench. Although not quite *une salope*. Nakedly exposed to the staggering value of my purchases, she is *turned on*— not just aroused, but desperate to seduce my monster, the unrepentant Dingle Screw. Now, she is panting frantically, desperate to glom a cheap and easy branglebump off my favorite bodily appendage.

She will attempt to disguise her intentions. By feigning normalcy and virtue in vain, trying to appear discreet. From my experienced vantagepoint, she is in the throes of multiple orgasms. Jollies not experienced by her since her greasy boy Gino, first slaked her primeval thirst for lust upon the clammy back seat of a rusty, ten-year old, red Firebird convertible. Notoriously screened with screaming, flaming yellow racing stripes.

I always get the jollies at checkout. Elation is not considered an official decretal, but I crack up every time I feed a new cashier this classic line. Right after getting complimented on my incredible bargains.

Almost like hitting The Trifecta. With bargain shopping, just do the math. *It's almost cheaper than shoplifting.*

CHAPTER FOUR

If you have ever sneezed, idling in traffic behind a Westchester County bee-line system bus, spewing smoke from its tailpipe, then you can grasp the billowing reputation of Alfieri Prestige Motors. I kid you not. As you must be aware by now, I love drama. Edgar Allen Poe realized that haunting is part of the story. The Great Pandemic is only one of the many challenges faced by Madame Beatrice. Several of these events are terrible tragedies.

The 'Golden Crown' has been displayed on local billboards for decades. As far away as Yankee Stadium, advertising luxury cars such as Volvo, Land Rover, Lexus, Lincoln and BMW. Every vehicle, new or 'preowned' regardless of make, model or year was 'Covered by The Golden Promise,' the symbol of confidence for Alfieri Prestige Motors.

This credo says more about character than economics. Madame Beatrice's father-in-law, Joseph Anthony Alfieri, touted it after launching his first BMW dealership in White Plains in 1970. 'Joey' added another one in Greenwich a few months later. Other dealerships followed until APM Inc. owned fourteen showrooms in the Tristate area. After shuttering Saab on Central Avenue, Joey replaced it with Lincoln, his first American car brand.

I swerved my peasant-gray Corolla off the extension of Old Sleepy Hollow Road into the circular parking lot at Beatrice's. Eleven in the morning, and I carried in both of my plastic shopping bags from Kohls.

Privet hedgerows girdled each flank of the mansion. 7250 square feet of Tudor Revival. Leaded windows hung over sloping mansard gables or sprouted out of white stucco walls. Weathered cedar shakes sat on pitted roofs that slung over both wings of a shambling country farmhouse, graced by a pair of red-brick chimneys. This 'Cottage', as it would likely prefer to be called, was crowned in the center by a single pyramid-shaped cupola.

The original owner, a prominent New York stockbroker had built it in 1929. He lost it along with his fortune on Black Friday. That's the unfortunate truth about wealth. It can vanish in the blink of an eye. The Madame's father, Thomas Brooks Wolcott III, who inherited it, paved over the smooth-pebble driveway in 1988, after his accountant told him that drastic budget cuts to household staff, who had raked it twice a day, became mandatory following Black Monday.

His grandmother, the former Abigail Roosevelt Willet, was so mortified by this premeditated abomination of nature that her heart palpitations intensified, which hastened her demise, short of a century. Black was my father's color of money. For Mondays and Fridays and every day of the week, including weekends. His book, *The Art of Contrarian Investing* even had a black cover. But his own investments were always bleeding red.

I clutched my bags from Kohl's, as I regarded the gigantic rear end of a huge silver Lincoln Black Label Navigator parked in front of me. New York license plate: Alfieri 666. I was looking at trouble. Big trouble for Madame Beatrice.

Franny never uttered a word, as he scurried past me. He only smiled and jumped into his Sherman tank, hit the ignition and barreled away, faintly signaling to me with a tap on his horn. I suspected he had finished a vicious bout with Madame Beatrice. A battle that had been brewing for weeks over their daughter, Emily's upcoming wedding in September. I could tell. There were eleven more calendar months left for this fight to continue.

Sorry— I forgot to tell you. Joseph Francis Alfieri is the former husband of Mme. Beatrice Wolcott.

Miss Emily Van Cortlandt Alfieri is one of their two daughters. Thirty-six, a graduate of Hackley and Trinity College, recently promoted to vice president at Burson, Cohn& Wolfe in Manhattan. Engaged to Mr. Peter Sargent Aldrich, once divorced— but happily without any children. Considered by 'everyone' to be 'a fine young man'. Acceptable to the respectable families like the Wolcott's, despite his first marital misstep. *Everyone* agrees Emily has chosen *well*.

The front door was unlocked. I stepped into the foyer carrying the shopping bags. I wanted to show some items to Beatrice before storing them in the basement. Chloe, our dearly beloved but memory-challenged cockapoo *de la maison* charged forwards, barking like a banshee to scare me away. I heard Roxy vacuuming upstairs in the master bedroom.

As I walked through the kitchen, I noticed Chloe had deposited a fresh dumpling of cock-a-poopy. I cleaned it off the quarry tile with a sheet of Bounty, although this was technically not part of my job description.

The house sprawls over two wings. Six bedrooms and five full baths. Powder rooms on each end of the ground floor. Madame and her older sister, Jill Roosevelt were raised here by their parents, Brooks Wolcott III and their mother Madeline. Brooks had inherited the estate from his father, Brooks Jr, so the home spans four generations.

Brooks III was called Brooky by his mother. She would have loved to call him Brooksie— if only he had been born a girl. Some say he might have preferred this epithet, as well as being born female. He accomplished almost nothing in his life, including his divorce, which 'everyone' said was inevitable. He fooled everyone and died young.

Brooky had tripped and fallen in the aisle, stone drunk, at The Plaza, while presenting Beatrice at The Junior Assemblies. The social scandal of the year amongst the Olde Knickerbocker crowd, a blemish that rarely travels beyond the social circles in Manhattan. Her older sister, Jill had no problems with her own debut, a few years earlier.

Beatrice was always the unlucky one.

I strolled past The Mirror Room, featuring an eighteenth-century mirror on a gilded frame, nearly covering the entire wall. It serves as my wrapping room prior to Thanksgiving as I move my storage bins upstairs for two weeks. Another wall displays rows upon rows of ancestor portraits—from both sides of the family. One observer commented that the power and magnitude of the family portraits might have staved off Brooky's inevitable divorce, until he died broke.

The wall over the fireplace features only one portrait. Anthony Wolcott Alfieri, Madame's only son, commissioned shortly after his death, bright-eyed and swarthy with sandy blonde hair, as a boy of fourteen. His dimpled smile dominates The Mirror Room. I look up to Anthony every day. Although, I never met him, I feel that I've always known him. In the same way, I know my long-lost brother, Jean-Baptiste. I feel the pain of Madame Beatrice every day.

I do my gift-wrapping on a huge oaken table. The Mirror Room is not only an antique mirror, but the reflection of a tragedy buried in the heart of The Madame, through no fault of her own. Beatrice endures and so, must I. To work smarter and harder on her behalf. In the words of Theresa May Alcott, I am 'Duty's faithful child' in her service.

I sauntered past the living room into the den. A crimson-curtained drawing-room on the far end of the ground floor where the rooms were aglow with the rouge warmth of the morning sun. Beneath cathedral ceilings, the white-potted philodendrons reposed on red-soaked Persian carpets, or on several raggedy Royal Sarouk scatter rugs.

An estate reeking of 'Old Money. But fading as fast as the worn-out carpets. Everything is *olden*—not *old*. Or just plain broken-down. Since the day that Joseph Francis Alfieri moved away for good.

CHAPTER FIVE

randfather Rochambeau was born Caspar Charles. His name is inscribed in black India ink on his Columbia College diploma, which hung on a wall in his study, with other framed certificates at his summer home in the Adirondacks.

This was the only place that I ever saw his name, fully spelled out.

His mail was addressed to C. Charles. Or only to Charles. His gravestone reads: Charles Rochambeau. His middle name, Charles might be the only affinity I ever shared with him. We were both called 'Charles' because both of us despised the Christian names which were inflicted upon us at birth.

Long before Grandpa became a big shot on Wall Street— the managing partner of Dillon Reed, he was a big man on campus. Phi Beta Kappa with highest honors in economics and political science. He captained the renowned Columbia fencing team and won the individual national championship with the Sabre, also the weapon of choice of French calvary officers. *Le Marechal* began his military career at seventeen, joining his first regiment in the French army.

Our family claims direct a lineage to Charlemagne. And to his grandfather, Charles Martel, who saved the vulnerable kingdoms of European Christendom from the ransacking armies of the Muslim empire. Charles 'The Hammer' defeated the Saracens on the banks of Loire River, near Vendome, where Chateaux Rochambeau stands today, in the decisive battle of Tours in 732 A.D. Grandpa revered our family history. Every Christmas Day, he raised a glass of fine French wine in his annual toast to Charlemagne. I have tried to instill Molly with an appreciation of our family's legacy to insure that these priceless traditions will be passed along to her three sons and six grandchildren.

Like his boss, Clarence Dillon, Grandpa preferred all things French. He trusted French names, bankers, lawyers and candlestick makers, including food and wine. He shared a bond with the legendary financier. Dillon's ancestor fled Ireland and settled in France during the Glorious Revolution, following the tumult in the age of Oliver Cromwell.

Theobold, Count Dillon became a colonel in an Irish regiment of the French Army. He fought in the American Revolution, serving as an aide-de-camp to *Le Marechal*. C. Douglas Dillon, Clarence's son was appointed ambassador to France, before serving President Kennedy as Secretary of the Treasury. My only cousin was named Clarence.

Grandpa started fencing at the age of eight, continuing it through Trinity School. At Columbia, he won the Alumni Association award as *the most deserving member of his class*, nominated by the faculty and voted by his classmates. A permanent class officer, he was charged to read the 'Class History' on campus, in the Fall following his graduation.

His summer place in Westport, N.Y had a name, 'Sheldon Manor.' Grandpa had paid for Clarence and I to attend Camp Dudley, where my father and uncle had spent parts of their youthful summers, in the same town. Several weeks were reserved for visits with my grandparents, either with my cousin or sister Molly. Sometimes, only by myself.

They led elegant but regimented lives. I had to fix bowls of cold cereal for breakfast at home, whereas Grandma served hot plates of bacon and omelets to order. Or French toast made with homemade bread. Crystal vases of flowers were placed on a large maple table with crocks of imported jams and fine English marmalades.

Grandma seemed content. She watched 'my program' with longtime housekeeper, Mary— *Days of our Lives*, along with tea and biscuits on weekday afternoons. She mended holes in worn-out clothes with her ancient Singer. Or directed Mary in her chores, while scheduling luncheons and outings with the ladies of The Westport Garden Club.

I couldn't resist but to eavesdrop. I overheard their conversations. Whispers of 'reverses' in the stock market. An ill-fated investment in 'Nemours'. Years later, I learned the details of the financial misfortunes that ruined my life.

Of course, my grandparents were snobs. But hardly aware of it. My father started losing money early in his career, while he bragged about his friendship with Warren Buffet. He was a pathological liar, among other misgivings, but I will concede to you, my father, Richard, was *never* a snob. Mainly because he couldn't afford it, like everything else.

Mary Kapisovsky, the housekeeper was the biggest snob of them all. She decried the lack of civility amongst the latest crop of new summer residents. Grandma disparaged the 'awful new people' in Bronxville— the tiny village in Westchester County where the former Cynthia Tether Dusenbery was born and raised. She married my grandfather at Christ Church on Sagamore Road, where they dutifully belonged for the rest of their lives.

Grandma always said to Mary or Grandpa: "Mr. Lawrence would be turning over in his grave."

William Van Duzer Lawrence, a pharmaceuticals magnate, founded the village as an investment. Also, as a social experiment. Him and his wife Sarah had met my great, great-grandparents at a formal dinner in Montreal in the 1880's. Their daughter-in-law, Victoria, became one of Sarah's closest friends. Tory claimed that 'Painkiller,' a patent medicine developed by Mr. Lawrence, was the 'miracle drug' that cured her rheumatism. She insisted it even saved her life.

My forbears were guinea pigs for Lawrence's latest invention— the Village of Bronxville. They were invited to become residents by Lawrence himself. Apparently, they were considered 'the right kind of people' to help him realize his ideal of an enlightened suburban community. They purchased a five-bedroom Tudor adjacent to his estate later bequeathed to become Sarah Lawrence College, following Sarah's death in 1926. The college purchased our house in the early 1960's, when Grandpa decided to move his family to a larger home on the other side of town.

Sheldon Manor was a perfect summer place. Two centuries-old, minimally updated, almost frozen in time. Summering in the Adirondacks was kept simple. My grandparents eschewed the live-in help normally relied upon in Bronxville, or at their winter residence in Delray Beach.

A spacious white colonial. Trimmed with green and perched on the slope of a hill. The front porch leaned over a hillock with a glimpse of Lake Champlain, surrounded by three acres of lawns. A slate patio in the back had a full view of the lake, framed by a stack of pines, furnished with white wrought-iron furniture and a blue striped umbrella. The grounds were cut and trimmed by a crew of gardeners arriving every Monday, with riding lawnmowers.

The walls inside—original horsehair plaster, light green, untouched for decades. Gated in front by forged steel fences, painted green. I remember the negro lawn jockey who proudly held out his lantern by the front gate.

Cocktails were served promptly at five p.m. on the front porch. Accompanied by cheese and crackers and bowls of macadamia nuts from Hawaii. Bartenders or servers were often hired. Everything for munching, chips and onion dips were spread out on little white tables of wicker furniture. My grandfather's cocktail never varied: Dewar's White Label on the rocks. Mine was a Coca Cola with a cherry. With the dusk falling in the evenings, the fireflies appeared, mingling with the descending twilight as they scintillated the panoramic from the front porch.

My grandparents entertained dinner guests with cocktails. Then retired to the dining room at a table surrounded by mahogany chairs with needlepoint cushions. Candles were lit on silver candelabra, flickering over embroidered linens. Racks of lamb were served by Mary with mint jelly, fresh green salads, croissants, petite roast potatoes, peas and carrots. Only French red wines were allowed, including the vintages from the cellars of Chateau Haut Brion. This exquisite *premier crus* red Bordeaux was imported directly from Clarence Dillon's private estate in Graves.

Dessert de le maison: homemade cherry pie with Howard Johnson's vanilla ice cream. Followed by cordials of rare Cognac or Le Bon Pere William, a French brandy, where the fruit was grown inside glass bottles, hanging from the living branches of pear trees. Childhood summers to remember—except for one unforgettable incident.

When I was seven, three elderly couples joined us as guests for a formal dinner. The dinner went late. I had weak bowels as a child and couldn't hold it, as dessert was served. The wife of the couple sitting next to me started coughing. After the guests left, I ran upstairs to the bathroom, took a bath and put on my pajamas. My father slammed into my room before I slipped into bed. First, he yelled at me for not excusing myself from the table. Then he unstrapped his belt, stretched me across his lap and gave me a wicked spanking.

This scars my pristine memory of my summers in Westport. Otherwise, I felt completely entitled to a life of privilege. But it was only a mirage. My family was forced to move six times in Westchester County for financial reasons. I finally fled from our last rented walk-up in Dobbs Ferry. My father promised this move would bring our family luck. Dobbs Ferry was the town where General Rochambeau met Washington to begin their great march that won the war.

The real reason. My father filed for personal bankruptcy as his credit cards were annulled. We were living hand to mouth off old savings accounts and borrowings. And the cash he squeezed out of pawn shops in the Bronx.

I felt obligated to withdraw from Taft in my junior year. I had an attack of the dreads, returned home and worked parttime painting houses, earning money to purchase snacks, food, clothing and to pay for the oil and gas to keep my rattling Volvo beater running. Some things never change. I was waiting for my salvation. And it was coming soon.

CHAPTER SIX

Madame Beatrice was sprawled on a divan in the Family Room. The Tennis Channel flickered, a minor tournament in Monte Carlo, with the sound turned off. Beatrice was lounging in a white tennis dress under a standup lamp, reading a book. Streaks of red in her eyes.

"Chloe did her doodoo again," I exclaimed.

"Good morning, Charles," she murmured as she pulled off her glasses and set down the book. She leaned forwards with a trace of grimace on her face. "Where did she do it this time?"

"Next to her water bowl. Her little pond in the woods. She thinks she's a Shih Tzu".

I laughed at my riposte, but Madame didn't even crack a smile. My humor escapes her when she's not in the right mood. Too bad. Yet, I was the idiot who cleaned up the cock-a-poopy. Sorry, Beatrice. Time to chill out.

"I used a Bounty towel and Lysol. Roxy has no reason to bitch about watering the plants today. I went way above my call of duty, no pun intended. Feel free to remit my hazard pay, forthwith, Madame," I said with a chuckle.

"*Tres' droll, Monsieur, comme d'habitude.*" Beatrice smiled, albeit perfunctorily. Her fingernails were bleeding. She always bites them under duress. I decided not to mention that I saw Franny in the driveway. I wanted to avoid any needless discomforting palaver to start the day, so I yanked a golf shirt out of a shopping bag.

"This one's medium. Trey's birthday is in April. How much?" I asked her. "Extra length in a dark green pastel. Don't play games. Even *Monsieur Bon Marche* might have to pay bust-out retail for a perfect gift, sometimes."

"Is it all cotton?" she asked, secretly snickering at the absurd notion that I paid full price.

"No, but it's an Izod dry-fit. Trey won't show his sweat in it. I got the exact same one for Ryan."

"Dry-fit sounds like a euphemism for cheap polyester to me," observed The Madame.

"Rayon and nylon. In a nice, soft weave. Cool in the summer. Make a guess. How much did I pay?"

I handed it over to Madame and she fingered the fabric. "Well, it does feel soft. Give it to Renaldo for Christmas?"

My fellow Pilgrims, Renaldo is Roxy's calamitous boyfriend. "It's way too small," I answered, which was true, although I considered Izod too fine a brand to waste on Renaldo. "You see him recently? He's put tons of fat. He wears large. Even extra-large. I bought him a sweater and a short-sleeved polo for Christmas. Croft& Barrow. 60/40 cotton-blend."

"In what color?"

"Purple. Purple with white stripes."

"How hideous," replied Madame, shaking her head. "Roxy will hate it."

'You never know. Maybe Renaldo went to Williams or Amherst. Roxy will love it, unless you tell her that I bought it. Technically, it's *your* Christmas present to him. It's the thought that counts," I reminded her again, as I always do.

Renaldo Lopes is the worst. His only motivation in life, besides pomposity is laziness. Yet, Roxy insists on subsidizing his aspiring proletarian lifestyle. And The Madame has been extremely unhelpful on this issue.

"Make me a guess, Bea, on both shirts. How much do you think I paid?"

She answered. "Four dollars for the Izod. Two for the Purple People Eater," then laughed at her meager attempt at humor. I was annoyed. I paid five dollars for the Izod only hours earlier. I was insulted. After discounts, coupons and allocating Kohl's Cash from a previous shopping trip, my net cost for the Purple People Eater was $2.67 pretax.

The game was over. Whenever Madame Beatrice says *Two Dollars*, she has capitulated, signaling she's not in a bantering mood. Something was bothering her big-time today. And I knew exactly who *he* is.

"What's todays reading?" I asked her.

She raised her copy of *The Norton Anthology of Poetry* and answered, "E.E. Cummings. *The Cambridge ladies who live in furnished souls.* I must have thought this poem was by Eliot," she said. "Sometimes, I mix them up, Charles. I think they both went to Harvard."

"Almost all post-modernist, anti-Semitic, atheistic intellectuals went to Harvard."

I should never flaunt my literary knowledge. Madame majored in English at Vassar whereas I was obliged to take English courses with illiterates of The Wharton School. I read only classic *literature*, not any current crapola.

Years ago, Bea mistook a famous line by Eliot in *Prufrock*: *In the room the women come and go. Talking of Michelangelo* with his most famous poem: *The Wasteland.* I felt obligated to point out her mistake.

She considered Eliot an Englishman. He was a British subject when he won the Nobel Prize. But I consider him American since he wrote all his seminal *poems*—not songs, sorry Bob Dylan— as an American. He is the only American *poet* who received it for Literature. I hate to wax pedantic, but I can only tell the truth in my confessions.

Beatrice was called the 'the smart one'. Born a brunette, she went to Vassar like her mother. Her older sister Jill was 'the pretty one,' with braided blonde pigtails as a girl. Jill dropped out of Denison after two years. And she was born a witch. Which rhymes with something even nastier, but more accurate. I'll skip over these grim details, until later.

Madame tips forwards and starts reading, "*the Cambridge ladies who live in furnished souls are unbeautiful and have comfortable minds (also, and with the church's protestant blessings daughters, unscented shapeless spirited) they believe in Christ and Longfellow, both dead....*"

She stares at me and yawns. "These words are confusing. Do I have a furnished soul, Charles? Jesus lives in my heart and Emily is beautiful, don't you think?" Sunlight burst through windows, as a teardrop dripped off her eyelid.

"Of course, Emily is a beautiful girl."

Beatrice winced. "I find this poem cruel and disturbing. Francis just told me that his mother is insisting on another Catholic wedding at St. Gregory's The Great. Just Like Francis and me and poor Charlotte. With that awful Bailey. Is it a coincidence both of those marriages ended in divorce? I want to hold this wedding at St. Mary's."

"St. Gregory's isn't so great for Peter, either. He's a protestant, Bailey was Roman Catholic. Although not *in reality* as we found out. Peter is a devout Episcopalian. His great-uncle was a former Chaplain at St. Marks School."

"Does that matter?"

"Not really. Does Lucy want to hold the reception at Westchester Country Club, again?"

"Francis says she'll pay for everything, including the reception."

I laughed. "Westchester's too big for a small reception. Final head count will be under a hundred. Hold the ceremony at St. Mary's and the reception next door at Sleepy. Like your sister Jill did a century ago. Especially after what happened to Charlotte. Bailey cheating on her. What a disaster."

"Sorry, Charles. I can't think about any more disasters today. At least, Lucy's paying for it."

"Franny could pay for it with his spare change. After all, Emily is his *other* beautiful daughter."

"The problem is Lucy. Stubborn as ever. I told Francis I must insist on doing the flowers. I'll pay for all the arrangements at the church and reception."

"Definitely no more Niko's Flowers," I said in agreement.

"Charles— don't be nasty. Nancy means well. She's still Lucy's oldest childhood friend."

"It wasn't just the flowers, Bea. That wedding was like going to St. Peter's at Easter, an insufferable high church spectacle. With four priests and six nuns broiling alive in Hades."

"At least they got the fans going. Who could have predicted hundred-degree heat in June?"

"Cardinal O'Brien was sweating buckets. Lucy should accept 'the church's protestant blessings' for Emily's sake, like in your poem. Except with fewer blessings in a *smaller* Episcopalian church."

"The Catholic ceremony is important to Lucy, but it's just too long."

"This will be Episcopalian— not Hindu. Nobody will be racing around flaming piles of sacred cow dung, but it'll be a typical Protestant ceremony— short and *sweet*."

"And beautiful, I hope." Madame raised a finger and moistened it on her lips. "You have a good point, Charles. I'll discuss this with Francis and..."

"Charlotte's *marriage* was a disaster. Bailey couldn't even keep it in his pants six months..." I blurted.

"Nevermore," she said, squinting. The Madame had signaled she was officially pissed off and wasn't joking.

"Quoth the raven, *nevermore*," I said. Lucy will be on board by May. Longfellow lives and Christ will be with us."

Portentous words. Madame Beatrice was trembling. But I just couldn't think of anything else to say.

CHAPTER SEVEN

Clarence Valcour Rochambeau is my only cousin, three years older than I. We shared bunkbeds at Sheldon Manor, while spending summer sojourns visiting our grandparents.

He was raised in Westport, Connecticut, where my uncle Francois and aunt Amanda spent summers sailing at their yacht club, or in regattas along the coast. Clarence was sent away to boarding school in sixth grade. His parents moved into their ski chalet at Stratton in Vermont every winter. Except for their provisional expeditions to Palm Beach, their house in Antigua, or Gstaad for two weeks after Christmas. Or the obligatory Easter Week in Sun Valley.

I forgot to tell you. Uncle Francois never worked a day in his life.

After graduating from Columbia, he volunteered as an assistant coach for the fencing team, teaching epee— his weapon of choice, for two years. Then he married Amanda. After Clarence was born, they retired to lives of leisure.

If my father had been a typical redneck gambler, addicted to horseracing, lotteries, sports betting, casinos or the dog track, our family might have survived. Gamblers Anonymous could have intervened and limited the damage.

My father, Richard was a Rochambeau— not a proletarian. He fancied himself a 'private investor,' but was a failed day-trader. There are no limits to the money you can lose on Wall Street. Dad battled my uncle over the valuations in grandfather's estate. Franc legally blocked the disbursements to my father. When my father died in a motorcycle crash on The Saw Mill River Parkway, he had never collected a single dime of his inheritance.

Typical of his 'bad timing.'

Clarence knew about wealth and money. And our family secrets— at least more than I did. He was well informed about our secret treasures. He must have overheard discussions of his parents and took mental notes. He swore that Sheldon Manor was haunted. And Grandpa kept a stack of *Playboys* hidden in the breakfront of his study, beneath a leather-bound volume of Alexis de Tocqueville's *Democracy in America*. He informed me that Grandpa owned a gun, a pistol for shooting red squirrels that invaded the barn where he garaged his white Lincoln Continental.

I snuck into his study one day and verified the *Playboys*. But I never found the ghost or gun. Nor did I ever dare to ask Grandpa about his pistol. Much less about his secret stack of *Playboys*.

Sheldon Manor had a 'Victory Garden' in the backyard. A flagpole overlooked the house and barn, next to the butt-end of the driveway. Grandmother tended to her herbs and rhubarb on a plot next to the flower bed. Grandpa's daily ritual included hoisting the American flag every morning after breakfast and strolling into town past the library to pick up *The New York Times*. He lowered it every evening. I 'd seen this ritual so often, I never gave it a second thought.

One Friday morning, in mid-July when I was fifteen, I had overslept again. I was at the age when it was impossible to wake me up in the morning. Grandma had given up trying, so she left me plates of sausages and scrambled eggs to heat up after I eventually dragged myself out of my bed.

I was starting my first year in prep school in September. As a tenth grader, called *middler* year at the Taft School in Watertown, Connecticut. My father was in the throes of his usual financial difficulties. Another one of his investments had filed for bankruptcy and was recently de-listed on the American Stock Exchange.

I suspected Grandpa would be paying my tuition at Taft. He had done the same at Exeter for Clarence and paid for summer camp for both of us, even though my uncle Francoise hardly needed the money. My parents were scheduled to arrive with Molly, later in the evening for a long weekend, with a family dinner scheduled Saturday night on Mirror Lake. Unfortunately, the beloved Lake Placid Club, where our family had belonged for decades had shuttered a few years earlier. We were all returning to Dobbs Ferry on Monday after breakfast.

I got dressed and scuttled to the kitchen. Both grandparents had left for the day, so I poured myself an orange juice and retrieved my breakfast plate from the fridge, ready to heat it up.

Then, I heard a gunshot.

I raced into the driveway. The barn door was open, but the big car was gone. Grandpa was standing in the garden, staring up at the flagpole. He turned and signaled to me with his right hand.

I waved back to him.

"Charles. Come here and I'll show you," he shouted, smiling as I trudged up the crooked rock steps to the garden. Something strange was going on. Grandpa wasn't flying Old Glory, but another flag of red, white and blue. The French flag, but I wasn't quite sure. He was flying it at half-mast.

"Who died? "I asked him. "Somebody important in France? "

"Very good, Charles," he replied. "You are familiar with the *Tricolore*."

He holstered his pistol, placed his hand on my shoulder. "Yes, we all did." Grandpa squinted, then looked me in the eye. "Charles, you are almost an adult. Do you know what day, today is?"

"Friday?"

"Also, *Bastille Day, Juilliet Quatorze*."

"The French Fourth of July. Why are you flying that flag at half-mast?"

Grandpa gazed at me sternly, his eyes narrowed.

"*Not* like Fourth of July in America. Le Marechal had returned safely home with his son, the Viscount in 1783, two years after the British surrender at Yorktown. At first, he sympathized with the revolution. But it wasn't the same. Not at all. This revolution wasn't about freedom. Only the mass slaughter of the *Ancien Regime* by the *Sans Culottes*. We *never* celebrate Bastille Day, Charles. No more than a Jewish family would celebrate the Holocaust."

At that time, the Jewish bloodlines on our family tree were unknown. I would learn the truth, decades later after Clarence took an Ancestry. Com DNA blood test. The current Rochambeau dynasty is rightfully traced to James Mayer de Rothschild in 19nth century France. He was a direct descendant of Nathan, the richest man who ever lived.

If the Lake Placid Club had been aware of that fact, my grandfather might have been blackballed. Even as a Rothschild. The club was renowned as a bastion of antisemitism.

Like Moses, I felt ennobled my Jewish ancestry. The realization my family was resilient enough to survive two momentous centuries, with revolutions

in both America and France gave me hope for my own survival. We even survived The Holocaust. I am blessed to be descended from many immortals in
the annals of World History.

I followed him, as we trundled down the craggy rock steps onto the
driveway.

"Grandma drove to Elizabethtown for groceries. Hope she doesn't forget
my favorite ice cream."

"Howard Johnson's vanilla?"

Grandpa tilted his head and replied, "*Le Marechal* turned against the
terrorists. He was imprisoned. After his release, he returned to our chateau
in Vendome. If Robespierre hadn't died, Jean-Baptiste would have been guillotined. Along with his son, The Viscount. I fire my gun to protest that *devil*
Robespierre. And the regime that beheaded thousands during The Reign of
Terror. They wanted a new world order. Tried to outlaw using names of the
days of the week."

"I didn't know that." I replied, shaking my head. I followed him to the
back door.

He turned to me: "I fly the *Tricolore*. Only at half-mast. Not as an act of
patriotism, but for the remembrance of French patriots murdered by terrorists...... I will show you, Charles. Something *important* in our living room."

He opened the screen door and I followed him into the kitchen, past the
breakfast nook and into the dining room. He stopped in front of the fireplace
in the living room.

"Look at this,'" he said, pointing to a rococo decoration. It was two feet
wide and three feet long, adorning the rose-colored French marble mantel.
The glass face was enclosed by filigreed gold leaf, resembling a clock with
a pair of lion's paws, clasped to the bottom. I had noticed this curiosity for
years. And never gave it a second thought.

"What's this crazy clock, Grandpa? It doesn't even tick."

"It's not a clock, Charles, it's a Napoleonic barometer. For testing atmo-
spheric conditions. In the nineteenth century, it was considered the latest
new technology."

I hadn't yet acquired my anathema for technological rages. Nor had I
suspected Grandpa would die of a stroke three months later. I remember his
death on October 19. The same date, back in 1781, when Cornwallis surren-
dered to Washington and *Le Marechal* at Yorktown. I never imagined how
grandfather's death would impact my family.

"Seems pretty cool to me," I had answered him, oblivious to my future.

He grabbed my finger and traced it over a black band on the face of the barometer.

"See this band. It honors the dead from families who lost loved ones during The Reign of Terror."

He let go of my finger, whisked his mustache and smiled with a concentrated gaze.

"Our family has served in many wars. Viscount Rochambeau fought in the American Revolution alongside his father as a teenager. He died for Napoleon as a young man in 1813 at the Battle of Leipzig. Other Rochambeau's sacrificed their lives under Bonaparte and in the fields of glory of The Great War," he said. "This barometer honors you, Charles. And our family's military history. It also proclaims the eternal glory of France... *Vive L'Ancien Regime.*"

CHAPTER EIGHT

I couldn't stop thinking about Emily. Or her troubled wedding. Madame worried about Emily's health, since her bout with anorexia in seventh grade. Her eating habits returned to normal after six months. This happened long before her parents' divorce. Or the tragic drowning death of her little brother, Anthony.

I was thinking about Emily, while driving to work on Tuesday morning. Then I saw an animal carcass lying by the side of the road. A dead deer, I thought, until I pulled off onto the shoulder and stopped the car. The mangled body I saw reminded me of a bull, rather than a deer. In truth, I've never really seen a bull up close, dead or alive.

It was no bull. The curved horns and body were too slender. Perhaps a beefalo escaped from the organic farm in our leper colony. I wasn't sure. Lepers are extremely health-conscious, nowadays. And major political activists. I knew I recognized the animal from somewhere. Maybe from my college days, as a frequent visitor to The Philadelphia Zoo.

An eighteen-wheeler barreled up the road. I got back into my car and continued to the estate. As I walked through the door, Chloe-Monster started barking from her cage. Roxy was doing the laundry in the basement. Beatrice had left me a note: 'Please have the bills ready." I pulled out the checking register from a drawer in the kitchen cupboard.

Bea wrote she was having 'luncheon' with the 'girls' at Sleepy Hollow Country Club. Which normally follows tennis with her group of 'girls' — all in their late sixties. Please note this subtle class distinction. Females of her kind, however elderly they are, refer to themselves as 'girls.'

Or sometimes 'ladies.' Only proletarians are called 'women'. The 'Girls' or 'Ladies' of her tennis group were enjoying the last vestiges of outdoor tennis. Until they relocate inside a bubble for the winter. Or so they had assumed. Shakespeare forewarned us in *Julius Caesar* to 'Beware the Ides of March'. Nobody could have presaged the Coronavirus that would arrive in March. The Pandemic that changed the world.

I sifted through piles of mail. Separating flyers, catalogues and bills into piles. In controlling her impulse spending, which I insist I have, Madame Beatrice yet remains on every mailing list in the shopping universe.

Bills, bills, bills. Water, electricity, telephones. Cable television, including a surcharge for The Tennis Channel. Essential, even in the off-season, until the Australian Open starts the season in February. Bea adores John McEnroe and his brother, Patrick. Never dare diss either one of them in her presence. I already told you but must remind you.

Many bills from Shamrock H-Vac. You've seen their trucks, if you live nearby. White Mercedes Sprinters with a glowing bright-green logo. I've seen them running on 84 West north of Hartford or as far away as Sturbridge Village. Shamrock was founded in the 1950's by William Ryan Keneally, a local plumber, whose father had immigrated from County Cork, Ireland. The Wolcott's were among his first loyal customers.

His son, Ryan studied nightly on heating and central air conditioning systems. Followed by accounting courses at Pace, after working full-time shifts. He took over Shamrock in his late twenties and married later in life, like Beatrice. He moved Shamrock H-Vac from Briarcliff Manor to a facility on the riverbanks of Croton-on-Hudson.

Ryan was more than a plumber to the Wolcott's. His son, Trey—William Ryan Keneally III was a classmate of Anthony Wolcott Alfieri at Hackley, before he drowned off Long Island Sound. Anthony was leaving for early soccer practice at Groton the next morning. The headmaster dedicated his first chapel sermon as his memorial.

I tore open four bills from Shamrock H-Vac:

Repair and replace slate on front walk. Slate $7. 87. 1/5 bag cement, per Berger's Hardware, including tax, $1. 77. ¾ hrs. labor $14. 35. Total: $23. 99 less $2.40 trade discount. Remit: $21.49

September. four trips; lawn mowing, weed whacking etc. two hours labor each trip. $139. 50. Replacement of dead potted plant $19.65 including labor $5. 45. Less $16.00 discount. Remit: $143.

Replace and install new KitchenAid 15" Built-in Trash Compactor in Stainless Steel # KTTS505ESS. Display model, scratch and dent— per contactor's pricing at Berger's—$1200.00, includes five-year extended warranty and applicable taxes. Please remit: $1200.00

CREDIT— $ 34. 59 Rain prohibited weed whacking on two Saturdays in August.

The prices were too cheap. Dirt cheap. So cheap, I referred friends looking to save money to call Shamrock H-Vac for quotes on landscaping and snowplowing. They were told to look elsewhere. My barber told me that the estimates he got from Shamrock for heating and air conditioning were 'a total rip-off'.

Something strange was going on. During my initial months working for The Madame, Roxy had told me to call Shamrock immediately after our ancient KitchenAid dishwasher died.

Twenty minutes later, I swear, maybe even twelve— Ryan Keneally, in person, swooped into the driveway and hopped out of a Mercedes truck in a blue suit, shirt and tie. Attended by a pair of smiling Spaniards wearing sanitary hairnets and dressed in immaculate white uniforms.

Ryan sat in the living room and talked to Madame Beatrice for almost an hour, as the Spaniards drove off for parts. Only one returned and he fixed the dishwasher in three minutes. Ryan, well into his seventies, retains the brash look of a handsome Irish youth with dirty-blond hair, sea blue eyes, tall and slim and still well-muscled.

An ice storm hit us all in early November. The next morning Ryan and my favorite landlord, the implacable Mister St. Ninny Poop dropped off twenty, fifty-pound bags of calcium chloride and a spreader from Ryan's Mercedes SUV. Hundreds of power lines went down all over the county, many roads closed. I was forced to stay home.

Madame Beatrice lost her electricity for the next two days. Yet, Ryan and Clodhopper plowed her driveway, shoveled her entrance and blanketed ice melt over the entire premises with spirited help from young Clod Jr.

Ryan was more than a friend to Beatrice— much more. His son, Trey was Anthony's closest friend. Beatrice was an eligible divorcee, but Ryan Keneally was happily married. Something was going on. It was obvious.

CHAPTER NINE

November arrived. I begged Madame to put Emily's wedding aside until next year. No reason to ruin the Yuletide spirit which I call The Holly Jollies. For anybody, not even Franny. Nobody had foretold a pandemic. My Christmas shopping was finished, and future trips would be curtailed until June, when Macys reopened in The Danbury Mall.

You will never see me in a department store from November to March. These 'sales' are fraudulent or outright scams. Stores charge 'bust out retail prices.' By Thanksgiving, retailers gradually withdraw discounts and promotions, mark things up and insidiously bolster their net selling prices and profit margins. A Holly Jolly season for retailers.

But a 'dreads' full one for an enlightened C.P.S like me, The Bargain Shopper.

The decretals of bargain shopping rule. Proletarians follow them instinctively, out of necessity. I have had problems buying from Macy's in recent years, due to drastic changes in pricing policies. They prohibit customers from using coupons to agglomerate extra discounts on items marked 'Last Act', 'Deal' or 'Final' on their clearance racks.

Kohl's has a few 'exclusions' on its coupons— but nothing like Macy's. Certified Professional Shoppers must maintain an average shopping 'mark' of 87.5 % to maintain official CPS accreditation.

Shopping is a battle of attrition. In the ever-changing retail landscape, since long before The Pandemic. Remember when the late, great SYM's closed its stores. Only several years ago— or so it seems. Bargain shoppers are always seduced by 'the thrill of the deal.' I can affirm 'It's almost cheaper than shoplifting.' The Bargain Shopper must be a *whore*. Precisely the kind of 'educated consumer' retail stores secretly *deplore*—or even *abhor*. Get it?

Here is my worst nightmare. This letter is my destiny.

KOHL'S CORPORATION
N56 W17000 RIDGEWOOD DRIVE
MENOMONEE FALLS, WISCONSIN, 53051

Dear Mr. Rochambeau:

We regret to inform you that we have canceled your credit card. It will no longer be honored, either on-line or at any of our 1159 nationwide retail department stores, effective *immediately*.

This unprecedented decision was initiated by our credit department, validated by our CEO, and ratified at a special meeting by a unanimous vote of our board of directors. On behalf of 122, 432 full and part-time associates, we would like to express our heartfelt appreciation for your participation in Kohl's MVP rewards club and our incomparable *Friends and Family* discount program for over two decades, with your impeccable payment history.

Unfortunately, and as our legal department insists, we must inform you our decision is *irreversible* —despite your A-Plus credit rating. This decision carries a *lifetime* sentence. We concluded a study of millions of Kohl's credit cardholders in 49 states over the decade. Our customer base generates a positive net gross margin of 36.7 % including normal overhead allocations for labor, plant, utilities and the absorption of costs associated with our net margins, like coupons, sales and promotions.

In every case, *except for you*, nationwide, this strategy has been profitable for Kohl's. We are a publicly traded, New York Stock Exchange (NYSE), symbol (KSS) corporation. Our loyalties are to our shareholders. Certainly not to you.

By contrast, an analysis of your purchases over the past decade is deeply disturbing, resulting in a negative gross margin of 29.837 percent for Kohl's. This number, adjusted to include other costs, including overhead, returns and allowances for inventory shrinkage, including shoplifting has resulted in even greater losses, not to mention the cost of the free shopping bags and gift boxes we sometimes provide.

Coupons and extra discounts linked to store credit cards are designed, as *loss-leaders* to encourage robust in-store traffic and stimulate incremental purchases by our customers of merchandise that carries higher profit margins.

Unfortunately, in your case, this strategy has failed miserably.

We estimate the adjusted full-cost losses to Kohl's on your purchases at 35 percent— even if you never use our bathrooms. This results in losses to Kohl's shareholders of thirty-five cents on every Rochambeau dollar spent. Since we compete in the private sector, it is necessary to inhibit inflows of deleterious **R** dollars, unless stripped of these incremental discounts. This will enhance our net profits and shareholder value. You are an *unprofitable* customer.

If you are considering legal action, our legal department refers you to the small print disclosure that accompanied your signature on your original *Credit Card Agreement*. It clearly states: *Kohl's retains sole discretion on the future use and eligibility of said card and can revoke such license or use by any person, for any reason whatsoever.*

Unfortunately, Mr. Rochambeau, we do not regret our decision. We prefer losing you as a customer forever. We encourage your patronage elsewhere. At our competitors, like Macy's, Nordstrom's or J.C. Penney, for as long as they can afford to stay in business.

RESPECTFULLY SUBMITTED,
MICHELLE GASS
CHIEF EXECUTIVE OFFICER

⚜ ⚜ ⚜

MY WRAPPING SEASON BEGINS. Our dumbwaiter, never too smart to begin with, decided to croak on me, instead of creaking. I only employ him once a year to move my hampers from the basement to the kitchen.

This year the pulley was stuck. Roxy Valdez, Beatrice's vigilant semi-live-in Chilean housekeeper was cognizant and nearby, so I yelled up the chute for some help. She started wailing. My mistake. So, I called Shamrock on my Jitterbug. As always, Roxy prefers to ignore my wrapping ordeal which she considers my silly pet project, rather than as an essential household responsibility we share in the service of The Madame.

I beg to differ. Roxy resents me. She hates watering the plants and begs me for help. Sometimes, I make a trade with her and do it myself. She complains about her 'tennis elbow', since she once heard Madame Beatrice use it as an excuse for skipping out on something. I am the undisputed *major domo* of this estate. And I must firmly draw the line.

Performing manual labor is optional for me in Domaine Wolcott. I do not water plants unless obliged by Mme. Beatrice. Roxy feels crucified and prefers to blame me rather than The Madame for the scores of thirsting philodendrons. I also sign her paychecks which makes me much easier to hate.

She curses me every day. In broken Incan or whatever pig English she mutters under her befouled breath. With three children, she is a major beneficiary of my annual Christmas booty call. Despite the remonstrations of *rigor mortis* over my dead body, Madame capitulates and wheedles me into wrapping gifts for her children. And boyfriend *du jour*.

Ryan's disaster *du jour* is to fix our dumbwaiter. I need to get my goods upstairs and into The Mirror Room assembly line ASAP. Then I spread them out and wrap them up scientifically, over the huge oaken table.

Ryan arrived in a larger truck with a crew of three men. He said that he had 'no clue how to fix 'a friggin' medieval contraption'. Two men were Spaniards. Mr. Kelly was an elderly man with white hair. He diagnosed a problem with the steel pulleys. It took them over an hour to remove the ballast and grease the assembly before testing it.

Ryan smiled, scrawled a bill, handed it to me. Mr. Kelly told me he was a retired carpenter from Tarrytown, living alone in his eighties. He had contracted hundreds of jobs for Ryan's father. I glanced at the invoice—$99.99 including tax. Shamrock never itemized taxes on invoices. Prices so cheap, I wondered how they stayed in business, much less afford a fleet of Mercedes? Cheap labor or illegal aliens. Maybe everyone was paid off the books?

The Chloe Monster started barking. The door swung open, catching us all by surprise.

Madame's older sister, Jill Roosevelt Wolcott Paulson rushed in and dropped a Big Brown Shopping Bag from Bloomingdales on the counter. She snarled at Ryan, curtly, as if she preferred to ignore him.

"So, the big boss *comes* again. Business must be slow?" Jill says to Ryan.

"Try doing repairs on an elevator from the thirteenth century."

Jill looks younger than Beatrice, but only artificially. You can tell that Jill tries very hard to look young. Her hair is blonde, except for the roots, double processed by Elizabeth Arden's in New York City every month. Her facelifts show dark lines. Then Jill sneers at Ryan and rushes into the powder room.

Ryan shakes his head in disgust as Bea barges in carrying two more Big Brown Bags, one in each hand.

"Hi Ryan— What misfortune has befallen my humble homestead today?"

Madame abandoned doing her hair colorings at a local hair salon years ago. Her headdress grows naturally in a brightly ennobled lily-white hue. She uses makeup on occasion, but only sparingly.

Ryan answers, "Your dumb waiter was shot. Thanks to Mr. Kelly here, I think we fixed it for another century. I think Donavan was the guy who repaired the catapults during The Siege of Jerusalem."

"Thank you, Mr. Kelly," Bea says, before turning to Ryan, as he followed his crew out the door. Madame looked over to me and winked "Don't worry, *Monsieur Bon Marche*," she said. "Jill bought all these 'minimum value' presents for Chip and herself. I never spent a single penny of my own money. Where's Jill. Hiding in the living room?"

The engine roared. Jill stepped back into the kitchen. But only after Ryan had driven away in his truck.

CHAPTER TEN

My fellow Pilgrims. I need to set things straight. I never flunked out of Taft, but I was *forced* to leave *voluntarily*. I can explain this apparent contradiction in terms. Halfway through 'upper-middler' year, after rooming for three semesters with Jameson Twombly, I chose, of my own free will and accord to return to Dobbs Ferry High School.

Nobody believed I hadn't been expelled. The headmaster and Jameson knew full well that I had never been caught with a girl in our room or was I ever busted for booze or drugs. Jay and I reunited in college. We still talk on the phone for hours, no texts or E-mails allowed. There is a tradition at Taft where students rub the nose of a statue of Abraham Lincoln in the lobby of a dorm for good luck. Jay and I promised to forgo this ritual entirely, unless we did it together. Jay is super competitive about everything, yet he remains my Vulcan brother.

Only cynical bastards believed the fake news that I flunked out of Taft.

Not that it matters. Flunking out of prep school has been a badge of honor among the elites, ever since it was romanticized in *The Catcher in the Rye*. Privileged students are wont to buy into the myth of a world besotted with 'affluenza', parental neglect and adult duplicity. This justifies not 'applying' yourself and 'getting the boot' in prep school, like Holden Caufield did. It has been accepted ever since as a legitimate excuse for failure.

Several guys got the boot during my first year at Taft. Neither was stupid nor lazy but possessed like a vampire with a Holden Caufield death wish. Was

Holden simply pandering to himself or was he suicidal? Did he have a problem with his parents? Why does it appear in the novel that he needed to flunk out of Pencey?

Some guys are rich, or so super-rich, they wear torn tee shirts and tape up the worn-out heels of their Weejuns. Their parents spend fortunes on purchasing 'shrinks.' The new normal in a brave new world of ultimate status symbols. Even trendier than owning a Bentley or a private airport. Some guys *want* to flunk out of school, like Holden Caufield. To authenticate their primal screams and existential distress. You know the type. Hiding behind the persona of an artistic, mildly rebellious nonconformist in a black shirt affecting a Jack Kerouac kind of coolness.

I'm sorry. I laugh at these guys. My problem was only *money*— the lack of it. Lacking the shekels to maintain respectability amongst my peers. I couldn't tolerate *anybody* feeling sorry for me. After all, I am a Rochambeau, regardless and I was *forced* to act *voluntarily*. It would be better for *everyone* if I dropped out of Taft.

Yet, I resented returning to public school. A big step down in the status quotient of my infuriated but confused teenaged sensibility. I worked part-time and full-time for three weeks, painting houses, after school closed in June. Then I packed my 1965 Volvo beater and drove to Atlantic City, at six in the morning on the Fourth of July.

I left a note for my parents. Otherwise, they might call the police. Two days later, I phoned home after finding a job and a place to live. I was barely seventeen but realized like Thomas Wolfe: *You Can't Come Home Again.*

I unshackled myself. Weary of relying on my father, listening to his promises. He never failed to disappoint us. Molly and Mom resigned themselves to living with his lies. Sorry, not for me. I've lived on my own ever since. Without even the dubious benefit of a high school diploma.

My first job in Atlantic City. A busboy at The Goose Head Tavern in Bally's Park Place, one of the newly built hotels. The job came with a cheap room no larger than a closet. With a tiny refrigerator on the ground floor of the utility annex. Public bathrooms, hot showers and a coin-op laundry were emoluments for hourly employees. An 'employee parking fee' was deducted, along with my weekly rent. I learned how the proletariat gets nickeled and dimed.

Restaurants were swamped. From a building boom since Atlantic City reopened for legal gambling a few years earlier. Labor was short, despite endless flotillas swarming into town on buses to perform menial day jobs. Dealers and pit bosses were blue-collar aristocrats of the casinos. I was too young to qualify but would have loved giving it a shot, working blackjack tables or roulette wheels. I started at rock-bottom wages on the local food chain.

I worked graveyard shifts. Hotel restaurants were open twenty-four hours. In November, as traffic slowed, I was promoted to waiter, working regular lunchtime and dinner services. Tommy Pagano, my boss, was middle-aged and married with two young sons. Soft-spoken with an operatic voice that barely registered above a whisper.

His daily trips from South Philadelphia were an hour each way. He told me listening to 'oldies' on his tape deck shortened the commute. I heard him humming Paul Anka and Bobby Rydell. He really appreciated me, I think, as he sometimes brought me cannoli from Termini Brothers bakery in his neighborhood.

Tips made a huge difference. Not to say they provided a living wage. Or I didn't need more money— a lot more to afford an apartment. I knew how badly I needed money, whenever I revved up my Volvo wagon with 210,000 miles and an oil leak. I started checking out want ads in The Inquirer for South Jersey, along with local papers.

I forgot to tell you. Yes— my parents were pissed off at me, especially after I didn't return home. But I spent Thanksgiving with them and Molly but told them I was skipping out on Christmas. I promised to return next summer and graduate from Taft after finishing 'my year-off.' I also informed them I needed to save money to pay for college.

A pack of lies. Things never work out the way you want. Nothing ever does.

Reading the papers, each day, it was impossible to ignore the headlines. The murder of Angelo Bruno topped the news on television and radio. Gaudy reports in the papers. The Philadelphia crime family was intertwined with Atlantic City. I could hardly keep track of the grisly details. Reports about hit jobs and murders popped up every week.

I had been to Quaker City only once. On a day trip with my fifth-grade class to Independence Hall and Liberty Bell. Tommy Pagano told me his brother Vincente ran their family restaurant in West Philadelphia. His wife was previously married to a soldier in the Philly mob. She kept him up to date. We killed idle time between shifts, talking about headlines, along with the latest scoop on the Flyers. I asked Tommy about the killings. The first time,

he squinted, but ignored me. The next day, he told me, shaking his head, that
'a major league mob war was in the works.'

I ended up finding another job. When I first arrived at Scarf, Inc. the
only thing I was thinking about was money. I was ushered into a sparsely
furnished conference room for an interview at ten a.m. It was generic but
immaculate, featuring a framed portrait of Rocky Marciano on one wall. The
opposite wall displayed a movie-sized poster of Sylvester Stallone, duking his
fists in the air in black Everlast boxing gloves. Rosemary Fozardi, the 'executive secretary' stood up to greet me and I sat down at an oblong table. She
smiled kindly. Then in a bizarre display that startled me, she erupted with a
barrage of apologies. There were literally tears in her eyes.

I had called her about the job yesterday, but she refused to discuss com-
pensation over the phone. The position was 'entry level' she asserted but
they were seeking 'a hungry up-and-comer' to join 'a growing family business.'
I scheduled the appointment and she asked in a whisper, how much money I
was making. I gave her an exact dollar amount. Of course, I lied— just as I had
lied about my age to qualify for the interview in the first place.

She let out a sigh. Every job at Scarf Inc. paid more than double what I
made, she said, even as I had inflated my earnings. Since New Year's, my tips
had been in decline. Rosemary's bleached blonde hair was garish, over the
top, but her soft features and smile compensated. She informed me the company's main business was 'concrete foundations.'

I scratched my head. I was so focused on money I forgot to ask for details. She had only spoken in generalities on the phone. Like, 'The company is
expanding ancillary enterprises' or 'utilizing special services with casino part-
ners.' Now she informed me, flush with pride. Scarf Inc. had recently agreed
to a 'major contract' to build the foundation for a 'luxurious new casino' with
'a famous, young New York real estate developer.'

Rosemary smiled at me, luxuriously. Then arose from her black, tufted
vinyl padded chair and intoned, "Please wait here for a few minutes, Charles."

Five minutes later, a tanned, middle-aged man in a dark blue suit literally
kicked the door wide open. Amazingly, he sat down like he was The Tower
of Babel. Talking and jiving with me like an old friend. He kept blabbering
away with his pitch-black hair, puffed out in a bouffant and streaked with
patches of gray.

He told me to call him 'Little Nicky.' Although, he said, he had several
other nicknames.

I assumed I was hired. This was a miracle, because I knew exactly nothing about concrete, except that I walked on it. My expeditious hiring was a miracle to me, as much as Christ walking on water. He kept on jabbering about 'opportunities in Atlantic City for an ambitious, young man.' If he was 'a sharp thinker with all the correct loyalties.'

I must have passed the secret Scarf Inc. acid test to get the job.

I told him I needed a place to live. Where I could live on the cheap and save money, so I could afford college. I had lied to Rosemary and told her I was over eighteen and graduated from Dobbs Ferry High School. Not that I expected she would check it out. Little Nicky's ears pricked up with the talk of my future ambitions. Yet, I sensed that little details mattered even littler to 'Little Nicky'. He laughed, clapped his hands together and promised: "No problem on my end, Charles. Even for a buck a month. I have no problem. I got something here."

He picked up a pen and notepad and wrote down an address. It turned out to be a fine location, a couple of miles from the Boardwalk. "Remember— only for nice guys like you, friends and family. I treat my employees right." He tightened his hands into fists and started shadow boxing the air. "Unless, they go really, really *bad* on me."

He kept on talking. Around in circles for twenty more minutes. Talking about 'loyalty' and 'respect in the local community' and so on. Then Rosemary stormed in, interrupting him with news of an upcoming meeting.

I had no idea what he meant. Or the skills I possessed, so essential to concrete.

I felt lucky to get out of that room before I blew it. I was afraid that if Little Nicky ever stopped bloviating, he might start thinking better, then change his mind and renege on his generous offer.

I felt sad telling Tommy I was leaving. I waited until the lunchtime until shift was over to offer the customary two weeks of notice. We shook hands, but he was too busy to press me for details. He'd assumed my new job was waitstaff at another restaurant and told me I could keep my room for an extra month. But I could start my new job anytime. He even volunteered to help me move. I thanked him, but I already had a new place lined up. Friday would be my final workday at The Goose Head Tavern at Bally's Park Place.

I called up Ms. Fozardi. I was ready to start. She gave me the address of my 'site location' in Atlantic City. My house key would be placed in the mailbox next to the front door.

Friday was busy. After the luncheon shift finished at two-thirty, Tommy waved me over to a table, recently cleared, and handed me a white box containing a baker's dozen of cannoli.

"Where are you going, Charles... Harrah's... Golden Nugget?"

"Into the concrete business. Business is booming, as long as they keep building new casinos."

"Which company.... United or General?"

"Neither one .... Scarf Incorporated."

Tommy furrowed his brow. His face became pale.

"Holy shit, Charles.... Haven't you been reading the papers... That's Nicky Scarfo from the Philadelphia crime family, you know, the Mafia boss... The kingpin of our union, Local 54. My brother was a year behind him at Ben Franklin High in South Philly. Everyone in the neighborhood knows he's a *made* man ... Get the hell out before you get into trouble. He might be behind the murder of Bruno.... if it wasn't Testa... Get out, Charles."

I nodded in agreement. "Okay, I'll be careful. He's the guy who hired me, but I don't know.... seems a nice enough guy to me." Then, I winked. "He told me that I should call him Little Nicky."

"Charles.... Scarfo is no nice guy. He's a wise guy. Known on the street as *Lethal* Nicky... or The Killer..."

Tommy got up and patted me on the shoulder. "You're a good kid. Just be careful."

My new place was a huge room in an old Victorian house, slightly smaller than a suite. My only valuable was my Bang and Olufsen stereo a Taft classmate gave me after I proofread his term paper on Baron Von Metternich.

If I had known how expensive it was, I never would have accepted it. He got an A on the paper and his father was rich as Midas. He was getting the latest model for Christmas, anyway. Other than my tunes, I hardly owned anything. A few boxes of clothes which fit easily into my Volvo. The move took one trip. Thanks to Little Nicky, I was moving up in the world. I had my own bathroom and shower, a kitchenette with a stove and a full-size Kenmore refrigerator.

I got an incredible bargain for my 'buck a month'. Fifty dollars was deducted from my bi-weekly paycheck at Scarf, Inc. I finally had spending money in my pockets. My room overlooked the street with a picture window. It lacked an ocean view, but had street parking and was only a twenty-minute jog to the Boardwalk along the beach.

I could live like a human being again. In daylight, instead of a dungeon, like a prisoner. My rent covered utilities, except telephone. The room was furnished with a table and two chairs, a loveseat in front of a color tv with rabbit ears against the wall. I promised Tommy I would heed his advice. So far, so good. Little Nicky was treating me like family.

My first day on the job, all I did was squeegee water off the cement foundation of a new mini-mall. The noise was earsplitting. Everyone wore hardhats, protective masks and earplugs. A layer of concrete had been laid out, rough and striated in many areas. The floors had to be smoothed using heavy grinding machines. Diamond studded rotary pads wore out quickly and were replaced intermittently. The foundation became red-hot from the abrasion and had to be cooled by an onrushing flood of cold water.

I wasn't allowed to touch the heavy equipment. My job was menial at best, requiring hard work and elbow grease. My back stiffened from the sweeping. But Pabst Blue Ribbons eased my aches and pains at lunchtime.

The job finished near the end of February. Nobody told me about my new job location, although I overheard a couple of guys griping about getting laid off. I was worried. Very worried. I got a phone call from Rosemary a few hours later on my last day of work, a cold and rainy Friday evening in March.

She told me that *Nicodemo*— not Nick, or 'Little Nicky'— the only time I heard his first name fully pronounced—'requested' I meet her at headquarters at nine on Monday morning. Her formal tone alarmed me. I asked her if everything was copasetic. Especially with me and Mr. Scarfo.

But Rosemary had already hung up the phone.

CHAPTER ELEVEN

You may have heard the tales circulating about 'bargain shoppers' with superior results. On reality cable, like *Extreme Cheapskates* or *Extreme Couponing*. Trust me. I can easily disprove these frauds. All they reveal is the ungodly state of our nation's bottomland. Gaudy spectacles that display the unscrupulous rebirth of P.T Barnum. *My 600 lb. Life* or *Dr. Pimple Popper*. A plethora of programs about 'Little People.' The circus carnival in America never really disappeared. It is alive and well and unsubtly recast to showcase the dregs of our cultural abyss on cable television.

Do you believe in charlatans? Then set up a 'Go Fund Me Page' for being a total moron. Or apply for reparations, since you were born an idiot. Obviously, you are a fool. Play Lotto.

I am The Bargain Shopper.

Several decades ago, I fired Mickey Drexler. The former CEO of The Gap. The visionary genius of retailing, a legend. Founder of Old Navy and C.E.O of J. Crew. In 2001, after 9/11, retail traffic disappeared. Nobody was shopping. Even after the stores reopened the following week. Old Navy was stuck with boatloads of men's Bermuda shorts. Six-inch hems, twenty-eight to forty-eight at the waist. The TRV was $19.99. Blue, red, orange and yellow plaids were off-color.

Sorry, Mr. Millard. These shorts were hashed out to five bucks— 75% off the TRV. Stacked into piles at the Peekskill store next to a Walmart.

Downscale. Marked down twice already, to the max. Yet, they would still not sell through.

Late in the season. Consumer confidence lagged. Old Navy needed floor space for the Holly Jollies. I followed my budding instincts as The Bargain Shopper. A concept not yet formally defined. I waited for an optimal moment. I had begun learning to maximize my utils. As I waited, these shorts were hard marked to ninety-nine cents.

By the end of October, the price was cut to 49 cents a pair.

I went into action. I had discovered the first decretal of The Bargain Shopper, although I dare say they are all essential: *If the deal seems too good to be true, then it's time to stock up.*

With discipline forged by Drexler's blunder, I began developing modern bargain shopping. I bought six storage bins at Walmart. I purchased sixty-four pairs of Old Navy shorts in a variety of sizes and colors. I sorted them out and stored them into plastic hampers. I officially transmogrified myself into The Bargain Shopper. I gifted these shorts for the next five years. Some recipients received as many as four pairs. Including all three Goldstein nephews, who grew into various waist sizes, slim as 28 and finishing up at size 38.

I still feel terrible for poor Mickey.

Only *slightly* off on his colors. The Gap disappointed on their next quarterly earnings report. I plead guilty as I had ruthlessly exploited Mickey's mistakes for my benefit. I maximized my utils, as I realized The Bargain Shopper assimilates the primal instincts of an animal. Like sharks, bottom feeders, or buzzards. In *Song of Myself*, Walt Whitman explains, *'I think I could turn and live awhile with the animals...They do not lie awake in the dark and weep for their sins...They do not make me sick discussing their duty to God.*

I pray for my sins. As I transmogrified into The Bargain Shopper, I fired Mickey Drexler, 'The Merchant Prince'.

⚜ ⚜ ⚜

NINE HAMPERS OF CLOTHES went up the dumbwaiter. After a trip for supplies at Dollar Tree in Peekskill, my wrapping was finished by Thanksgiving. Three boxes remained with gifts for birthdays or other occasions. The Madame's main job is to check all the addresses, since most gifts are sent to her friends. She dropped them off at UPS in December.

I forgot to tell you. Bea stores hundreds of boxes in her basement. Bloomingdales, Lord & Taylor and Bonwit Teller. From Best & Company, long gone, but with boxes interred by her mother. Or grandmother. Sturdy orange cartons from Richard's of Greenwich. She prohibits me to send out presents in these boxes from J.C. Penney, Kohl's, or Macy's.

She considers it a cheap trick. I never try to dupe, hoodwink or bamboozle my recipients. I believe fine boxes add value to the gifting process. Maximizing utils is a way of life. I simply have not yet convinced her of the value of marginal utility. Sadly, hundreds of fine boxes must fester in mold, mildew and dust in her basement.

Jill was hanging out, more than usual, with Bea in the Fall prior to The Pandemic. They met often over high tea, served by Roxy in the den, as I was toiling away, wrapping the gifts. I felt lugubrious, like Edgar Alan Poe. Remember *The Fall of the House of Usher*? His life's tragedy loomed over me in The Mirror Room. Directly over my head, as I peered at pallid Wolcott ancestor visages on ancient portraits. Or handsome, young Anthony Alfieri, staring me down.

The sisters were discussing Emily's wedding. Whenever, I heard the *Hallelujah Chorus* blaring from Jill's cellphone, I knew an A-lister was calling. Programmed to allow six full rings for DEFCOM ONE before vanishing into voicemail. Most of us organize our data, like names, alphabetically, for simplicity. Or geographically. Or other criteria. Jill Paulson created a Dewey Decimal System with a pecking order based on wealth. When she transferred her phone book from paper to digital, she customized her smartphone. Her directory was divided into five sections with different ringtones. DEFCON ONE, TWO, THREE, FOUR, or FIVE. Categories rated by the net worth of the caller.

DEFCON ONE had the ringtone from Handel's *The Messiah*— a hundred million plus. Several billionaires, but luminaries like Alyssa Milano and Chelsea Clinton or any Soros. DEFCON TWO required wealth of the fifty-million mark. Jill keeps abreast of business news. Relying on invaluable Greenwich gossip to realign the fluctuating financial rankings of her friends. Her phonebook is continuously updated with the current DEFCON status of her entries.

DEFCON THREE was assigned *We are Family* by The Pointer Sisters. Designed for calls from her son, Slayton, out on parole since his conviction for vehicular homicide was reduced to manslaughter. Jill spent an extra million on legal fees. Or her daughter, Alexis, married three years, following a million-dollar extravaganza at The Met to Gloria Alamode, National Executive Director of the ultra-feminist *Lavender Legionaries of the Sacred Pudenda*.

In many original and vicious ways, Jill displayed her unique, corrosive sense of humor. DEFCON FOUR includes the butcher, the baker and the candlestick maker. Even her lawyers and doctors are proclaimed by *Everyday People* by Sly and Family Stone. Assigned a paltry two rings, before swallowed into voicemail. DEFCON FIVE is for spam and 'undesirables' which are summarily blocked. Jill practices Witchcraft, also spelled with a B.

Jill Paulson lives in Greenwich. So, of course, she is rich. Which rhymes with bitch and witch, because she is three in one. She 'married well'. A euphemism of the upper echelons. I refrain from saying, 'upper class.' I forgot to tell you. Jill got rich by selling her soul to the devil, like Faust. You may dare to laugh at me, but I can prove it.

Nobody says, 'she married money.' Marrying 'well' insinuates class, professional or financial status. Used to disguise filthy lucre. Or insinuate wealth. Whatever. Yet, it must be approved or dignified by an allegedly competent body of jurisdiction. Like a family or 'proper' society. Take your pick.

Here lies the difference: Everyone agreed Jill married *well*. Nobody said that about Beatrice. Even though The Alfieri's were richer than the Medici's. And pricey automobile dealerships were only part of the story.

Joseph Anthony Alfieri started as the poor son of an Italian immigrant bricklayer. When he died, he served on the boards of hospitals, schools and savings banks. A pillar of the community. He owned landscape nurseries, a commercial real estate empire, cleaning and building contractors. Honest, but nevertheless blue-collar industries.

His reputation was impeccable. Franny and his younger brother Demetri—their mother was a Greek named Laskaris, graduated from Iona Prep. Which doesn't quite cut it amongst preppy elites. If an Alfieri had gone to Georgetown, their family might have received an indulgence from 'polite society.' Franny went to Fordham and Demetri to Manhattan College. Most Catholic institutions are not considered the 'right schools' to old WASP families, like the Wolcott's.

The Alfieri's were *not* 'the right people or did they belong to the 'right' clubs.

Jill had her wedding reception at Sleepy Hollow Country Club. Eight years prior to her sister's marriage to Francis, but long before her father,

Brooks III experienced financial disaster. Beatrice was the unlucky one. When Francis married Beatrice, Joseph Alfieri bailed out The Wolcott's and literally saved the family from public disgrace.

Not only did Joey pay all the bills. For both the wedding and reception. A lavish rehearsal dinner at the Four Seasons included fifteen Fugazy stretch limos transporting scores of guests to afterparties all over Manhattan, all night long. He also gave Brooks a huge unsecured loan that was never repaid. Brooky rarely spent a dime on anyone except himself, even long before his final impoverishment before he died young, as many society wags have observed.

The wedding was held on Joey's terms. Dictated by Lucille, devoutly Roman Catholic. Beatrice's aunt Ellen— ever alive, alert and still dancing in her nineties, nearly balked at attending the reception at Westchester Country Club. "I haven't been there for a luncheon, since it was taken over by all those *wop* contractors in the sixties," she remarked. Revered as the guest of honor at the wedding, Evelyn publicly referred to the arrangements designed by Nancy at Nico's Florists as 'Ginny La-La.' Apparently, she didn't realize that Nancy was Greek.

Sorry. I would like to be charitable. But I saw photos from the wedding album. And I must heartily concur.

CHAPTER TWELVE

With money to spend at stores and restaurants on the boardwalk, life in Atlantic City was a pleasure. Except for the fact, now I was worried about losing my job. I made a point of ignoring action in the casinos, where I saw signs of desperation beneath the bright lights. Somber faces of people going broke in a heartbeat. I chowed down at buffets in the casino's but snubbed the tables and slots. Open gambling only reminded me of my father. He preferred calling it investing. The rattling noises in my Volvo alarmed me with every mile, so I rarely drove out of town.

I kept 6 quarts of motor oil in the back since my cylinder head was cracked. I carried gallons of water, radiator and washer fluids. The radiator leak was minor. I had painted the car's exterior with gray primer last June before running low on cash and the door with the skeleton of a fish, using a pint of black sample paint for Black Fish Painters.

If Little Nicky had to lay me off, I was totally *fucked*. I would lose my subsidized rental. I considered dropping by to see Tommy Pagano at the casino. I hadn't seen or spoken to him, since I left The Goose Head Tavern. He worked Saturday nights and I wanted to ask him if I could get my job back, if necessary. I ruled this out at the last minute and settled for a long constitutional along the Boardwalk.

Stories were coming out every day. Mob killings in Philadelphia were ramping up. 'Little Nicky' was mentioned by name, but his involvement was rumored and considered speculative at best. I blocked these stories out of my mind. I realized I was just a civilian prole who wore a hardhat to work. But I suddenly regretted ignoring Tommy's warnings.

I didn't sleep well Sunday night but arrived at headquarters well ahead of schedule. I sat in my car for twenty minutes, rather than risk walking in too early. I didn't want to appear nervous. Rosemary's Cabriolet was parked in her spot. I crossed the ice-scarred lot to the front door. Scarfo's parking space was empty, so I breathed a sigh of relief.

Rosemary was dressed for Spring, in a bright pink and green resort tunic dress. I took a seat at the conference table. A large black coffee with some creams and sugars and a box of Dunkin' Donuts was set in front. For me, I hoped. I opened five packets of sugars and creams and stirred them together.

"Well, Charles, I have some good news and some bad news," Rosemary said.

I was dreading bad news. I grabbed a jelly donut and took a bite with a sip of coffee.

"I only like good news. Hit me with the bad news, first."

"Only good news for you, Charles.... Unless you're not interested in making more money. And I'm talking a lot more with all the extras," she said, with an eager smile. "Not just little tips. I'm talking big cash bonuses. You'll have to be more flexible in your hours and in a few other ways. You'll learn the game very quickly."

My eyes brightened. "I'm excited, Rosemary. What's the bad news?"

"Nothing relevant. You're not planning on staying a laborer, anyway. We lost that contract to build the foundation for an Indian-style casino. Nicky's furious at the asshole who reneged on the deal. Some guy who hasn't learned how to play by the rules, here in Atlantic City." Rosemary shook her head in disgust, as her eyes glared. "He's the son of a developer, some bastard rich kid from New York." She lowered her voice. "Nobody will ever trust his ass ever again."

"An Indian casino— you mean like a giant teepee?" I asked her.

Believe me, I choked on those words. But they still rolled out of my asinine mouth. I wasn't trying to joke about our company's latest misfortune. I was so coiled up and over-tired. Rosemary excused my inexcusable blunder by answering me with a thunderous peal of laughter.

I learned soon thereafter that the 'Indian casino', she referred to was 'The Taj Mahal.' And the 'rich kid, asshole, bastard from New York' was none other than Donald J. Trump.

"You're a funny guy, Charles.... Nicky and I have confidence in you. He's promoting you to the service sector of our business, the growth division. We partner with casinos to keep clientele loyal to the brand. Loyalty is critical. Unlike a commodity trade like concrete. He's directing a major reorganization of the family....... the family business. Nicky's very busy. Otherwise, he'd be here with us today. He sees your potential.... How's your car running?"

This odd juxtaposition of words alarmed me. "It's running okay— good enough, I guess. What's my new job involve, anyway? Not watering down concrete?"

"Relax, Charles. Sit home and wait for my call. Check your phone messages and mail. I'll keep you up to date." She pulled open a drawer and handed me a small black device. "This gizmo is called a beeper."

"What's this for?" 'Motorola' was imprinted with the company trademark. I fondled it in my palm.

"From now on, you'll carry it everywhere. Put it on your night table, before you go to sleep. It's a paging device. When it goes off, just call the number on the screen. Quick like a bunny, wherever the *fuck* you are. Call me collect... Comprendi? It's a critical tool in your new job."

"I'll get used to it."

"Don't worry. Nicky's taking care of you. Any problems, you call me. We'll take care of everything."

"Even when I'm not working, I'll still get my full paycheck?"

"Yes, Charles. And I almost forgot. Nicky's giving you a 25% raise."

My phone rang at seven in the morning on Wednesday. Rosemary whispered my assignment. I was meeting some guy at noon on Thursday in the lobby of the Holiday Inn, next to Philadelphia International Airport. Later in the afternoon, I got a telegram at home, with additional information.

The 'guy' I met at the hotel turned out to be an attractive Hispanic female carrying a brown leather suitcase. She instructed me to drop it off ASAP at Scarf Inc. headquarters.

I delivered it to Rosemary an hour later. She nodded, eking out a smile, but never even said hello.

She didn't call me again until Tuesday. I was instructed to pick up a briefcase at Scarf Inc. and exchange it at International Departures the next day. I got another telegram at home. The contact was a short muscular Columbian with a mustache. On my drive back to Atlantic City, my car started blowing out smoke and steam from the hood.

I pulled off the road after crossing the bridge. The engine was overheating, the thermometer bleeding red. I pulled out two jugs of water and a gallon of radiator fluid. It took half an hour for the engine to cool off. I filled up the radiator with fluid and water. It kept overheating. I stopped four more times, before limping into a service station on the outskirts of Atlantic City. My beeper had blasted three more times.

I was running well over an hour late and had lost track of time. As I finished talking to the mechanic about a new radiator, my beeper went off again. I called up Rosemary, collect at the Scarf Inc. headquarters.

She was breathless, in a state of panic. She ordered me to stay put, cautioning me not to do anything. Except never let 'the fucking briefcase out of your sight'. Then, she relaxed with a sigh, saying, 'Everything will be taken care of.'

In twenty minutes, a tow truck arrived. The driver, a laconic black dude who must have been ordered to tip the mechanic grandiosely—a hundred bucks in cash. I rode on the passenger seat back to headquarters. He smiled at me several times on the way, but never uttered a single word.

Rosemary was waiting for us, next to her car in the parking lot. I handed her the briefcase. She never said 'Thanks.' Or even acknowledged my presence. It felt weird. I guess nobody was talking to me.

Then, he drove me home. I asked him when I would get my car back. Or the estimate for a new radiator. He replied with a wink, "Don't you worry, Charles.... everythin's bein' taken care of."

And so, it was. Everything. Bigtime. At nine in the morning on Friday, I peered outside as a late-model Cutlass was being parked out front. The black dude came to my doorstep, his tow truck idling in the driveway. He passed me a package with title, tags, insurance cards and registration for the Oldsmobile. It had 9752 miles. All the documents in my name, signed with a replica of my signature. He handed me a leather-fobbed key chain, with both car and trunk keys. And a 'special key' for the glove compartment.

Rosemary called me later. She apologized profusely. She told me due to recent accounting adjustments, my paycheck would arrive a day late. Via courier on Saturday. It arrived the next morning and my raise was intact. But the fifty-dollar rent charge had been forgotten. Or was it forgiven, I wondered?

CHAPTER THIRTEEN

Jill's husband, Andrew Paulson Jr., known as Chip, was a 'late bloomer' who prepped at Avon Old Farms, graduating at twenty and six years later from The Cornell School of Hotel Administration, the only school at Cornell that admitted him, even though his father was a rich alum and trustee, who had majored in Astrophysics. Chip majored in Salad Bar Management and Technology. One of the 'right' schools because *technically*, it qualified as Ivy.

Andrew Sr. became CEO of American Food Processors, Inc, once listed as AFP on the New York Stock Exchange. He had also received an MBA from Harvard. When he died a widower, his only child, Chip, inherited his fortune. AFP was founded by the son of a redneck tobacco broker in Atlanta, who diversified by acquiring various brands of processed foods like SeaFine fish sticks and Dagwood buffalo wings. AFP also became infamously known as 'Big Junk Food' across the entire globe. And scorned as badly by The American Medical Association as 'Big Tobacco.'

Following Harvard, Paulson became a consultant for Booz Allen, assigned to the AFP account, before hired as an executive of AFP. Within a few years he was promoted to president and continued to reposition the company. When Boyd, the chain-smoking founder of AFP died of hardening of the arteries at sixty, Andy was named Chairman and CEO. He issued a huge public offering of convertible debentures and borrowed heavily from the banks. Then he started acquiring a string of regional fast-food franchisors, such as

Fido's Doghouse, Gaucho Burrito, Winkies Fried Chicken to expand the fast-food operations of AFP throughout America, Europe and Asia.

Thankfully, for me, like most other industry moguls, Paulson overlooked the opportunity to develop lucrative restaurant franchises for my idea, *Humble Grilled Cheese*. Please keep mum. An unintended consequence of Covid- 19 has been a delay in the commercial development of The Fartidalator, as proletarians have since been discouraged to congregate. I require large populations of mobile deplorables for my product to succeed.

Paulson's strategy was failing miserably. An outbreak of salmonella at Fido's was traced to dirt-cheap Mexican sauerkraut. Chip, who considered his twelve-hour work week, a distraction from the golf course, was promoted to Vice-President of Quality Control for Tummy Tum Hospitality Systems, the new restaurant division of AFP Inc.

Things got worse at Tummy Tum. Problems at Gaucho Burrito. One problem was customers biting into live maggots inside the burritos. Another was guests getting sick from eating the maggots, dead or alive. And puking buckets of vomit over shiny linoleum floors. For some reason, business slowed. Seven or eight customers died of food poisoning from the burritos, according to the CFO. The Chief Counsel argued that the little Asian girl who died had only eaten a single bite of *Chalupas El Grande*, so the correct number was seven.

AFP stock plummeted. From forty-five to seventeen. Ratings on AFP bonds and debentures were cut by Moody's and S&P to Triple C junk status. Word on the street was that Paulson had made gross miscalculations. Jill started worrying about money. She was calling up Beatrice to commiserate with her every day. Only a few years earlier, Chip had sold their modest home in Katonah and moved into a marble mansion in Greenwich with a gatehouse, heated swimming pool and four acres of Japanese gardens on Round Hill Road.

I visited the house once— once too many. Weeks after I started working for Madame, I met Jill for the first time in Briarcliff Manor. Jill had left her overnight bag with a silk jewelry pouch which contained a double strand of black pearls. Jill was planning on wearing them in a few days with a new gown from *Razooks* to a benefit at Greenwich Hospital.

I found it behind a table lamp in the den and volunteered to Beatrice to deliver it, in person, to Jill in her home and left swiftly for Connecticut in my Escort. I rang the bell and waited on the doorstep, expecting to be greeted by a uniformed housekeeper. Or as I fantasized, a livered footman in a white wig resembling an English barrister.

But it was Jill—Mme. Paulson herself in a ratty bathrobe. Peering at me from behind the front door, only half-open. You'd think she'd be cheerful or relieved. Smiling appreciatively for her necklace. Wrong again. Play Lotto.

She glowered at me with her unique scowl of deprecation. I can't remember the exact order of her slurs. Only the words of her last sentence that ended with: 'the servant's entrance is in the back of the house.'

I should have jammed the fucking purse through the door, before she slammed it in my face. Or turned on my heels and drove off. But I didn't. I hiked to the back of the house, where a housekeeper awaited me, unsmiling.

Unsmiling, I handed over the neckless.

Heracles, the Greek philosopher from Fifth century B.C. implored *Your character is your fate*.

I do not wish to drown in eternity in the Phlegethon, a river of boiling blood. I am many things, but primarily a gentleman despite many flaws. Madame Beatrice helps me service the classic ideals we share. I was newly appointed in the job and didn't want anything to upset The Madame. I never told Beatrice. She would have agreed I was treated like a dog by her wicked *bitch* of a sister. Perhaps, I should have confessed this episode to her, long ago. I have learned to appreciate the plight of the proletariat as well as the primal instincts of our species, as I am a Man of Science. Eating, Shitting and Fucking. Whatever. I hope that The Madame is reading my confessions right now.

The Wall Street Journal reported Paulson Sr. was doomed. He would be summarily fired at a secret emergency meeting of the AFP board of directors. The article noted his stock options would expire with his dismissal, per his employment contract and thereby become totally worthless.

The report rallied the markets for AFP securities. The CEO of *Big Junk Food* was marked down to zero.

Jill became suspiciously repentant. She hadn't seemed so contrite since the fourth grade, after she flambeed a litter of baby gerbils in a metal wastebasket. Now, she was confiding with Beatrice. Driving from Greenwich on Sundays to attend church, even praying in the pews of St. Mary's. Was she praying to God for deliverance from evil penury?

Or perhaps, praying to something ungodly?

Her husband, Andy Jr. would be fired alongside his father. Ending their careers in a blaze of industrial infamy. Chip would be forced to sell *her* new home on Round Hill Road. Was Jill praying to Lady Luck? Wrong again, it was Lucifer. Satan flew out of The Inferno in a rage, flapping his batwings, slaughtering every avenging archangel in his path. Jill had agreed to a deal with the Devil and sold herself cheap. Prior to the AFP board meeting, a private equity company suddenly tendered an offer to purchase the maggoty shares of AFP at a huge premium.

Lucifer smiled as things even got better for Jill. Shares of AFP soared as one the worlds' *biggest*—I can't say whom— private equity firm started a bidding war and won the battle, by doubling the premium on the previous offer. In 'A Pyrrhic Victory' by *The Wall Street Journal* 'Big Private Equity' grossly overpaid to acquire 'Big Junk Food.'

The Devil danced again and cuddled the bosoms of her craven bodice, as Jill accepted a Faustian bargain price for her cheap, rotting soul. She closed the transaction in the nick of time. Another aspiring witch—or bitch, take your pick, was sworn in by the devil as a minion of the underworld for the rest of eternity.

The next day, Big Private Equity announced a 'spinoff' of Tummy Tum Hospitality Systems, soon to be listed on the Nasdaq as TTHS following an IPO. A rising star from McDonalds was hired to turn around TTHS as president and CEO. To provide the young executive with 'experienced guidance' Andrew Paulson Sr. was named Executive Chairman. Zillions in salary, bonuses, equity kickers and options were offered 'to retain his invaluable business leadership.'

Paulson, the son of a grocery clerk, had only one ambition in life. Growing up in a fetid trailer park, he often wept as he watched his thrombotic, carbuncled mother scrubbing his ragged, filthy, smelly underwear on a rusty washboard in Moose Lake, Minnesota. But he dreamed of becoming a billionaire. After his death, The Forbes Four Hundred revealed that the formerly budding young astrophysicist and architect of 'Big Junk Food' had fallen well short in his earthly quest.

Jill Wolcott Paulson, his daughter-in-law and friend of the devil, would succeed in hers. With her pockets full of his money, she would become the finest specimen of a rich witch bitch that has ever been spawned in Hell.

CHAPTER FOURTEEN

Just so you don't think I'm crazy, the animal carcass lying by the side of the road wasn't a deer. Or a beefalo from the local leper colony. It was a water buffalo. I kid you not.

It escaped from The Stone Barn Center for Food and Agriculture, a few miles down the road, part of the Rockefeller Estate in Pocantico Hills. The scientific name is *Bubalus bubalis*, a species rarely seen in America. I saw the story on Channel Twelve news. The buffalo was killed by an F-150 pickup truck. The driver had forgotten his cellphone and returned home to Ossining right after the collision that morning, before reporting it to The Tarrytown Police.

Peggy Rockefeller maintained an organic farm. It continues today with a gourmet restaurant called *Blue Hills*. Wild game is an important staple of the menu. Everything is charged sky-high Rockefeller prices, which translates to *minimum* value. They maintain barns for the animals and a petting zoo. Don't ask me if water buffalo is served. I never pay an extra penny to eat organic. I Follow the Science and realize that all food is converted by our stomachs into tiny molecules of organic shit. Ergo, it's a waste of money to eat, digest or shit anything expensive including *Bubalus bubalis*. I used to eat water buffalo spare-ribs in Philadelphia, where they ran wild, but I still preferred cheesesteaks.

I decided to stay home for Thanksgiving. I finished wrapping, but I was planning a trip to Vermont to spend Christmas with Molly and family. They live on twenty acres off Upper Hollow Road in Dorset. Twelve bedrooms and four kitchens in four adjacent buildings. Mom resides a few miles down the road in her assisted living facility.

Christmas dinner is served formally in the main house. It's funny watching mother hobbling around the kitchen, like *she* owns it. She spends the morning scolding Pierre, the head chef, who had retired three years ago from Michelin's four-star, La Tour D' Argent in Paris. Mom orders him around like a peon, using remarks disguised as questions, while dipping her fingers into all the bowls of sweet potatoes, cranberry sauce and turkey gravy.

As you surmised, Dr. Goldstein, the psychiatrist is rich and famous. He graduated from Harvard, Yale Medical School and served his residency at UCLA studying under a professor with some funny long name. You've seen many of his articles on the cover of *Psychology Today* as well as other psychiatric journals and popular magazines.

Jeffrey is semi-retired. He focuses more on his research but has been a god-send to our family. Especially when Mother goes off the rails. Molly might have even married Jeff, due to Mom's chronic mental illness.

They have three sons, all married. The two younger ones, with wives and children will be spending Christmas with us. My godson, Dylan and his wife, Lauren are staying in Maui, as she is expecting her second child in mid-January. I wrapped over sixty presents in forty-five boxes to outfit The Goldstein Army this season.

Madame invited me to join her for Thanksgiving dinner. Emily will be driving to Worcester with Peter to spend it with his parents, but Charlotte is flying home from Atlanta with a new boyfriend. He's divorced. Nobody in the family has met him yet, so I declined the invitation. I want Bea to forge her own first impressions, unfettered by mine.

I left work early Wednesday afternoon and picked up a cooked turkey breast at Shoprite on the way home. Then I called up *Zachy's*, a wine store in Scarsdale to help curate my annual extravagance—four bottles of wine to grace the Christmas dinner table at the Goldstein's and toast Charlemagne. I decided on Chateau Mouton-Rothschild.

I refuse to disclose the vintage. Or how many francs I splurged. It is the *maximum* in minimum value, like dining at the Rockefellers. Last year, I brought Chateau Lafitte-Rothschild, a similar *premier crus* Bordeaux and its brother from Paulliac, a little town in the Upper Medoc in France.

I encourage Molly to foster family pride, including our connection to the French branch of the Rothschild family. Even if it costs me a king's ransom.

Legendary vintners, like Baron Guy and Phillipe de Rothschild are as important to us as Charlemagne. They are part of our history. A legacy Molly should be proud to share with Jeff and her offspring.

The Rochambeau military heritage is prominent on two continents. Pride strengthens family *bonds*, far more than a dreary *bondage* to the past. A glorious, rather than effete homage. My choice of wine is worth every penny.

Mother denies our legacy, a flat-out rejection of our Rothschild and Rochambeau heritages. Obviously traced to my father, Richard and her own unstable mental condition, which compels her to block out the names and dynastic achievements of my ancestors. They seem provoke tragic memories of my father's failures.

Back to my confessions. I ate a turkey dinner and called up Jameson in Wellesley. I left a message on his voicemail.

Speaking of whom, I first met Jameson Bigelow Twombly while I was *pissing*. After I first moved into my dorm at Taft, I had to go to the bathroom. A preppy dude dressed like Gatsby in a pink polo and pink and white-striped seersucker shorts, stepped up to an adjacent urinal. Then he looked me in the eye with a wicked grin and said:

"*I'll do business with anyone. But I only sail with gentleman.*"

I didn't get it. I figured the *business* part was the *pissing* part. You know—doing your business. The worst thing you can be at prep school is a straight arrow or doofus, so I needed a comeback. *Anything* that would work.

"*I'll piss on anybody, but I only shit on pink gentlemen.*"

My *riposte* seems lame. But it cracked us both up in the high prurience of our youths. We were condemned to be roommates. Humor helps you make friends as long as the jokes work. It always helps to make friends.

Bathroom humor is the lowest form of comedy. According to the pedantic colleges of academia. Ruthlessly devalued by every discourse since Aristotle's *Poetics*, right up to Henri Bergson and his essay, *Of Laughter*. I heartily disagree. The time is now ripe for an update. To demonstrate bathroom humor to the intelligentsia, not just the proletariat. To develop a framework for a *nouvelle* epistemological platform, The General Theorem of *The Scatological Sublime*.

A philosophical debate will emerge between nominalist and empiricist factions resulting in a dichotomy between opposing *analytic* and *synthetic* derivatives. Scholars and literary artists will debate the assumptions and tenets of a 'New Aestheticism.' Interpreting bathroom humor a *priori* through a didactic filter of conflicting axioms and absolutes.

Oscar Wilde raised the decibel level of this controversy. And the conscious-ness of *Literati* after publishing *The Picture of Dorian Gray*. The arguments continue to this day. Yet, The Academy prefers to retain at will, the impe-rial audacity to summarily reject many verities well-proven in The General Theorem. Our world is a living Hell. And I can prove it. I was born from half a zygote as 'The New Adam.' Please excuse my French. I don't give a shit. No pun intended. I devoted my life as an epicurean of *The Scatological Sublime*. I am a Man of Science who tells the truth. Many consider me puerile. I prefer 'young at heart.' Fuck them all. It is of little consequence on Planet Moribund. Like Dorian Gray, I find no pleasure aging ungracefully. We must face the incon-trovertible truth about gender and proclaim: 'Boys will be boys.'

I will only tell the truth. I am The Bargain Shopper. Not a literary *ar-tiste*, like Dylan Thomas, Gerard Manly Hopkins, or Shakespeare. I consid-er *South Park* a comedic masterpiece. The anguished Mr. Hankey, famed as The Christmas Poo, is a concrete *ad hominem* parody of despair. *Gestalt* like Hamlet but resembling Macbeth. At least, physically. A caricature, albeit a mushy one, masquerading as a merry, yet tormented figment of a fully secular-ized modern turd.

I will follow my bliss.

Jay Twombly dressed like Gatsby and quoted J.P. Morgan. Like my cousin, Clarence, he understood Money and Society. We shared fantasies about hot chicks and were screwed by coaches for crummy athletics. Or by the faculty for our shitty grades. Fragrant sticks of votive incense burned through the arms of The Buddha on our windowsills. The blasphemy of religion, masking smoke from our pipes and bongs. I hung out in The Tabernacle with Jay and others after lights out, pitching pennies under the peeling plaster next to the urinals , or Fart Lighting into oblivion in The Inferno.

Our temple for nocturnal discourse, despite our microaggressions and transgressions, we represented democracy in action. Pennies rolled into the uri-nals at night. Losers were sons of privilege and obliged to fish them out of a stinking abyss. America lacks a hereditary nobility, Jameson explained. Every family, no matter how wealthy or august diminishes over time. Revitalization occurs through marriage. New wealth from aspiring families must be pumped into the veins of old, ossifying American lineages. Lest they vanish from his-tory. Families become effete over time. Only one moneymaking genius occurs per century in any family, Jay explained. Except for the Dupont's of Delaware.

J. P. Morgan would 'do business with anyone.' He fought off *arrivistes* and *parvenu* in drawing rooms, *tres gauche*. You *must* do business with *nouveaux riches* in this class struggle, if your desire is to 'only sail with gentlemen.' I call this The Twombly Conjecture. A theorem combining Darwin's Theory of Evolution with the political abstracts of Rousseau and *The Philosophes*. You may also call it 'The Evolutionary Social Contract.'

I will summarize Twombly: wealth is the insurance for the 'Survival of the Species.' You must marry money if unable to make it yourself. Jameson considers us 'The Species of the First Estate'. He once told me: 'To marry advantageously beneath oneself is merely taking dung to manure one's acres.' So be it. I must heartly agree.

✤ ✤ ✤

GRANDFATHER ROCHAMBEAU DIED IN OCTOBER. He had only been billed for my first semester at Taft. At Christmas break, I overheard my father talking to my uncle Francoise. Grandpa had split his estate into two parts, with half bequeathed to Grandma. The other half was to be shared equally by his two sons.

My uncle had discovered a shortfall in the estate. Millions invested in a portfolio called 'Pledge Accounts' under the auspices of a bankrupt Wall Street firm called Nemours Securities. Investments still listed as part of the estate, but they had been liquidated years earlier, he explained, in a lengthy memo to my father. Nemours was connected to the Dupont dynasty. Yet, another case of 'bad timing', for my father. Apparently, the Dupont's had exhausted their rightful allotments of geniuses. Just in time for me to come romping along with my empty piggy bank.

I confided to Jameson when I returned to Taft. Grandma was doing better, adjusting slowly, but facing unexpected financial concerns. My father had bounced the tuition check for the semester. My mother was furious. But my father was screaming and cursing at her, as his investments continued to get hammered. In a burst of rage, he even called my mother a *whore*. Not only was his inheritance delayed, it was many millions less than he expected.

Money. My apocalyptic vision and attacks of the natty dreads. I never knew I had a twin brother, until I was enslaved by The Archangels of Golgotha. With the love of God, Jean-Baptiste saved my life and I escaped from this cult in my middle thirties. I'll tell you later in my confessions. Unbelievable. I only tell the Truth in my confessions.

I never graduated from Taft. A full scholarship would not have helped. My father was always a dollar short. The only son he ever loved was named after *Le Marechal*. But the tender heartbeat of my brother had stopped long ago. And I was born to live during The Great Pandemic. And damned to burn into ashes forever in the Valley of Jehoshaphat.

As for my father, Richard. He was nothing but a born deadbeat.

CHAPTER FIFTEEN

I never saw Little Nicky again. I followed his story for decades in newspapers, after I heard he had been sentenced to over forty years in prison. He died in custody, a few years ago. I might appear to be blasé and naïve about trafficking in cocaine. I must confess I wasn't in the least innocent. I was a teenager with nowhere to go. Nothing to do. Praise the Lord, I survived. This experience has given me permanent attacks of the dreads.

My new car was equipped with a tape deck/ radio. A fuzz buster on the dash. The glove compartment opened with a 'special key.' Inside was a switchblade, a box of Puffs and a loaded twenty-two Beretta. The trunk was outfitted with jumper cables, brass knuckles, a spare tire, and an official Mike Schmidt baseball bat. Little Nicky showed his civic pride as a Phillies fanatic. Later, I learned that wooden bats were standard accessories in the trunks of mobster cars.

After my initial pick-ups, and another exchange at the airport, Nicky moved me into retail. I became a 'mule' making 'house calls' in private suites of 'Whales' at Resorts International and Golden Nugget. I delivered cocaine by the kilo. Bundles of cut powder marked blue. Or uncut rock, marked red, wrapped in brown paper. Whales were the ultrarich clients who wagered thirty-grand on a single roll. Even more in chips at the craps tables.

'Toot Parties' ran fulltime. Hookers in silk lingerie or black lace panties, like in the saloons of old-time cowboy movies. They were cute with me. They smiled and pinched me on the cheeks. Or on the crotch, stimulating my erogenous monster, Mister Dingle Screw. They whispered sweetly, pleading for hot fun, fluttering jet-black eyelashes.

All the stereotypes were correct. On return calls to these lavish suites, I brought gifts of long-stemmed roses. Along with extras like hash pipes, Quaaludes and dime bags of pot. I'm not telling specifics. My insatiable monster could have fucked them into oblivion or got sucked off *gratis* more than you could ever imagine in my most succulent dreams.

Hookers weren't worried if I was underage. Some of them were younger than me. I decided not to snort my profits from the gram bags of coke I got in tips. Rosemary convinced me to trade them for thick wads of cold, hard cash.

In April, following a cash drop and pick-up at the office, Rosemary handed me my first bonus in a brown wrapper— a $5000 cash bundle of twenty-dollar bills. Three weeks later, my bonus doubled. And I was averaging $700 a week in 'tips' without any deductions for rent. My car insurance was prepaid for the next few months. I was rich.

Rosemary called me one Friday afternoon. *Nicodemo* requested I meet her for another conference on Monday afternoon. She told me not to worry, "Everything was being taken care of."

This time I didn't worry. Maybe I should have.

After brunch on Sunday, I ran into Tommy Pagano, walking right out of a coffee shop on the boardwalk. I had intended to go over to my old haunt some night for good food and palaver. Like other things in life, I simply never got around to it. Or maybe I just forgot. "How's concrete treating you?" he asked me.

"Hard as hell," I answered, with a wink. "Scarfo treats me very good, Tommy. My new job is a lot more stimulating. I got a promotion and a big raise. I'm in the service sector now, dealing directly with customers."

"That's wonderful Charles... but word on the street is Nicky's not doing too good in concrete. He lost the Taj Mahal and most of the majors. I heard his cement work is very substandard. Sure, he gets little jobs, here and there. Probably just enough to keep his name on the shingle."

"Are you sure, Tommy? I've been very busy. They've delivered on everything they promised me."

Tommy stared at me for an interminable minute. Then he started shaking his head, from side to side, directly into my face, as he moved closer. "Get your ass out of there, Charles, before you wind up in jail. Or wake up sleeping in cement pajamas. Haven't you been reading the papers? Everyone knows

Scarf Inc. is a cover for the extortion rackets. And the front for his dealings in prostitution and drugs."

"I'll keep an eye on it. So far, so good, they treat me like family. They take care of *everything*."

We shook hands and walked off in opposite directions. My appointment was at two on Monday afternoon. Rosemary was sharp-eyed and went straight to the point. "We're having a problem with our main supplier, Charles...... I mean, our supply chain. These fucking foreigners are sending us shitloads of adulterated crap."

The oddity and magnitude of her language caught me by surprise.

Rosemary squinted at me and continued, "Nicky's just found a new guy he thinks we can trust. A young guy, a college type like you, who's learning how to become a dentist in West Philly. We need to move you into a safe house we own, right next to his dental school on a college campus."

"You've been giving me free rent. Give me the same deal, I'll be packed and ready to go in a week."

Rosemary issued a wan smile. "Absolutely.... Actually. The truck with your stuff is halfway to Philly."

I frowned visibly. Then I almost choked. "What about all my—"

"—Don't worry about your bonuses, Charles. They found all your cash under your bed. All three bricks. We're depositing them into a safe deposit box in a local Philly bank. Call Ernie at the branch and pick up the key. Set up an account. He's changing the license plates and registration on your car. He's a friend of the family. The only banker we trust there. Here's your new address and phone number. Your phone is connected. Here's the rest of your info."

She handed me a house key and three index cards. My new address was on 48th and Larchwood. One card had Ernie Palumbo's address and phone number. The other had a phone number for my contact, Dr. Snowden Lawrence.

"Don't worry, Charles.... Relax. After move-in, take a few days off and check out the city. There's a beautiful drive along the river. You'll love the cheesesteaks. Nicky's taking care of everything."

My new house was a row home, three stories high and furnished. A king bed was already made up in the master suite with four pillows. And a blue plaid comforter thrown over matching dust ruffles. I breathed a sigh of relief. I was moving up in the world. The windows were adorned with plush burgundy curtains and matching cornices. The blinds were shut, so I opened them to invite the fading daylight. The house smelled harshly of disinfectant,

as if it had been recently fumigated by professional cleaners. An uncapped
bottle of Ajax had been left in the sink.

After returning with groceries, I called Dr. Lawrence. He never picked
up, so I left him a message and unpacked cereal, maple glazed donuts and
Doritos onto the counter. Before I loaded them into a cabinet, I had to remove all the contents: four Arm& Hammer baking soda, six boxes of baggies,
metal bowls and sifters, a set of Pyrex glass bowls, two tiny sterling silver
spoons, an electronic digital scale and a pair of walkie-talkies, unpacked in
the original box.

I took Rosemary's advice and drove around the art museum and past
boathouse row along the Schuylkill before exiting by the statue of Ulysses S.
Grant on horseback. I turned a hard right towards Strawberry Mansion and
noticed a Frisbee golf course in the woods, outfitted with steel baskets. The
next day, I purchased two 165 grams discs at the University Bookstore and
returned to Sedgley Woods, as I learned the course was named. I played two
successive eighteen-hole twin rounds of disc golf and even broke par by two
shots on one with a score of fifty-three.

⚜ ⚜ ⚜

DR. LAWRENCE WAS BORN with a *simper*. The best description of
what he flashed me in April, when I first met him. He reminded me of *Doogie
Howser*— too young for a doctor. But a lot more like the Doogie on drugs in
the *Harold and Kumar* movies that came later. He was certainly the classic
druggie, only he was dressed in a white lab coat.

His personality matched his character. He wasn't yet a doctor or a dentist, but a student. At University of Pennsylvania School of Dental Medicine.
His coat pinned with an impressive-looking badge. His name engraved on it,
so I wouldn't have known if he was a doctor or a quack. Yet I must admit, he
seemed to me, a very nice guy.

We exchanged identical black Halliburton briefcases in the lobby. He
asked me in a whisper, if my car was 'clean' and I stuttered 'yes' since I had
just taken it through a carwash, since I had left Atlantic City. I had parked it
a dozen blocks away from the dental school on Larchwood. After I made the
switch, I jogged home through a drizzle carrying the briefcase and locked it
into the trunk of my Cutlass. Then I drove off immediately to Atlantic City.

The following week, we made the exchange at Allegro's on Spruce Street. A campus restaurant where he offered to buy lunch. We sat down on a table with a plaid tablecloth and chowed down on Italian hoagies, a large order of French fries and two Cokes. Snowden was wearing his civilian garb, blue jeans, slightly shredded at the knees, along with a faded maroon Exeter sweatshirt.

I told him my cousin Clarence had gone to Exeter. And I went to Taft, but I never graduated.

His answer surprised me but confirmed his adolescence. "Either did I. I got caught smoking pot in my room a few weeks before graduation. I think I vaguely remember your cousin. Did you flunk out of Taft?"

"No. I left on my own accord. My father really couldn't afford it."

"Either could my mine, but I had a full scholarship, before fucking up. I learned a valuable lesson in life, Charles: Don't be careless, but whatever you do...don't ever get caught," he bellowed, as I noticed his fair skin was imbedded with freckles. "What a bummer. That blunder almost cost me my admission to Penn, along with my scholarship."

"How did you pull it off. Most colleges, especially prestigious ones, withdraw their acceptances if you get busted or get booted out of high school, especially without a diploma?"

"Elementary, my dear Watson, I bullshitted my way out of it. To an admissions officer, like I always do," he said with a smirk. "How do you like A.C? I love The Golden Nugget. What a comeback for sex, drugs and rock and roll. 'Things go better with *coke*,' he said with a laugh, as he lifted his cup of soda, along with his level of bullshit. "PCP with angel dust hurtling outta my fuckin' brain. Wowwwweee. Dude. We gotta do some freebasing."

I paused to process his request. "I don't know. You can't be too careful, Dr. Lawrence. I don't do drugs, but I need the money, so I stay sober," I continued, sounding like the only adult in the room. He was becoming evasive.

"Shit on Shinola.... What am I going to do?" he shrieked. "I fucked up bigtime... Now I'm getting fuckin' married.... How crazy is that?" He sighed. "And I'm getting fucked in the music business. How old are you anyway, Charles? Tell me your whole story. Don't lie. Tell me the truth."

"Old enough to rock and roll, but too young to die. I just don't want to die broke."

He seemed to appreciate my humor. The following Wednesday, he asked me to meet him in the heart of campus. We sat down together on the pedestal beneath the statue of Benjamin Franklin.

After exchanging briefcases, he surprised me by handing me a cardboard box.

"Try these on for size, Charles. You live in the student ghetto. Start looking and acting the part."

The box was full of shirts. Penn sports jerseys. In the school colors, red and blue. Three tee shirts, two sweatshirts and a stained white polo, inscribed with the University emblem. I laid the polo flat on my lap. Four concert tickets were appended to the pocket by a roach clip. Tickets for a concert by *The Dead Milkmen*, a local punk-rock band.

"You mean, I should look the part of a starving student?" I asked him.

"Not around here. Nobody starves in the Ivies, Charles. Everyone lives like royalty, even if they get a free ride. Don't bullshit me. You come from money. Old money that ran out. Don't lie. I got my doctorate in bullshitting, *summa cum laude*. I went to fucking Exeter, for Chrissakes. I know old money when I see it. How did your family go broke?"

"The usual way. Bad investments. Laziness, stupidity. Something like that."

Dr. Lawrence nodded. "I get the picture. Another poor boy held hostage in a rich kid's world. I know that syndrome very well, Charles. Just stay incognito around campus, like you're a student. You have the right camouflage in this box. Change your name, so you can't get traced by the police. Rochambeau screams of prominence, loud and conspicuous."

"I'll think about it."

He squinted his eyes. "What do you *really* want out of life, Charles?"

"To bark at the moon. But I'll settle for becoming rich. Poverty sucks."

He escorted me to Houston Hall, and we sat down for lunch. I insisted on picking up the check. Then he gave me a walking tour of the campus. He asked me about my cousin, Clarence, but I didn't answer. We looped past Franklin Field and up the steps past the Furness building. Strolled over to the library again. As we turned onto Locust Walk and past 36th street, he pointed to his old fraternity. Snowden was an incredibly nice guy. Especially, for a cocaine dealer.

We turned into the walkway of the house. The living room was vacant. Oak paneled walls were covered with plaques and framed composites. I followed him into the basement and allowed him to beat me in a game of ping pong.

After we departed and crossed the 38th street bridge into Superblock, we split up on the sidewalk near the dental pavilion. Snowden never stopped simpering. "Don't look suspicious and you'll be fine. You're a good man Charlie Brown. And I must admit that for a preppie, you really got *balls*."

CHAPTER SIXTEEN

Jameson finally got around to returning my call on Friday night after Thanksgiving. His wife and kids had gone traipsing through all the shopping centers in Newton and Wellesley. They could have done it on-line, he complained. I reminded him that I considered Black Friday 'Amateur night in Dixie'. His family was lying in front of the tube, playing video games and had finished all the leftovers. Except Jay, who refuses to eat leftovers. He had just grilled himself a Porterhouse.

"If Trump lived in the gilded age, he would have died of excessive venery like Vanderbilt," Jay said.

"What the hell is venery?"

"Too much sex. That's how Vanderbilt's doctor explained it to his family. That his enlarged prostrate was due to gonorrhea. Cornelius Vanderbilt died in his mid-eighties."

"Trump is venal, not venereal," I replied. "How could you ever vote for Trump?"

"Most pundits say Trump is more like Andrew Jackson, an imperial populist. Read Vanderbilt's biography. With his whoring and arrogance, Trump reminds me a lot more of The Commodore. I don't like Trump any more than Vanderbilt. They have too much in common with Trilmachio. They are both vulgarians."

"J.P. Morgan was just as arrogant," I said. "But you love his ass."

"Morgan had taste. And *noblesse oblige*. Absent in Vanderbilt or Trump."

"All the robber barons are burning in Hell. I know you voted for Trump. Admit it. You only vote Republican."

"Actually, I'm a registered independent. A classic liberal in the true sense of the word."

"Give me an example."

"I'm liberal on social issues. Like Roe versus Wade. I vigorously support Planned Parenthood."

"Of course. Margaret Sanger. Eugenics and legal genocide. So, the ghetto won't plunder Wellesley."

"Race has nothing to do with it, Charles. It's about freedom of choice."

"That's a crock, Jay. You said Obama reminded you of Dr. Zaius in *Planet of the Apes*."

"I never said that, you idiot. I said he displayed the same *kind* of arrogance and condescension as the head ape in the movie. Obama was always talking down to *everyone* from his bully pulpit."

"Human or monkey?"

"Simian. Monkey is considered a slur in our new age of political correctness. The answer is both species, Charles. Obama is an arrogant human bastard. You can't trust him. Ask Dershowitz. I ran into Alan in Aquinah last July, bouncing along untamed on Moshup Beach. He told me that Obama owns one of biggest estates on Martha's Vineyard, but he's never even been invited over to his home, ever since Barack stabbed him in the back."

"I thought Obama was his former student at Harvard."

"He was. And they used to be friends. Until Barack broke his promises on Israel, right before he left office."

"Jameson. Have you ever considered that perhaps, *you're* the racist?"

"Absolutely yes.... and positively no. I am not, nor have I *ever* been a racist."

"You sound racist to me. How can you be so sure?"

Jameson paused to clear his throat. I thought that his phone went dead, but Jay only had a brain freeze. "I was a huge Knick's fan, as a kid," he uttered weakly. "The Knicks won two NBA championships under Red Holtzman."

"So what? Plenty of racists watch the NBA."

"......But my favorites were Frazier and Reed. There were also great white players on those teams, like DeBusschere and Lucas. My father went to Princeton and worshipped Bradley, even though he wasn't a basketball fan.

They were all inducted into The Hall of Fame. Frazier's son captained Penn basketball. If I was a racist, my law firm would fire me."

"No way. You bring in too much lucre. You can be a racist without realizing it. Remember what you said about Eddie McDowell, after he gave that speech bashing Taft as a bastion of white supremacy. You called him 'a professional black' who made his living, just by *being* black. By 'mau-mauing the flak catchers' of the liberal establishment, like in that old book by Thomas Wolfe. This was long before the rise of Jesse Jackson or Sharpton," I reminded him.

"The book was by *Tom* Wolfe and *Radical Chic* was in the title," Jay replied, slightly perturbed. "The Black Panthers raised money at a party hosted by Leonard Bernstein in Manhattan. Obama learned his trade at Punahou, the Andover of Hawaii. Just look what happened to Eddie at Taft. Elected president of the Black Student Union and praised as a 'black student leader' in the Ivy admissions offices. He sucked in athletics and academics but punched his ticket to Harvard."

"Are you admitting you're jealous of Eddie. We're you rejected by Harvard, Jay?"

"I didn't apply to Harvard. I got nuked by Princeton. My brother, Teddy went there in the sixties, before dropping out and moving to Quebec. My father insisted on driving me down for my interview. I was familiar with the campus because I had marched in the parades as a kid at the reunions."

"Maybe it was an excuse for your father to revisit campus?"

"He gave me the classic tour of Old Nassau. The eating clubs like Tiger Inn, Cottage and Ivy, where he belonged. He loved the Princeton of Amory Blaine in *This Side of Paradise*. Never thought too much about the *other* side."

"So, they nuked you anyway? You must have had the grades and board scores to get accepted."

"Charles, my numbers were well ahead of their averages. My father waited in the lobby, wearing his black and orange tweed vest and an Ivy button pinned to his lapel, like F. Scott Fitzgerald. He pounced on the admissions officer after my interview and asked him, as 'a concerned alumnus.' To my utter horror about 'recent trends in admissions'. The dog whistle for asking if Princeton was still enforcing their secret quotas on Jews, Asians and Blacks. Kikes, Gooks and Coons in my father's mind, if not his parlance. The admissions guy knew the code and pretended to bite the bait, although I'm sure he was secretly puking. He knew how to read between the lines."

"So, you're admitting to me that your father was racist and antisemitic?"

"No more than anybody else in *his* world. He was mostly a snob. One time he placed a big sign on the tennis courts at our club in Prout's Neck, near our summer place in Maine. As newly installed tennis chairman, he was infuriated by players wearing garish stripes and loud colors onto the courts. The sign he posted read: 'Whites Only.'"

"So, he wasn't racist. Only insensitive. Did the club have any black members?"

"There weren't any blacks back then within a hundred miles, except for Portland. My father wasn't prejudiced, just clueless. When the admissions officer at Princeton replied, 'Native Americans' my father answered, 'You must be kidding.' He laughed in his face. Even as a qualified legacy applicant, I knew I was *fucked*."

"What's your problem with Obama?"

"Nothing. All I'm saying is that Obama is a race hustler like Sharpton. Maybe worse. He learned how to game the white liberal establishment in prep school, just like Eddie. And he did it to the whole country in politics."

"What about that dick, Mosley? I heard he only got 500's on the SATS but still got into Harvard?"

"His real name is Rich, short for Richard," Jay corrected me.

"He might be rich. But he's a total dick. Did Mosely deserve to get accepted to Harvard?"

"Are you kidding. He sucked at everything. Even worse than McDowell. Mosely had four generations of family money, legacy and big donations to Harvard fundraising campaigns."

"Look at it this way, Jameson. Rich Mosely didn't suck at everything. He excelled at getting his sweet ass into Harvard, early decision, like Eddie. They both sucked at everything. Little dick overcame the prejudices of the Harvard admissions office, despite his blatant stupidity, academic inferiority, and as the epitome of white privilege. They normally reject applicants like him in the first round."

"He was just lucky to be born with the right suck points to get into Harvard."

"So was Eddie McDowell. He was born black, rather than rich and connected. He played the game by shooting off his big black mouth to his advantage. Mosely played the birthright card. McDowell played the race card. They both got accepted. Why shouldn't Eddie use black privilege as his competitive advantage? Mosely used his. College admissions is a *Game of Thrones* disguised as a game of craps. The opposite of an honest craps table. Face the facts, Jameson, college admissions has *always* been a rigged game in the real world of *The Game of Thrones.*"

"You've made your point, Charles. But I'm no racist, either consciously or subliminally. Neither was my father. Whatever you may think about Trump, there's a conspiracy in this country dedicated to using race as a political weapon. Coming soon to a theatre near you. And it will be a disaster for this country."

"Obviously, you've been listening to Rush Limbaugh."

I don't listen to Rush anymore. I work my ass off every single waking hour of daylight. I wish I had nothing to worry about except long lines at the stores in the malls, like you."

"*Touche* to you too, Jameson." I winked as I realized I had destroyed Jay in the argument *du jour* and his trite repartee was merely a pathetic admission of his utter surrender.

"How's Beatrice doing, still watching the Tennis Channel?" he asked.

"As always, even in the off season. And I'm sure you still watch Hannity?"

"I'm so tired from working I nod off right after Tucker Carlson."

"That preppy guy who wears a bowtie?"

"That was on MSNBC, decades ago. Give Tucker a shot, Charles. He gets it. When Trump fucks up, Tucker never glosses it over. That's been a major blind spot with Sean and even with Rush. That Trump can do no wrong."

"Sorry, Jay. I can't stomach any more alt-right political punditry."

"Tucker has the knowledge of Rush. And the brain. He reminds me of Dr. Baltzell in that course we took at Penn. He sees the issues from both sides, so he keeps his arguments in the neutral zone of constitutional history. He's also funny as hell. He can be as satirical as Jonathan Swift."

"Sounds as delicious as your leftover turkey," I said sarcastically. "Merry Christmas to Sarah and family. I look forward to seeing you in July. Your presents will arrive with Santa. Call me after Christmas, if you need any exchanges."

"I certainly will. By the way, Sarah never returns your presents. They only gave her ten bucks for five shirts and two shorts at Old Navy, years ago. Hardly worth the hassle. You should ask for gift receipts."

"Oh...yeah...I forget, because I'm always in such a rush. Stores always screw the customers on returns. That's how they make their money. I'll try to remember next year, Jay, I promise."

"Tucker's *one of us*. Happy Holidays to the Goldstein's. Merry Christmas to your mom, Beatrice and Francis. To hell with Jill. You wouldn't believe the connivances she's been using on my old friends at The Round Hill Club. I hope they end up blackballing her again this year. What a *bitch*."

CHAPTER SEVENTEEN

My fellow Pilgrims, I am not a criminal or a lowlife. I am a loyal American. A Soldier of Truth born from the rib of *The Ancien Regime*. The blood of nobility and royalty, including Charles Martel and his grandson, Charles the Great, renowned as Charlemagne. Crowned as the Holy Roman Emperor of Europe by Pope Leo III on Christmas Day in 800 A.D. I follow my grandfather, as I raise a glass of the finest French wine to honor his legacy every Christmas day.

I am a direct descendant of *Le Marechal*, who shared in the American victory at Yorktown. I am a dedicated Royalist and claim four degrees of pedigree on my father's side alone, going back twelve generations to the royal court at the Palace of Versailles, during the illustrious reign of the Sun King, Louis XIV. *L'Etat. C'est moi.*

John Greenleaf Whitter, the great American poet once chimed in verse:

> *Shine knightly star and plumed snow*
> *Thou too art victor Rochambeau!*

Napoleon Bonaparte awarded General Rochambeau the Legion of Honor in 1805.

My life has been fraught with challenges. Yet, I believe in the existent secular national religion known as The American Dream. Which dissipated due to the ineptitude of my father. I was forced into the ignoble life of a proletarian, almost like the *Sans Culottes* and became a drug-running high school dropout.

But I lifted from memory, the immortal words of Ralph Waldo Emerson from a course on American literature course that I took at Taft: "*Fall back on your own genius. New powers will emerge.*"

I had abandoned my education after dropping out of high school. I had lied to my parents and everybody, except for you, as I redeem myself by telling the Truth in my confessions. To continue my story, I was living at 48th and Larchwood in West Philadelphia and trafficking cocaine for Little Nicky, while expatiating the Penn campus.

I would stop by Houston Hall and read the *Daily Pennsylvanian*. I patronized stores and restaurants on and off campus, including Pagano's. I nearly introduced myself to a waitress as a friend of Tommy's but chickened out as I remained *incognito*. I focused on my drug pick-ups with Dr. Lawrence, shuttling deliveries every week, back and forth, to and from Scarf Inc. headquarters in Atlantic City. By June, I sensed that change would appear on the horizon.

Rosemary took me aside one afternoon. Strangely, she started grilling me with questions about my future, as she handed me another brick of twenties. Something *big* was going down. I knew she was shielding me from it, trying to protect me, like Tommy Pagano. I started thinking. Maybe, it was Rosemary, *not* Little Nicky who had championed my welfare. She was my guardian angel with my best interests at heart. Rosemary was the one looking out for me.

I wore my Penn sportswear and blended myself into the campus crowd. Perhaps, my new *persona* inspired this premonition. If I had found my genius, it was by reimagining myself. I stared into my mirror one morning, sporting the colors of the red and blue. Perhaps, it was possible for a high school dropout, an unindicted career criminal like me, to jumpstart his ambitions. With the help of a college education. With or without a diploma.

Only in America. The answer was 'definitely maybe'. I snuck into summer college classes in July. Six at Penn and two at Drexel. Just for the sake of giving it the proverbial 'old college try' and reboot my luck.

Maybe, some secreted new powers within myself would emerge.

I took stock of my assets. Besides looks, brains and personality, I tallied ownership of a four-year old Cutlass, a healthy bank account and enough cash bundled in Jacksons to pay for rent, food and living expenses for five years. Of course, I was living frugally, without any allowance for tuition. But I had plenty of time to find myself a new path.

I was shocked. Amazed how easy it was to execute my audacious plan. Nobody checked me for identification. Not even once in the eight lectures I crashed. Even in smaller classes, I grabbed an empty seat, smiling at my classmates. I jawboned, jived and participated in class discussions. I raised my hand to ask questions. I waited an extra hour to gabble with a teaching assistant following an Anthropology lecture in the University Museum auditorium.

I was focused on my education. I transmogrified into the model student by accident. It was simple. Cheap and easy. Nothing is cheaper than free. It didn't require a spark of *pneuma* to discover my inner genius. I could get my life back on track by *thinking* of myself as a college freshman. Then it dawned on me. Maybe I *did* graduate from high school.

I decided I wanted to go to college.

It might be bad for the soul, but anybody who can swing it, goes for it anyway. Higher education is a bulwark of The American Dream. It could provoke a return to normalcy for my ambitions. Better than a drug dealing desperado. I could resume my upward mobility, long-lost after my father's financial malfeasance had left my family shipwrecked.

Summer classes ended in mid-August. I asked Rosemary for a meeting, following my latest drop-off in Atlantic City. She turned to me and quietly nodded. Then, she pulled me aside and steered me into Little Nicky's office. She locked the door and sat down in his black leather swivel chair, behind his carved mahogany desk.

A pile of unopened mail lay there. Untouched by human hands for months.

"Hello Charles. I assume you have important news."

"I've saved up enough money, Rosemary. It's time for me to go to college."

She blinked and stared at me. "Don't do anything until I talk to Nicky," she whispered. "He's been out of sorts, lately. Getting more and more pissed off with Dr. Snowden, your dentist contact."

"Quality issues with the new rock coming in?"

"He's been jacking up his prices...Nicky thinks he's bullshitting us and getting greedy. This happens with all these guys. Nick might have to teach him a lesson. And bust his chops. I want to help you, Charles. But you can't just walk in here and decide to give notice. Things don't work that way around here... You know that .... Comprendi?"

"I get it. So, how do I handle it? Write Nicky a thank you letter with an explanation?"

Rosemary visibly restrained herself from laughing. "No, Charles... you *don't* get it. Nicky never trusts anything in writing. That kind of crap is for judges and lawyers. Just turn in your beeper and move out of the house. Mail me the keys. You can always trust my brother-in-law Ernie at the bank. Nicky's busy as hell and very pissed off. But I think I know how to deal with him."

"I want to thank you, Rosemary......for everything."

Tears trickled her cheeks. "Don't worry, Charles. Everything will be taken care of."

I was a free bird. Ready for college and not just any college. The University of Pennsylvania. Founded by Benjamin Franklin in 1740. I was ready to prove myself worthy of higher education.

I moved into one-bedroom apartment at 40th and Pine. I'd pay a fortune more in rent, but it was six blocks closer to campus. I felt safer now in the student ghetto, since I wasn't toting drugs or cash. I wanted to *feel* like a college student. I ordered two dozen red and white roses for Rosemary. She sent me a thank you note, which was also signed by Little Nicky, wishing me 'All the *correct* best of luck'. I was certainly relieved.

Another mob killing was in the news. The wise guy who got whacked, dared to call Mr. Scarfo 'Little Nicky' in public. Nicky despised the name, so I wondered why he ever told me to use it. Unless he always had a contingency plan. If things didn't work out 'too good', he would have dressed me in cement pajamas and tossed me into Schuylkill.

Nicky was busy, out of sorts and ticked off. Yet, I worried about Dr. Lawrence. I had taken his advice and changed my name to Charles Dodgson, while retaining my real identity on my lease, credit cards, driver's license, bank accounts and the safe deposit box with the stacks of cash at PNB.

I considered warning Doctor Lawrence. I didn't want to see him get his pearly whites busted. Nicky mustn't have found the time to teach Snowden a lesson, as I often crossed his path the following year. He simply nodded and simpered to me. With all his pearly whites intact. I covered my tracks by paying my bills with twenties.

Don't ask me how I conjured my pseudonym. If you can't deduce it, you're dumber than Tweedledum. Here's a clue for ignoramuses: I am dominated by fabulist delusions and fantasies, like Charles Lutwidge Dodgson. Except for his infatuation with prepubescent girls Through the Looking Glass. Here's a hint. The answer is *not* Hubert Humbert.

Although Reverend Dodgson would have enjoyed sharing close quarters with Lolita.

Academically, I played it safe. Four courses in large lectures, including Microeconomics. I considered Financial Accounting, but dropped it, like I did with Calculus. I could deal with quantitative courses better after gaining confidence in my abilities. I settled on Russian History, Environmental Biology and a film class the SCUE students guide referred to as 'Monday Night at the Movies.' I decided to play it safe.

I earned my education the old-fashioned way. I *stole* it. Not exactly. I *extracted* it from a 'Not Penn State' institution in West Philadelphia. Like great-grandfather Rochambeau, who graduated from Princeton and my grandfather from Columbia. Now I had arrived on the campus of an Ivy League University.

Not that I allowed this dubious distinction, go to my head.

Decades ago, clever people, ahead of the technology curves figured out how to hook up television sets into cable systems to *extract* free service. Illegal yes— but it never hurt anyone. A victimless crime, if even a crime at all. Then cable companies shut down the technical loopholes. I must elucidate a simple, but crucial semantic distinction here. Regarding my usage of the word *extract*. I am The Bargain Shopper. I have never been a shoplifter. I have never *stolen* anything. Yet I have *extracted* things. Like we all do, for instance, the air we breathe. You can't blame me that a renowned university, like Penn fails to monitor the attendance inside their own classrooms.

Air and bathrooms are free. So are water fountains. I am free to drink from the public wells on the environs of an open campus. Along with my attendance in lecture halls. Free for the taking for people like me. Even for wild dogs and buffalos, because the air is free. I didn't need to register as a human being to receive my free college education.

I got myself a great deal on a product. Free, like the samples from Colgate and Proctor& Gamble. A product called a college education although I admit it may be 'basically useless.' But I was spared the torture of going through the agonies of the admissions process. Oh, how they kill themselves to get in. Through so many different doors.

The front door means you are a valedictorian with perfect test scores. You volunteered twenty hours a week at a local hospital or a crummy food bank. You're a saint or heavenly angel sent by God to change the world. You might even have a snowball's chance in Hell of getting in.

Many side doors: Athletics, legacies, minorities. You know these deals. Each one is different. Many potential paths to plow. Mostly through exclusive routes managed by expensive consultants.

The back door is hidden from view. A door reserved for billionaire offspring. Or big-time politicians, movie stars or celebrities. Clientele who can donate big bucks into the coffers of prestigious colleges. Even tens or hundreds of times more in cashflows than the outrageous tuitions these institutions charge their privileged customers.

I got into Penn through a secret door. Way off the radar. I *skulked* through it. More accurately, I walked through it with the *genius* of insolent chutzpah. Remember the old song by The Rooftop Singers, "*Walk right in, sit right down, Baby let your hair hang down.*"

That's what I did. I walked right in. Right through the *cellar* door. Then sat down as Charles L. Dodgson. But I never let my hair hang down. I was never awarded a Penn diploma, although I had earned it by dint of my diligence and hard work. I got an Ivy League education, 'basically useless', as it has since proved to be. Keep in mind, I got it for free.

There are other reasons Charles L. Dodgson got a better deal as a consumer at the University of Pennsylvania than other academically brilliant, but regular paying student customers:

I designed my own curriculum.

Any course I requested was graded Pass-Fail.

No grades were issued without my permission.

Class cuts were allowed for any reason. Or no reason at all.

I was allowed unlimited class cuts.

No doctor notes were required for the cancelling or postponement of tests, papers or exams.

No exams or term papers were required. Unless I felt like it.

I had unlimited 'drop and adds.'

No academic restrictions. No required forms for me to file.

I decided my grade in every course I took. I chose my own cumulative grade point average.

I graduated *Magna Cum Laude*.

CHAPTER EIGHTEEN

I was curious how things had gone on Thanksgiving with The Madame. It was raining buckets as I arrived to work on Monday, but she greeted me with glad tidings. Good news, I could tell, and I was eager for details. Her eyes lit up as she told me that Michael Cutter was a handsome marketing exec for Coca-Cola. Raised in Lynchburg, Virginia by a single mother, he attended SMU on a football scholarship and started at left cornerback. Most important, he was divorced.

His ex-wife, a former SMU cheerleader, lived in Stone Mountain with their two daughters. She remarried a surgeon. Michael's father was a Baptist preacher who had succumbed to alcohol. Beatrice raved about Michael's politeness, saying he reminded her of Rhett Butler.

The Holly Jollies were here. I dropped off the last package for Dylan and family in Maui at UPS. Six unisex layettes for a baby due in January. Early Thursday morning, Hell broke loose. Beatrice called me at five, so I was afraid of a terrible accident and woke up frantic with the dreads, rolled over and grabbed my cell phone in a panic.

No big deal. Madame had lost her electricity. Her boiler had shut off and the cold air awakened her. She had called Ryan on his cellphone. No answer. Then she remembered he was away in Ireland this week with his wife, Mary. I told her to call Shamrock and dressed myself for the Yukon in a turtleneck, flannel shirt and heavy sweater. I pulled on my Barbour topcoat and headed to Briarcliff Manor in my Toyota.

I will not bore you. Everything got fixed. Beatrice apologized grandiosely for waking me. She had panicked when Ryan didn't answer. When I arrived, A BMW from Alfieri Prestige Motors was parked in her driveway. It
didn't belong to Franny. The rear window had a bulldog sticker: 'Yale Men's
Lacrosse'. Trey Keneally was talking to Beatrice in the kitchen, as I flung
through the door and The Chloe Monster started barking me into oblivion.

Trey left ten minutes later. When he returned at four, he was wearing
a white Shamrock uniform, as he checked the boiler again. He only lived a
few miles away in Sleepy Hollow. A town called North Tarrytown until the
galloping Headless Horseman was ensnared to raise property values for the
entire community. The Madame, sleep-deprived, retired for a nap. She awoke
in time for a bath, before leaving for tea and bridge with the 'Girls' at Sleepy
Hollow Country Club. Trey and I meandered towards the living room, as he
tried explaining boilers and heating systems. Then he abruptly turned into
The Mirror Room. We sat on two dark green leather chairs facing the fireplace. Suddenly, he whistled. "We just ordered three more Sprinters. We own
fifty-two trucks. Dad never uses leases, except long-term. Like our property
from Metro North. If we keep growing the business, we might need to lease
a bigger lot on the Hudson."

"Business must be booming. How can you afford Mercedes trucks...Cheap
labor?

Trey squinted, shaking his head. "Those days are long gone. Can't run a
business of any scale using illegals. Maybe you can sneak in a few here and
there. Not worth the hassle if you get busted."

"I audit our bills. Your prices seem cheap, I dare say. Are you sure you're
not losing money?"

Trey smiled broadly and I imagined how his father, Ryan might have
looked in his thirties. "We don't give away anything at Shamrock," Trey replied. Then he paused. "Ohhh... I forget...... Your account. The Wolcott's get
our friends and family deal. My first job after college was doing billing. We
were very late switching our books to computers. I told my father we were
losing money on a few small accounts and needed to raise some of our prices
to break even."

"But you didn't. Not even to cost. Something else might be going on."

"You may be correct," Trey said with a smile. "No reason to talk about it."

"Why not?"

"Dad gives discounts to Beatrice. We bill her goods at fifteen percent below cost. Labor at twenty below. No markups or profits allowed. We lose thirty to thirty-five percent on every invoice."

"Just like Kohls and the retail stores do with me," I replied with pride. "I'm a Certified Professional Shopper. Beatrice calls me *Monsieur Bon Marche*. But I work very hard to find the bargains that earn my results. How do you justify losing money on purpose with Beatrice?" I paused and took a deep breath. "Maybe your dad is secretly in love with her?"

Ryan smiled. "Of course, she's a friend. And I know he admires her. But he's only in love with my mother. But you're very astute, Charles. There's a missing piece to the puzzle but I just can't justify any reason to talk about it."

"I'm sure there's nothing to be ashamed of."

"Alright, Charles, The Hammer. There is something. I only learned about it after Anthony's funeral." Trey pointed to the portrait over the mantel. His face flushed red, as he held back a tear. "I saw Jill Paulson giggling at the flowers sent by Joe and Lucy. She made a wisecrack at the wake as she stepped down. I couldn't believe my ears."

"My God. Anthony was her own nephew."

Trey rubbed his chin. "I'd never seen my father drunk until that night, when I was fourteen. I told him what I overheard. Then I cried on his shoulder. I can't repeat it, a slur that denigrates Italians. My father loved Anthony as much as I did. He had kept a secret about Jill. But he was so angry that night, he broke down and told me. I freaked out."

"Anthony's death must have been traumatic for everyone," I said.

"Catastrophic. For both families. Bea filed for divorce six months later. She never used the Alfieri name again, except her listing in The Colony Club directory. Their members always list their married names, even if they're divorced."

"How do you happen to know that little factoid?"

"My mother-in-law is a member and I thumbed through the book. I married into Old Money by accident at Yale since Lily's the greatest girl I ever met. But she's a Stillman and a Livingston and related to everybody like the Wolcott's. When she started at Groton, she was in the chapel at Anthony's memorial service. They would have been classmates."

"I didn't realize the divorce happened so fast after Anthony's death?"

"Francis blamed Beatrice. Maybe unconsciously, but he made her life unbearable."

"But I heard Anthony swam past the danger flags at Manursing."

"Just like the other guys, but he slashed his knee on a shard. The cramping started because he'd been playing soccer all day in the heat. He panicked as his leg cramped in the current. He was a strong swimmer. The lifeguards arrived a few minutes too late. It was a freak accident."

"How could Francis possibly blame Beatrice?"

"She convinced Anthony to go to Groton. Otherwise, he would have been on a canoe trip with me and guys on the Lower School Lacrosse team. His father wanted him to stay at Hackley, so he could go to all his games. Beatrice wanted Groton and Francis believed her main reason was to redeem her family's reputation at both Groton at Yale, which had been tarnished by her father."

"I heard her father was a ne'er do well, who never had a job. So what?"

"Brooky had another reputation."

"As drunk and a deadbeat. My father was also a deadbeat. So what?"

"Brooky was a *maricon*. A gay man, as I decline to use a slur. He was in The Uranian Club at Yale."

"Like Skull and Bones?"

Trey laughed. "Not exactly," he said. "A secret society for male affinities descended from British schools like Oxford and Trinity College, Dublin. It goes back to the glory days of Walter Pater and Oscar Wilde in Victorian England."

"So why did Brooks get married?"

"Procreation. Social norms dictated obligatory lineal descent for the aristocracy. 'Coming Out' is a relatively new thing. Oscar Wilde married and had two sons. Brooky had a "Boston Marriage' like Cole Porter. I heard he hung out with John Cheever, the writer, who was also married with children, but gay, along with other 'boys in the band'. They met regularly at the Yale Club and other places in the city like Studio 54. Another major haunt was some bar in Ossining."

Trey looked up to the portrait of Anthony. His eyes flooded with tears. "Did you know that kid could punt a soccer ball three quarters of the field in the seventh grade?

"Definitely the picture of a handsome jock."

Trey's face brightened. "He wanted to become a sportscaster. He was hilarious doing his shtick mimicking Chris Berman of ESPN. Anthony idolized him. Chris also went to Hackley. Anthony found his middle school yearbook from 1969 when he was the goalie on the soccer team. He was skinny as a rail back then. So, Anthony switched to playing goalie in soccer and lacrosse. He had the reflexes of an alley cat. Nobody could beat him in ping-pong."

"And he was one of the smartest in his class."

"Valedictorian of the Lower School. Just like Chris Berman. He also loved The Eagles— the rock band, not the NFL team. He was a huge Jet's fan and he wanted to go to Brown and work for ESPN, like Chris."

"Tell me, Trey, what's really going on with your father and Beatrice?"

"It was never about Beatrice. It was always about Jill."

"You must be kidding," I answered, but the revelation hit me like a ton of bricks. I felt like a fool. There had to be some reason Jill despised Ryan so wickedly other than she was a bitch. I stared into Trey's eyes.

He scratched his forehead and took a breath. "Dad was going into his senior year. Shamrock had two trucks. He worked for my grandfather on weekends and summers. In July, the central air conked out at the Wolcott's. My grandfather stopped by, located the problem and called my dad, who was home, working out in the basement. Grandfather told him to drop off the parts, so he could stop by and fix it before bedtime. It was hot and humid."

"What does that have to do with Beatrice?"

"Let me finish. The house is empty. Jill is lying in the backyard on a beach blanket in her bikini. Dad was in gym shorts, sweat rolling off his torso. He handed her the bill of lading and she jumped off the blanket and wrapped her arms around him, pulling him down between her legs. She even yanked off his shorts."

"God Almighty. Jill raped your father."

"He twisted off her but couldn't stop himself from ejaculating. Beatrice had been playing under a laurel tree in a meadow. When my father looked up, Bea was staring at him, as he lay next to Jill. They were buck naked."

I wiped my left hand over my face. "How old was Beatrice?"

"Eleven. Dad was seventeen and still a virgin. Jill had quite the reputation at Masters. Ask your sister, Molly. Jill supposedly lost her virginity at thirteen. When she tried to seduce my father, she was already on the pill."

"How could Molly know about this?"

"You know why. She was Beatrice's best friend at Master's."

"I forgot. Jill still treats your father like dirt. What a bitch."

"My father and I refrain from using slurs. Even on Jill. He feels he owes a debt to Beatrice. She never said a word to anyone—especially her parents. That's why I didn't want to tell you. We try to keep it a secret."

"If Bea was eleven, she might have been traumatized. Did she ever talk this over with Ryan?"

"Never. Not even after fifty years. He doesn't even know if Bea ever said anything to Jill. But he is determined to pay Beatrice back. If she said anything, she could have ruined Ryan's reputation at age seventeen."

I nodded to Ryan, arose from my chair and stepped into the kitchen. I grabbed two Molson ales from the fridge, along with a couple of frosted mugs from the freezer. When I returned, I noticed that a shield was pinned to Ryan's uniform, as I handed him his beer. Resuming my seat, I asked him, "Is that a fraternity badge? I'm a brother too, a former Knight of Brotherhood in The Peace House at Penn."

"It's the coat of arms of University of Edinburgh. My grandmother was Scottish. She asked me to visit the Bogle family graveyard outside town before she died. I spent a semester there as an exchange student in the Fall of sophomore year at Yale, before I married Lily in June. Mom was proud of her Scottish heritage and kept carpet balls on the mantel. Her passion in life was The Ardsley Curling Club."

"You mean that crazy game they play on ice rinks, sweeping it with squeegee brooms."

"Exactly. You probably saw it on television during the Winter Olympics."

"My true passion was Frog Bowling. I love barbecued frog legs."

"Don't ever go Frog Bowling in your sneakers."

"I tried doing it in my loafers."

"You must be crazy."

"That's how I ruptured my groin. Frog Bowling in loafers. I needed a hernia operation last year. The doctors had to amputate my entire belly button."

"Typical Frog Bowling injury. At what hospital?"

"Sleepy Hollow?"

"I bet Doctor Chow Mein did the operation?"

"He was the anesthesiologist. His brother, Lo Mein performed the surgery, along with Doctor Ravioli. They work together as a team."

"Just like at an all-you-can-eat buffet."

'Exactly. But I'm afraid there's no more Frog Bowling in my future."

"Too bad. It's destined to become a sport in the Winter Olympics. Just like Curling. Give Kitty Croquet a shot sometime, just for the hell of it. Lily and the kids love it. So, it works for me."

"I'm planning on going back to Frisbee Golf."

CHAPTER NINETEEN

I became a *faux* freshman at the University of Pennsylvania. Unlike 2372 classmates, I had not decided to which undergraduate school I belonged. Much less my major. I never enrolled in any of them. Neither did I address this fact until I left a lecture in Environmental Biology and ran smack into the smiling face of Jameson Bigelow Twombly.

I had never kept up with anyone from Taft since I withdrew. Including Jay and my 'asshole buddies.' If you leave anyplace place for the wrong reason, you never belong again. You want to forget about it. Hard to explain unless you've been there before. But you *know* it. We bought cheesesteaks and sat down on College Hall Green for over three hours to catch up. We kept talking and talking, like the old days. We still do. Jameson *gets* it. He's a 'quick study'.

I told him why I changed my name. And what happened since I left Taft, except for my drug work in cocaine. I feared somebody from his social neighborhood might not justify renewing a friendship with an employee of 'Little Nicky', no matter how elegantly I spun the merits of concrete. Memories of dealing drugs haunt me today.

Jay mentioned Taft students I might run into. Fortunately, I kept Charles as my Christian name. He promised to keep my secrets *secret*. I knew I could trust him. He was the first kid I met at Taft and last one I saw the day I left. Life is full of ironies and goes in circles. My first semester at Penn exceeded my 'Great Expectations.' As I invoke the optimism of Dicken's classic about aspiring youth. I got a bargain on tuition but paid a stiff price because of my isolation, always on guard to conceal my identity and more tiresome than I ever imagined.

I never turned in term papers. I *did* write them but graded them myself on a generous curve. I took several quizzes but absconded from the classrooms with them. I thought it prudent to cut class on exam days. In early March, Jameson waved to me, as I passed him on Locust Walk in front of 'The Castle'. He caught me by surprise when he asked for a 'big favor'. I gulped. Then, out of the blue, he asked me to join a fraternity with him.

I told him, *no dice*. I was keeping a low profile as an invisible man on campus. I wasn't socializing even if I wanted to. Exposing myself to the klieg lights a fraternity generates was crazy.

Jameson never quits. He begged me to reconsider. He had his own clandestine reasons, I learned, after he was cuckolded, openly and ignominiously by his former girlfriend. During the Fall, he had signed a bid to join St. Anthony's Hall, the prominent preppie house on Locust Walk. After pledging, he had caught a future brother *in the act* of hornjacking this perfidious slut on his waterbed, upstairs in house. For some inexplicable reason, Jameson went apoplectic over such a minor brotherly infidelity and vowed to quit St. Anthony's Hall forever.

Common decency prohibits me from revealing his savage retaliation against this brother or his former wench. Brilliant and onerous, Jameson *fucked* them both excellent. Trust me. He needed a frat, any of them, as a convenient hangout between classes. He hates giving up entitlements. Including his divine right to cheap sex.

He knew the rush chairman of 'The Peace House' from sociology class. A skinny, pompous dude known as 'Sir Drekstain of My Alba.' Rho Alpha Chi members sprouted odd fraternal names as 'Knights of Brotherhood.'

We agreed to meet Drekstain at the house. A black mongrel Labrador and beloved house dog called Mister E almost barked us onto the street as we entered. Nobody knew where Mister E came from. Perhaps a slum-dog puppyhood in West Philly. I identified with Mister E since I was also like a stray animal who had wandered onto campus one fine day, found myself a home, and stuck around for good.

Mister E barked harder at men of color or in uniform. He protected The Peace House from criminals who cruised campus. And surprise drug busts by the Philadelphia police. The only thing he hated worse was harmonica music.

Bob Dylan drove him into histrionics. Like *Cerberus*, the watchdog in *Dante's Inferno*, he guarded The Gates of Hell.

We waded through mountains of trash. Thousands of beer cans, bottles and pizza boxes, before clearing out space to sit on a torn vinyl sofa in the living room. I will never forget the smell of raw sewage wafting up from the bowels of The Abyss. Seaweed and dead fish washed ashore on a beach following a hurricane, baked by the burning sun.

An odor that suffuses your nostrils. Sticking like pine tar, lingering in cavities. I revisited thirty years later, and the house stunk with the same bouquet of shit, vomit, booze, pig sweat and piss, with a slight hint of crème de menthe.

Sir Drekstain was late. I picked out magazines and handed Jay a *Time*, addressed to Rosie Blosenfuchs. I read a current edition of *Sports Illustrated* subscribed by Mr. E. S. Balls. A petite, frizzy-haired girl in skintight jeans, clambered up the stairs into the foyer and peered into the living room. Then she yanked a guitar case out of a trash pile.

"Hi guys," she bleated. The case was emblazoned with a red and blue sticker of a fish skeleton: Campus Crusade for Christ at Penn. "Don't think we've met. My name is... everyone in these hallowed halls calls me Krazy Karen."

Jameson and I rose from our seats and introduced ourselves. I considered stepping forwards to greet this lovely coquette accordingly. Alas, mountains of fermenting compost inhibited my natural instincts towards politeness. Especially after I saw a monster rat nibbling on a crust of petrified pizza.

The young damsel seemed to be in somewhat of a hurry, anyways. "Are you guy's pledges? I haven't seen you guys hanging around here?" she queried, smiling at both of us.

I noticed the large animal over the fireplace was as large as a moose head but resembled a wild boar with antlers. "We're meeting with Sir Knight, My Alba," Jameson replied. "About joining the pledge class. I assume you play the Spanish guitar. I love guitar music. Can you play 'Classical Gas?'"

"Oh, let's just say, I do a little bit of picking and strumming here," she answered. "What I really dig is racking up games of eight ball with the guys. There's a pool table in the basement. If you want it, come here any time you feel like getting it on. Play me as much you want. Everyone in the fraternity does it with me. Please come. We can rap about Jesus. I'd be happy to do it for *him*, anytime."

A gaseous emission ballooned in my sphincter as I stared at Jameson. He nodded and replied, "I'm sure you would, Karen .... I mean Krazy Karen. That sounds very *cool* indeed."

Her eyes lit up, sparkling like champagne. "They have a classic Brunswick downstairs. All the pockets are handmade jobs with genuine cowhide. All leather." Then she winked and continued. "God gave Man an opposable thumb for a reason. I'd love to rap some more but I gotta go now. I'm late for class... Peace be with you.... Jesus saves."

Just after Karen left, Sir Drekstain, our tardy knight clattered into the living room. With a loutish smirk, he sat on a corduroy chair, crossed his legs and clasped his hands together. His shallow smile turned into a grimace.

Right off the bat, he gave us a hard time about joining. We both needed to be intensively vetted by the entire brotherhood for *three months*, he told us, shaking his head. To 'prove our virtue to the fraternity' he suggested we consider participating as contestants in a public jousting tournament on College Hall Green. In return for our hardships and labors, he told us he might consider waiving half of our pledge dues.

"We must ensure our initiates are devout Crusader Knights, free-born gentlemen well-bred in civilized company, virtuous, puissant, adroit on horseback and proficient in the arts of pikes, halberds, and crossbows. Well-trained in the strategic deployment of archers and engineering sturdy ballista and siege towers, with a strong will to fight the yokes of servitude, and if necessary, scale the highest rocks in the mountain ranges of every region of the known world."

Thus, spoke Sir Drekstain of My Alba. His drool bucket overflowed with the sweetmeats of a rat-infested mind. I peered at Jameson, ready to laugh in hysterics. And nearly jumped up from the sofa.

Jameson raised his right hand. Majestically, he spoke slowly, articulating that although he was previously pledged to join St. Anthony Hall, tragically he was forced to quit. A heartfelt decision driven by his own personal virtue.

'St. A's is a 'Hostel of Faggotry.' He told us that he dared not use the bathrooms for fear of getting gangraped.

Sir Drekstain paused. He was deeply moved by this stunning admission. Until now, he explained, he had never really believed the rumors of rampant buggery that infested 'The Hall'.

Jameson winked, as he palmed a twenty to Sir Drekstain to cover both of our pledge dues. Mister E stuck his big black head out of a couple of vagrant pizza boxes. He started growling, his jaw was clenched to a long, skinny bone. Possibly the tail of a cow. Or even an animal as huge as a mastodon.

Sir Drekstain stood up and imposed a brisk smile upon each of us.

"Gentlemen.......You might have possibly detected the distinctive odor of our Chapter Hall. Love it or hate it, you will be destined to go nose-blind to it within a week. We all do. All the Sir Knights here, including myself. Take a deep breath and enjoy it while you can. You will never forget the inimitable notes of this ever-refreshing peppermint scent."

CHAPTER TWENTY

The Goldstein Army encircled my mother at Christmas. Around Molly's enormous maple table.

Chef Pierre held his ground, ignored her orders and prepared a stuffed wild goose along with Chateaubriand. He finished it off with a dazzling maple crème brulee. As usual, Molly refused to join me in my annual toast to Charlemagne. But she had no qualms about guzzling her fair share of my vintage Mouton-Rothschild. Our mother, the former Sabina Ingersoll is growing old, slowly losing her mind. She forgets names and spouts absurdities. Her faculties are dwindling, and Molly and Jeff told me to save the date for her surprise ninetieth birthday, scheduled for late October with 150 guests. Unfortunately, I think this means, they expect this time, it will be her last.

I returned to Melville Corners and stopped at McDonalds on my way to work. Hungry for more than my usual MVR breakfast. I will be meeting with Franny and Madame Beatrice at noon to discuss Emily's wedding. I walk inside and scan the menu, flashing over the counter. I've *never* gone through a drive-thru window in my entire life, and never intend to, even if Hell freezes over. No more than I would purchase anything online, log onto a computer, or switch to a smartphone. It's a *dumbphone* to me.

I am writing these 'Confessions' in shorthand. In the tradition of Homer and Herodotus. I prefer the technology of Luddites, who write their scrolls of wisdom in cuneiform or using quill pens. I prefer truth over fiction. Emerson said, *'These novels will give way, by and by, to diaries or autobiographies—captivating books, if only a man knew how to choose among what he calls his experiences that which is really his experience, and to record truth truly.'*

Mister Ralph is correct. And I remain a Soldier of Truth as I promised.

Please understand why I 'refuse to use' drive-thru windows. Even observant Amish dine at fast food restaurants. I simply wish to avoid being ripped off. These windows are bloodless monsters, who shortchange the innocent. Passing out cheeseburgers without cheese. Serving medium French fries after charging customers for a large. Or forgetting to give out the free napkins or ketchup. Once I drive away, I'm the one who has been *fucked* over.

Hassles give me the dreads. The Bargain Shopper loves the jollies and lives by *Caveat Emptor, 'Let the buyer beware'*. I practice this *credo* and developed *Gnosis* over the decades, the occult knowledge to battle monstrosities like drive-thru windows. I plan on banishing them at every single franchise of Humble Grilled Cheese.

I look up at the menu board. Lights flashing, prices dancing. Undecipherable. I scan for breakfast sandwiches. A Sausage and Egg McMuffin is $3.89. But wait. The same one without the egg is $1.59. An egg biscuit is $1.19. I order both and save two dollars. I remove the egg from the biscuit and place it in the McMuffin. The biscuit is a bonus. I devour it with jam, along with my senior coffee and reconstructed Sausage Egg McMuffin. MVR dining. You need to look harder to find *More* food for *Less* bread.

Follow the Science. The decretals of The Bargain Shopper. *Learn the pricing of your entire inventory before buying.* Knowledge is Power. *Caveat Emptor.* Always compare your utils relative to the prices, just like I have shown you. The Bargain Shopper realizes that pricing is neither consistent nor necessarily rational.

Assume the opposite and you will *find* your bargains. 'Combo meals' are a trick play for the owners. Often more expensive than *a la carte*. Go figure. Price points are loaded with hidden discrepancies. You must ferret them out. The Bargain Shopper is a broker who identifies pricing anomalies using superior information. An arbitrageur who factors *utils* into quadratic equations and regressions for maximum value and realizes the intrinsic value of his own utils.

Do you think I'm crazy? *Follow the Science.* Dust off your abacus and do the math. Study the entire menu. At stores, you rely on scanners, *not* prices before checkout. Never forget this crucial decretal: *Scanner prices rule the day.*

✤ ✤ ✤

FRANNY WAS LATE— and in a big hurry, as usual. We sat down in the leather chairs in The Mirror Room. He had gained thirty pounds since the divorce. His father, Joseph Anthony was skinny when he died of lung cancer on New Year's Day, seven years ago, although he had quit smoking *Swisher Sweets* in his late thirties.

Franny wasted no time. "I have an announcement. Lucy had another bad fall in the dining room, two days before Christmas. Fortunately, Hildy was in the living room, but Demetri and I have decided to move Mom into assisted living. We hope to make this happen by the end of the summer."

"I think it's about time, Francis," Beatrice replied. "Then nobody will have to worry. It must be difficult for Lucille to give up her home. And leaving behind all her wonderful memories must be terrifying."

As usual, Beatrice, showed her compassionate self. I tried to follow her noble, altruistic lead, but sensed Franny could be holding back some hidden cards. "Have you found the right kind of facility?" I asked him. "Surely you're planning on selling the big house in Harrison?"

"The Osborn in Rye. Right down the road. She knows quite a few people there already including some good friends. We're going to rent a two bedroom as soon as the right one becomes available."

"Why does she need two bedrooms, Francis?" Beatrice asked.

"She needs a guest room. Otherwise, she might refuse to move in. We lack the authority to put her house on the market without her permission. Not that we'd ever do it without her consent."

"You mean you haven't told her yet?" I asked him, as I looked up at The Mirror, centuries old and slightly blemished which distorted my face, but not my rationale.

Franny laughed, shaking his head. "I haven't amassed the courage to ask her. Not by a long shot, even after the fall, which was bad. She hit her head on the coffee table and collapsed without even a whimper. She's tough as nails but it could have been disaster. Demetri thinks we should wait before we tell her. I'd rather wait until Spring. You know Lucy. Like the rest of the Greeks. Immoveable as the three hundred Spartans at Thermopylae."

"Right up until their deaths," I added, highlighting the drama with a touch of historical accuracy.

"Well, I think it's all for the best, Francis," Beatrice replied, scratching her forehead. "Have you spoken to Lucille about St. Mary's for Emily's wedding? You promised me, Francis."

"I tried to, Bea. I just couldn't get through to her. The timing is bad. I need your help. We don't need to kid ourselves. Lucy controls everything. We had to shut down Alfieri Cleaning Contractors last month. Demetri laid off everybody right after Christmas. We've never been forced to do this in any of our businesses. We gave everyone prorated severance pay out of our own pockets. Besides the cost, it's been traumatic for us. Stressful and emotional."

"The cleaning business could pick up again, by the summer," I said, hopefully.

"No Charles—it's never coming back. We're selling the building and liquidating everything. Trucks, burnishers, supplies and equipment. We've been burning up cash for the past decade."

"I suppose you haven't explained this to Lucy?" I inquired.

Franny winced. "Of course not. That's my problem. I'd love to hold the wedding at St. Mary's and reception at Sleepy Hollow. It would be terrific. The problem is that Lucy converted from Greek Orthodox to Roman Catholic when she married our dad. The testimony to her eternal love is St. Gregory the Great, as the great shrine of her filial memories with my father—powerful, sacrosanct and completely inviolable to my mother."

Madame winced. "I see, Francis. Charles and I still think St Mary's is a better venue for Emily and Peter. It's going to be a much smaller wedding. And Peter is a devout Episcopalian. I think Lucy will understand."

"Sure—if you can bring my father back to life, he'd agree with all of us."

"What's the bottom line, Francis," I asked him. "We need a decision from you to make our plans."

"I'm short on cash. Lucy's in her nineties, but razor sharp. I'm in no position to defy her, even if I wanted to. I hope you will support me. I will explain it to Peter and Emily. They will understand. Certainly, for Lucy's sake, if not mine."

"Perhaps, Emily could convince Lucy to change her mind? To consider an alternative," Beatrice said.

"Sorry, Bea. Here's the bottom line. I already reserved the date with large nonrefundable deposits at St. Gregory's and the club. What choice did I have? Lucy's my mother. At the end of the day, she still calls the shots in our family."

"Maybe, God will decide," I answered, staring up at the picture of Anthony, looking down on us with a cruel turn of the lip. Followed by a tear. I will always regret I ever uttered those words.

CHAPTER TWENTYONE

hartered at Berkeley in 1916, the Rho Alpha Chi National Fraternity reached its heights during the 1960's as it burgeoned to thirteen chapters. PAX was founded on the bedrock fallacy of some alleged but spurious relationship to The Knights Templar, who had been dispersed half a millennium earlier, uncoincidentally on Friday 13nth.

By the end of 1970's most Peace House chapters had disbanded. Like Parson's in Iowa and Windham in Vermont, the houses were shut down with the colleges. Only two remained: The Alpha chapter at Berkeley and Delta at Penn.

As pledges, we learned the sacred 'Landmark Motto' of the fraternity:

'To thine own self be true, but only in Brotherhood we trust.'

The pledging ceremony is revered as a symbol of God's invocation to Abraham. It demanded the unequivocal blind faith of every pledge to perform the ultimate sacrifice when called upon. This powerful drama, like the killing of a firstborn son, was considered by The National Fraternity as the most sublime moment in the mortal life of every postulant. An allegory to confirm that true faith in God must be sanctified by the ultimate trust in brotherhood.

Each pledge is called by his Peace House name and ordered to appear on the top floor of the chapter house, where he is duly blindfolded and led into the bathroom by his 'Big Brother.' He is told to drop to his knees next to the commode and grasp with his right hand, without any mental reservation within him whatsoever, the 'dark contents' floating inside of the toilet bowl. Then he is commanded to smash 'the slimy contents' hard against his forehead.

This sacred ritual, known exoterically as the 'Banana Slam' is a sworn secret, intended to uphold the obligation of 'Faith in Brotherhood'. Every pledge must submit willfully or face the ultimate blood sacrifice prescribed by the Sir Knights of the Order. The Supreme Penalty: '*Castration of the entire genitalia prior to being boiled alive.*'

The pledges fall in line to recite the Landmark Motto from memory. And are obligated to keep flagons, goblets and tankards filled for the bibbing and tippling of brothers and their trollops, until duly passed on to the degree of Sir Knight. I chose 'Charlemagne of Frisbee' as my PAX name. 'Sir' was added months later, after my holy initiation.

As you are aware, my fellow Pilgrims, our family was descended from Charlemagne. I had been playing Frisbee golf with regularity at Sedgley Woods in Fairmount Park. I decided to combine these two references into my official fraternity moniker. Peace House brothers normally customize their fraternity names.

I was assigned with fellow pledge, Phildo of Pamphilia to monitor sanitary practices of knights and guests alike, inside the chapter hall, during sanctioned events including, poetry readings, naked quilting bees, senior roasts and our beloved orgies. Two 'Party Ponds' in the backyard were traditionally utilized to promote joyful hygienic hospitality consisting of a pair of inflatable kiddie pools. One was labeled *Puke* with a large oaktag sign. The other one was tagged *Piddle*.

Unauthorized defecation into the Puke or Piddle Party Ponds was sometimes frowned upon by accepted rules of order during public events. Particularly during the orgies, where a slothful lack of self-discipline was exhibited by many of the half-clothed, but fully inebriated partygoers.

Violations were frequent. Despite our vigilance, unhealthy incidents became a hot topic of debate during house meetings. Lethargy Lad of Sardinia opined we needed to maintain but a single large pool to accept both bodily fluids. This condition, he said, was found in nature. In lakes, rivers and oceans. High-pressure nozzles could be employed to mitigate congested effluvial odors. His argument was dismissed. Boisterous hollers and guffaws ended the meeting.

Lethargy Lad, I later learned, was considered by many brothers to be 'phlegmatic' on public issues. On several prior occasions, he had even been accused of 'Taking the easy road'.

Phildo of Pamphilia was an active voice in maintaining high fraternal standards. Inside the University's royal colosseum, he argued, a precedent had been settled on this vital issue. Deep in the dungeons of Franklin Field stood a huge *Pissoir*. A tall concrete wall doused by steel sprayers to service sports fans and visitors. Fathers and sons, alike, at football spectacles would line up, side by side, to irrigate this 'Wailing Wall of Tinkle'.

Supplicants removed their codpieces, protruded their penile faucets and urinated *en masse*, as was done during the efflorescent days of the great public bathhouses, many centuries ago, like in the Roman city of Caracalla. It was widely accepted that *public* defecation inside these venues, Phildo argued, was forbidden. Following six strenuous hours of heated debate, the brotherhood finally voted that our traditional 'Two-Pond' system must be maintained.

At our next orgy, honoring the Persian king Xerxes, Phildo and I faith-fully tended to our pledge duties. We monitored both Party Ponds for bla-tant fecal violations and hosed them down on schedule. Sorting through the inanimate bodies of the naked and the dead, we were also obliged to dis-pose of three leftover cadavers, including the decapitated remains of a Penn Phrenology major. His torso was inhibiting the egress between the foyer and first floor bathroom, and his bilious stench had overpowered the fine, minty-fresh odors, beloved by our Knighthood in The Chapter Hall.

Yet, his skull was singing energetic choruses of *Fight on Pennsylvania*. We stuffed his corpse, along with two fully domed ones into three large holes of the gigantic button sculpture, located in front of the library. Then we placed the quivering, phrenological, but charismatic head — singing tenor smoothly as Enrico Caruso— onto the lap of the statue of Benjamin Franklin. Throughout the rest of the evening, we enjoyed many opportunities to grope and cunny the scores of nurses and wenches before bringing our own quies-cent cods into play.

Vital pledging duties consumed April. I was assigned to answering the door with Mello of Santa Monica, a blond-haired surfer. We greeted Sir Knights and guests by name, answering the house phone within three rings, while keeping a log for messages. We served goblets of libations and platters of victuals, according to the requests of Sir Knights.

We served the *noblest* purposes of brotherhood. In every way, besides the libertine. The romantic poet, Shelley had observed '*The function of the sublime is to end the slavery of pleasure.*' I heartily concur with Mr. Percy, whose wife, Mary had also written *Frankenstein*. Whatever.

Krazy Karen, the most beloved slut in fraternity history announced one day that her priceless guitar had been stolen during a marathon evening of carnal jollies. While playing eight-ball with six different Sir Knights it had disappeared at halftime, as she showered to 'freshen up' between her trysts. A committee was discharged to search the Chapter Hall.

Mello and I, naked and fearless, scoured through trash piles in every room and hallway. For over three hours, but to no avail. But Mello did not easily yield to defeat. He retrieved a large black case from inside a hidden cubby hole on the far wall of the pool room. After our initial euphoria subsided, I realized it felt too light for a guitar case. Something else was jiggling inside, so I flipped the latches, opened it up and spilled the entire contents onto the pool table.

A guitar was not among them. Mello called up Karen to give her the woeful news.

"Hallelujah.... Praise the Lord......Jesus saves," she exclaimed. Our fear and fluster subsided as she confirmed that we had found the *entire contents* of her guitar case: Seven Ziplock bags with battery-operated sex toys, dozens of factory-fresh condoms and diaphragms. And two virgin jars of Pathmark Petroleum Jelly.

We were tasked to feed Mister E by shouting "Four... Four.. .Four." Our finest canine Sir Knight jumps to the sound of his beloved dinner bell command. Then he clatters into the dining room and chows down on his water buffalo chili, which is served to him by our Knighthood at exactly four-forty-four every afternoon.

Nobody could pronounce, much less spell, his lengthy Dutch-German surname. Other than Jameson, Mello became my best buddy. He reminded me of my father, athletic, blond-haired and perpetually smiling, with a husky but melodious laugh, but invariably flat-broke. He transferred to UCLA after our sophomore year, but I stayed in touch with him until I joined him in The Archangels of Golgotha. A fateful decision that nearly cost me my life as it had done to Mello. I realize that our friendship disguised my unconscious desire to forgive my father.

Has any son ever been born to hate his own father?

My father was killed in a motorcycle crash, before I returned from Santa Monica. Riding in a thunderstorm that qualified him as suicidal. His life insurance had lapsed years earlier. I can't divulge anything else about Sir Mello, The Archangels of Golgotha, or my father. Right now, I need closure and my privacy. Trust me. Play Lotto.

✤ ✤ ✤

PLEDGING WAS COMPLETED IN APRIL. One of our finest postulants, Leon of Czikowsky contracted Lyme's disease and withdrew before he transferred to Wesleyan, closer to his home in Connecticut. In a candlelit ceremony, attired in magenta robes and sporting flamboyant new codpieces, we were duly initiated into the grand body of Sir Knights of Brotherhood of PAX. Each of us signed the 'Doomsday Book' with our Peace House names as 'Sir Knight,' a venerable tradition that originated on 'Founders Day' in April of 1919.

The following evening, the Peace House community assembled for The Feast of the Neophyte Knights. I assumed my place amongst august company to commence dutiful servitude to our order as Sir Charlemagne of Frisbee. My heart and tickledingus visibly throbbed. With a charge of electricity only beheld by an adult male donkey's hot pizzle. According to Hippocrates, *"Youth is impatient of hunger, especially when lively, spirited, brisk, stirring, and lusty."* Our fabulous feast was the perfect way to gourmandize our lusty and gluttonous Knighthood.

Rich, steaming stews and soups were served in quantities and magnitudes. Platters of capons, pullets, and goslings stripped of succulent flesh. Carcasses of organic, free-ranging water buffalo, culled from wild, grazing herds, roaming on campus. Butchered, marinated, barbecued, and hanging on large steel hooks from the rafters of our dining hall.

We invited the crapulous Peace House of Temple, despite their scurrilous reputation. A chapter recently shuttered by the FBI. They were our first guests to arrive, like a cageful of baboons with ox flies and inculpated our dimmer switches as 'a vulgar display of Ivy League pomposity'. They hurled more deprecations at our goat cheese focaccia and other canapes, with a particular vengeance towards the genuine corks that sealed our wine bottles.

Victuals of fried tripe and macerated roast pig were provided. Woodcock saturated with sauces, relishes and mustards. Blood sausages garnished with platefuls of roast chestnuts. Kellogg's Pop Tarts, bushels of dried oats. Golden apples, Cheetos, sugarplums and jars of honey. Tankards filled from hogsheads of mead, Dr. Pepper and ale. Trayfuls of vegetables, interlarded with dormouse and Twinkies. Tureens of orange turnips and green chitterlings.

Our Knighthood is chivalrous, ravenous, full of fine trenchermen and lusty fornicators.

Our neophyte class of stout-hearted and gallant Sir Knights lined up, tall and erect for inspection by pledge class captain, the impetuous Sir Jameson of Greenwich. We displayed fine elongated codpieces to the brotherhood, securely fastened by hand-crafted commemorative golden buckles. Hundreds of guests showered us with applause.

Sturdy, ballocking lads gleefully larruping and frigging the cunnies of buxom harlots. We positioned a red-cushioned barstool and shouted in chorus: "Eeee fer a reefer. Eeee fer a reefer..." to invite our favorite canine to partake of his favorite knightly vice. Mister E loved to emulate our lecheries. He was exhilarated by animal spirits and barked three times to confirm a climactic humping of his regular concubine, 'Little Miss E,' the overused, visibly abused, badly shredded black velvet hassock, who always lay still, poised and ready for casual sex on the floor of the barroom.

Upon hearing his clarion call to oblivion, our dogmatic crusader clattered up the stairwell, jumped on top of his favorite barstool with his jowls slobbering. 'Mister Eeefer' was sporting the enraptured eyes of a frisky, newborn puppy, ready to suck a hot nipple. We celebrated seven birthdays for Mister E each human calendar year. Blowing billowing bong smoke into his delirious, wild-eyed face. Lusty Sir Knights, with much oil left in their lanterns, tickled his palate with rum-laced water buffalo chili as they tippled, bibbed and toasted him with scores of raised flagons and goblets.

Strumming and bum fondling.

Making hot cross buns, Sir Mello of Santa Monica, our dilly-darling joy boy, straddled the breasts of Krazy Karen while Sir Scuzbag of Brittania frigged her pelvic lamia on top of her beloved Brunswick.

Sir Country Bob of Turkey Foot awaited 'sloppy seconds' from a befouled 'Boston crème pie' lying voluptuously, poised in position, inside The Temple of Cannabis.

Sir Clitman of Carazia removed his codpiece, rectified his stout whangdoodle and dandled an entire lair of *mannetes* including a barbaric horde of Tartar wenches with his spermatic vessel.

Cods battered, tattered, shattered and bespattered.

Sir Semi-Tool of Calabria gammoned each widow and deflowered every virgin. As he sung the sweetest orgasmic timbres with the finest melodies from lute and lyre.

Sir Lethargy Lad of Sardinia lowered his breeches. Then he ramboodled his beloved, the lovely and lupine Lassitude Lass, who screamed with joy as he ransacked her insatiable labial.

With deep philosophical misgivings, a disbarred judge, belly-bumped a clap-stricken harlot and thwacked accordingly upon the sundry fruits of her corpulent twaddle.

An appointed magistrate, dismembered by a succubus, his dung-hole shorn of venereal dingleberries was rapt to perform many of his long-promised hymeneal acts.

Celestial trollops, weasels, polecats and shrew mice. Anal fistula.

The dotard University chancellor lay twerking in the Orgasmatron like a trollop. Sir Dim Hung Dong of Pyong Yang flogged her salacious butt-cheeks. She quacked like a duck, begging for more ravishment and brayed like a horny ass before finally farting *fortissimo*.

CHAPTER TWENTYTWO

ABANDON ALL HOPE YE WHO ENTER HERE

My fellow Pilgrims, as you remember, The Age of Pandemic started during The Ides of March. Life on Earth was transmogrified into a living Hell. I awoke one morning into the nightmare of *Selva Oscura* in *The Inferno*

Rumors of a Chinese virus, as deadly as SARS and Ebola had surfaced in January. But human transmission was never confirmed until the twentieth. I remember The Hong Kong Flu as a boy in 1969, which killed over a hundred thousand Americans. I was a teeny bopper, lying about my own pilgrimage to Woodstock. The festival had dominated all the headlines at the time, while this killer flu was generally ignored. Go figure.

I entered the Dark Wood of Coronavirus. I drove up the Taconic into the caverns of the Jefferson Valley Mall. The stores were deserted, reimagined as targets for thieves and kleptomaniacs. I wanted to see these ruins myself. Before our civilization reverted to cannibalism. Where are the primal caves, when you need them?

Only kidding. After the attacks of 9/11, I took the train into New York City and visited the site of the Twin Towers, the holocaust of lower Manhattan. I still feel the same way, today. God is Dead.

Allow me to confess. I never expected Covid-19 to last. The first cases in America appeared on January 21. Secretary Azar of Health and Human Services declared a public health emergency on the 31st as Trump cut off travel from China. I even heard rumors that it was abating in Wuhan. Late in February, Doctor Fauci said on *The Today Show*, no reason to worry. Or to change your behavior. I listened to the experts who told us to 'Follow the Science'.

What a call. Some experts were clamoring that the virus wasn't as deadly as the common flu. Educated idiots. I distrust politicians, anyways. The more I Followed the Science, the more I realized how Truth was repackaged to serve specific political interests. As a Soldier of Truth, I realized I had to verify everything myself.

I am The Bargain Shopper. I knew I could capitalize on this virus and the misfortunes of others, as I did with Old Navy after 9/11. I still feel guilty about getting Mickey Drexler fired. Yet, here I was, looking across an empty mall, desolate as the fortress that Lord Byron described in his alliterative poetic masterpiece, *The Destruction of Sennacherib*:

> *Like the leaves of the forest when Autumn hath blown,*
> *That host on the morrow lay withered and strown.*

I turned my eyes again to the parking lot. Miles and miles of asphalt were spread out, forsaken and abandoned. *The tents were all silent. And the idols are broke in the temple of Baal.*

> *For the Angel of Death spread his wings on the blast.*

I conjured images of the Leopard, the Lion and the Wolf. And of my own day of reckoning. Unforeseen as my destiny since my unholy birth, unstrapped from an anvil following Jean-Baptiste II out of our mother's womb. Beholden in the throes of the dreads. Ready to face the savage beasts in the Portals of Hell. I am The Bargain Shopper and I sat on the floor of this empty mall with my heart in hand as I wept aloud.

I prayed for the return of the Angel of God. As Byron had imagined Sennacherib, I saw the broken embattlements of empty shops. I scanned empty caverns with unbelieving eyes. I chanted cantos of woe and fear. As prophesied, I had arrived at my destination. Except a few years ahead of schedule into The Nine Circles of Hell.

To claps of thunder, I passed through The First Circle. Satan greeted me with a bright, squamulose smile with a pair of shiny horns on his head, his wings were covered with oily scales. A tiny black goatee adorned his chin. The infamous pedophile, Jefferey Epstein was pleading with a centaur for promotion into Limbo.

Emperor Nero and Caligula sat under the Sword of Damocles. Brothers in torture, sodomy, and incest, snickering with Hitler and Nazi brass, renowned for their satanic laughs. Alumni of the Third Reich bragging to Lucifer in The Third Circle about the virtues of torture and cruelty. And the crematoriums of their death camps. Even hotter than Hell.

Robber barons boiling alive in blood money. Wallets in hand, negotiating the tides of the Phlegethon. Jim Fiske and Jay Gould chatting obliviously with Crassus in a deep ditch under hailstorms. Epstein begging for a ticket to Purgatory, trying to bribe fallen Archangels and the Marquis de Sade to entice alluring young sexual prospects.

I never saw J.P. Morgan. But Vanderbilt was slurping cocktails with a Hooters girl in the trenches. If Morgan was in Hell, he might be on Stygian Lake, sailing with gentlemen. Or blackballing Epstein— certainly, no gentleman. Or buying a *Stairway to Heaven*. Anything but a one-way ticket out of Hell, which he most desired.

I will ask Jameson upon my return. I'll ask him about the fate of President Trump. Was he doomed because of his infidelities and business deals? Everyone saw the Billy Bush tape, yet he was still elected President. Did he sell his soul to the devil like Jill Paulson? Hell has a humongous waiting list. Zillions of celebrities and politicians. And recently overrun by gangs of pedophile priests. Ask Lucifer, although I've heard that he's sworn to secrecy on these lists.

I know the answer about Trump. I'll keep it to myself. Gangsters hang out in the three compartments of The Seventh Circle. Renowned for their silk suits and vanities. Sybarites, like Lucky Luciano remind me of Trump even more than Vanderbilt. Capone is brown-nosing Archbishop Ruggieri and Pope Nicholas V. As if his despoiled holiness has a snowball's chance in Hell of getting Capone into Heaven. Why does Al think these clerics were sent here in the first place? He is playing poker with Arnold Rothstein with an antique White Sox cap on his toupee. I heard he had fixed the World Series in 1919. Now, he's trying to cheat Capone at cards. Fat chance. Cash in your chips, Arnie. Play Lotto.

In the Eight Circle, lies a lake of boiling pitch. Full of peculators and thieves. Small time grifters who steal from the common man. You know them well. They swallow 'the salt of the earth'. Spineless snakes who suck blood.

Like William O'Neal, a nobody. Owned Tristar Chemical. A small-time pathological liar who bribed custodians and purchasing agents. Paid soft dollar kickbacks to the Archdiocese to sponge off their constituencies. Do not be fooled. Friendly alacrity and *bonhomie*, a smiling cobra who reneged on his promises to longtime employees. Thank God, there is a Devil. He will burn forever in The Inferno. Where Pol Pot eats live chickens with chopsticks. Where Idi Amin and Attila the Hun drink children's blood in goblets, carved out of human skulls.

To my delight, in the deep, dark, flaming abyss, I heard the call of the wild. The inimitable bark of Mister E— beloved canine crusader, Sir Knight of The Peace House. Finished with his doggy years on Earth, his bark sounding stronger with two more barking heads. I took Satan aside. How could such a perfect beast be condemned to Hell?

Satan laughed through his pink, suppurated cheeks. He wagged his dragon tail with delight but ignored my question. I followed him upstairs into the morning light. "How do I love pandemics," he emitted, with sulfurous breath. "Let me count the ways. First, I can finally take a vacation. Epidemics help me hit my quotas. I'd settle for an outbreak of Cholera until we get to World War III. It's been very exciting down here. Pandemonium. The bats in our caves have been going crazy by the River Styx waiting for the daily ferry to arrive with boatloads of newly-minted, atheists, who despise God and humanity. Pandemics can even work better than wars. I can hardly wait for the arrival of Covid-20."

"But will Mister E ever make it into Doggy Heaven?"

"Give my regards to Jill. What a perfect bitch," he emitted, as a cloud of black smoke billowed from his nostrils. "Looking forward to working with her forever in Eternity. Hey, Charles, you want to know the Truth?"

"Of course. Just tell me what's going to happen to Mister E?" I pleaded.

"Coronavirus is the best thing that's happened to Hell, since The Bubonic Plague."

CHAPTER TWENTYTHREE

homas Sowell, of The Hoover Institution at Stanford observed "*It takes considerable knowledge just to become aware of your own ignorance.*" Nobel Laureate poet, T.S. Eliot said, "*We know too much and are convinced of too little.*" Both of these geniuses are correct. As I started my sophomore year, I was *convinced* of only one thing. No university, no matter however prestigious, can do anything to ensure the teaching, much less the learning of *anything of value.*

The only thing I had learned was how little I know.

Benjamin Franklin, our university's enlightened founder would have agreed. Art History and Criminology were a waste of time and money. In my case, a waste of time, since I never spent a dime for tuition. The ancient adage remained true: *You get what you pay for.* I retained my digs at 40th and Pine but signed up for lunch at the fraternity to hang out and maybe knock down a beer or two. After Labor Day, we had our first house meeting.

Under Old Business, last year's philanthropy smashed previous records. Newly elected chaplain, Sir Groover of Eurypterid commended our hard work and generosity. After deducting for labor, overhead and other legitimate expenses, a check would be sent to fatten the coffers of Habitat for Humanity for $22.68.

Under New Business, the committee to 'Find a Bitch for Mister E.' was conscripted but a trip to the animal shelter in Haverford was postponed. We had reasonably presumed Mister E would be awarded complimentary 'tryouts' to evaluate candidates in their natural sexual habitat to qualify her mating skills but the lesbian director was 'a bigger bitch than her mutts.' The search for a lascivious Mrs. E and first canine ever elected to our harem was tabled.

In a critical agenda item, Sir Gunnar of Youth in Asia volunteered to play Santa Claus at the Christmas Festival in December. A huge honor and commitment. Last year, Youth displayed fidelity to the Landmark Motto. He was voted 'Pledge of the Year' and deemed 'duly qualified', nominated forthwith, seconded and elected by acclimation. He would need to study with the intensity of a Talmudic scholar to master *The Christmas Anthem*, a poem recited only from memory. Twenty-four verses of inspiration. Paradoxically the most lugubrious couplets of Yuletide ever written.

It was composed fifty years ago by a martyred, now legendary Sir Knight of The Peace House.

This brother was canonized four decades ago by our National Fraternity as Lord Rapier of Whangletool. He had recited his magnum opus only once, while playing Santa at The Christmas Festival, where he fell upon his knees, following an apparent beatification and confessed to a hideous mortal sin. He had desecrated his sacramental oath—inadvertently, during uncontrollable throes of romantic passion. In a venal exchange for a variety of unspecified sexual favors. Unforgivably, he revealed the inviolate secret of the 'Banana Slam' to his betrothed. Or engaged. Whatever.

He immersed himself in prayer, contemplation and penance. In search of divine and ontological truths of human existence, while studying the *Summa Theologiae* of Thomas Aquinas. He concluded that true faith in God was only coincident with a pure devotion to the Landmark Motto. Mercifully, he also realized his redemption could be attained. Even in this mortal life. But atonement would require him to perform the summary execution of the Supreme Penalty.

He removed his codpiece, unsheathed a paring knife, and slashed off his cock and balls. Praying to God for mercy, while begging forgiveness from the brotherhood, as he bled himself to death. This was the first time the Supreme Penalty was ever inflicted upon a Sir Knight— at least, voluntarily. Yet, Lord Whangletool escaped being boiled alive. And this was only the second or possibly third verifiable castration in fraternity history.

⚜ ⚜ ⚜

KRAZY KAREN NEVER STOPPED PLEADING with me to enjoin her in the pool room. Fortunately, Jay had warned me of her latest affliction, so I bleated back, "Sorry Krazy.... I don't know how to swim." She got the message and stopped trying to goad me into 'quickie' games of eight-ball every afternoon. The news that had already started leaking out became a flood. Karen was being treated at Student Health, along with three knights for pubic lice. Several crustacean antidotes had been prescribed and mandatory sexual abstinence was imposed upon all guilty parties.

I was spending less time with Jay, but more with Mello who lived near me on Spruce. Unlike more languorous Sir Knights, who preferred the safer pastures inside our portcullis, we liked to explore the amusements of Center City. We took the trolley down to the Italian market. Or to Pat's Steaks on Passyunk. Or engorged empty bellies with chow-down dinners in Chinatown on Saturday nights. Mello was always short on cash. We always checked menu prices in the windows before entering. I coined an acronym to describe the decretals of Bargain Dining and started awarding our favorites, like *Rainbow Ray* with the acronym *MVR* for 'Maximum Value Restaurant'.

Then one day, I saw an ad in *The Daily Drummer* for a lecture on Thomas Eakins at Philadelphia Museum of Art. A neoclassical temple that loomed over the Schuylkill River which was a subject for several of his major paintings. Mello passed on it since the 'suggested donation' was two bucks. His instincts were correct. The lecture was a bore, but I sat behind a cute, blonde ponytail in tight jeans. I strolled over to chat with her after the lecture. She was a sophomore transfer at Moore College of Art. And very hot to trot. Her name was Eleanor Atwood.

I'm sorry but I must warn you. I confess a tragic-pathetic story heretofore follows. Truth must prevail as always. But if you accuse me of 'bad taste' then consider yourself *jxzasshitncunt*. I invited Eleanor to share in the fine perversions of our upcoming 'Classical Roman Orgy' in honor of the late Emperor Sulla, scheduled at our chapter hall following the bloody Dartmouth football spectacle at Franklin Field on Saturday afternoon. Her eyes twinkled with libidinous desire, as she thrilled to accept my lascivious offer as befits any lissome, inquisitive sylph. I encouraged her to invite another innocent, yet not ineludibly virtuous maiden, to join in our festivities and be mercilessly ravaged by an entire corps of lusty Sir Knights. Also, for some legitimate security precautions.

Eleanor inexplicably ignored my request.

Long before any togas were torn off, or the whistle was blown to start the 'Galley Races' or the cavalcade of deviancies and unconscionable sexual depravities commenced, I volunteered to give her a ride home to her dorm at Moore following the festivities. In case, she still desired one, after being sexually plundered and abused.

But I could not find her. Until Sunday afternoon, passed out and stinking and lying on top of Little Miss E on a sticky couch in The Peace House basement. Her underwear was pitted, her dirty blonde hair matted down. She declined my offer for a ride and told me she had been invited back to the frat for 'more fun' next Friday night. One of our brothers, Jon 'something or other' who lives off-campus had invited her back as the official 'Guest of Honor.'

I thought she was bullshitting. She promised to bake chocolate chip cookies for the entire brotherhood. Then smiled at me obliquely, swiveled off the couch, trussed her molten hair and clopped upstairs to catch the next trolley.

I talked to Mello the following afternoon. Naturally, I assumed he had inadvertently fructified this nubile strumpet. He recalled bumping and grinding with a hot, naked, blonde for several sadistic dances but as usual, he couldn't remember her face, much less her name. He was positive about one thing for sure. He *never* had sex with her, except for a hasty, but adroitly delivered hand job. He was so boozed up he had left the orgy early. Long before last call for orgasms. But he couldn't remember anything about chocolate chip cookies. I was sure Eleanor was lying.

Wrong again. She started arriving weekly to the chapter hall. Every Friday afternoon, precisely at Four-Forty-Four as Mister E finished his chili bowl, she took over the kitchen and baked an extensive variety of homemade cookies for the Knighthood. Then she shacked up with a variety of Sir Knights, filling the void created by the cessation of carnalities once provided by the recuperating Krazy Karen. For the first time in years, the fetid, green felt on top of the Brunswick which had always stunk up the council room like rancid tuna, didn't even require a replacement.

Krazy Karen was furious. Sexually sidelined. Shunned by the Knighthood like a Mennonite heretic for her affliction with *crabs*—which was hardly *herpes* or *the clap*. 'What the fuck is the big deal', she conjectured, with the divinatory clarity of her beautiful mind. Crustacean remedies cure most of the painful symptoms. This kind of bullshit pissed her off. Considering all she had sacrificed for the Peace House. She plonked her anger into a box, braided her hair into little pigtails with pink ribbons and paraded around in a white pinafore dress, buttered with aphrodisiacal perfumes.

But to no avail. She wasn't asked to rack up for eight ball. Or was enjoined in a single tailrasping bumswink.

Not only was Karen furious, but jealous as hell. She'd secretly admired Eleanor's sincere commitment to promiscuous, casual sex but considered her an outsider, although a ruthless competitor who slaked the sexual hunger of horny knights with soft cookies, rather than playing them hard in eight ball. Cookies as addictive as cheese enabled her 'bait and switch' tactics. But Eleanor had never paid her dues and Karen believed that only she was the hobby horse who delivered the broiling provisions to an undernourished Knighthood. For the last three years, except for several voluntary 'lay-offs' during the heights of her raging menstrual periods.

Like Persephone, Queen of Hades, she enticed virginal Knights with sexually bereft scrotums, while lounging below deck, in her claustral boudoir. Faking orgasms to fecundate the concupiscence of lusty knights. To brighten the faces of sad cavaliers who craved hot lodging for their limber dinguses. She even managed to simulate a perfectly warm silk purse of ecstasy, while spread-eagled athwart that cold hard slab of fine green cushioned slate.

Her rage continued into the sublime date on the fraternity calendar. Then came the straw that broke the camel's back. Eleanor, *not* Karen, was selected by Sir Koala of New South Wales, duly elected as *Sow Rex*, to perform the cherished role of *First Elf*. Honored to service Santa Claus, during the Holly Jollies of The Christmas Festival.

As runner-up, Krazy Karen was appointed Second Elf. Perfectly well-positioned to achieve her terrible revenge. Her sinister plot would succeed. Eleanor Atwood's tenure as the most favored wench of The Knighthood would end in damnation. Along with the unfortunate and unlikely fall of the legendary Sir Gunnar of Youth in Asia.

Eleanor would never set foot in The Peace House again. The party was over.

CHAPTER TWENTYFOUR

New York City was completely locked down during The Ides of March and Governor Cuomo issued stay-at-home orders on the 20th. Madame asked me if I wanted to be laid off, as most clothing stores had closed except for Target. She knew I never shopped for clothing at Target or Walmart, except socks and underwear and *never* on-line. I appreciated her offer to collect unemployment but informed her I preferred to retain my position as *major domo* of the Wolcott household even as I ceased my duties as The Bargain Shopper. She was perfectly happy with my decision.

Many people were so terrified by the virus, they rarely left home. Others simply ignored it, ratifying the words of Bertrand Russell, '*Most men would rather die than think.*' Over 300, 000 Americans died by the end of the year.

Whether they were thinking or unthinking about it, they all died of The Coronavirus.

New York State reported five thousand new cases a day in March. These numbers multiplied as 'Flattening the Curve' became the new mantra. Hospitals were overrun with Covid patients. Beatrice never worried, except for her concern for the poor and elderly. She followed CDC guidelines and placed sanitizing wipes, face masks and gloves throughout the house. She posted the entire list of Covid-19 symptoms on the refrigerator. Both of us were prone to 'Follow the Science,' as I have always followed my Decretals as a matter of principle, along with all the rules.

Roxy never follows rules. She always breaks them and hides. Then she cries when she gets caught. Madame hinted to her not be wasteful. Roxy started double masking, spraying Lysol everywhere and wearing gloves for an hour, before trashing them. The Madame, a lady of character, hates waste and finally ordered her to desist.

As I've told you Bea loves tennis. Her interest intensified as a young ball girl at Forest Hills and continued as a lineswoman in her twenties. She was an umpire in the early matches of The U.S. Open. Fairness is part of her character. Jameson, who knows everything about everybody, told me she lost a singles match against Barnard by calling a foot fault on herself. Overturning the outcome after serving to win at *match point*. Her opponent had already walked off the court in defeat. Heraclitus would have agreed. Madame Beatrice was the 'unlucky one'. Born with bad timing like me. She deserved a much better fate in life, commensurate with her character.

"Charles. One of the girls in my tennis group at Sleepy says that Omega-3 rich foods are good for your brain. Especially during these lockdowns. There's been a terrible outbreak of depression and suicides."

"Everyone's worried about the economy. The stock market is crashing." I answered. "People are jumping off buildings on Wall Street like it's Black Friday. That's how your grandfather bought this place on the cheap. I read somewhere that the suicide rate is lower in close knit communities like the Amish."

"Also, in the leper colonies. We should eat foods with anti-depressive effects. I'm making a list."

"What kind of foods?"

"Fish and Beans."

"I hate fish, but I love barbecued frog legs," I said. "Do frogs qualify as fish as far as vitamins go?"

"I'll check the Internet, Charles. I do hope you like eating beans. They're very good for your brain."

"I've always heard that beans are good for your heart."

The Madame grimaced, got up from the chair and filled her glass from a bottle of Bogle Chardonnay. After taking a sip, she rolled her eyes. "I 'm still worrying about the wedding. If this pandemic gets any worse, it may have to be postponed indefinitely."

"Which could be a blessing in disguise."

"No, Charles. Peter and Emily need to move ahead in their lives. They're not getting any younger. Even if it's held at St. Gregory's The Great, I still want to get it done ASAP, so I can stop worrying. It's always on my mind."

"It's way too early to worry, Bea. We have plenty of time," I said. "The invitations don't even go out until July."

"I heard some of these covid tests don't work, Charles. They give the wrong results, which scares me even more. Whenever I cough or get a sore throat, I worry, because I'm not even sure I can trust the test results."

"Maybe, we have Governor Cuomo and President Trump to thank for *that*."

⚜ ⚜ ⚜

AFTER WORK, I STOPPED AT SHOPRITE, before returning to Melville Corners. The parking lot was packed. A long line of stolid shoppers clogged the entrance. Denizens of *Les Miserable*. But unlike breadlines during The Great Depression, nothing was free. The prices on everything were as high as ever. The free plastic shopping bags were long-gone and banned by the state to satisfy the Greeniac lobby. The paper one's cost everybody a nickel per bag.

Thank you, ShopRite. Thank you, Governor Cuomo.

The store was an emporium but only of commotion. The ambience of the old Soviet Union. Or current one, for all I know. I was wearing a facemask, thanks to Bea, because I had used up the ones from the leper colony. ShopRite would have forced me into wrapping a filthy scarf on my face. They couldn't have cared less, even I was starving.

I finagled a shopping cart. A five-pound bag of red potatoes cost $1.99. My tumblers of util maximization were lubricated, locked and loaded. I purchased eight items as I scrounged past rows of empty aisles, possibly ransacked by *Black Lives Matter*. I live alone and don't need many supplies since Madame allows me to take anything I want from her cupboard, including Roxy's casseroles, impounded like icy bricks in her freezer. I always pretend that I've forgotten them. When Bea coaxes me to take one home, I always end up tossing it into the trash before it even thaws.

I steered my shopping cart into checkout. Jacked up prices, few deals or discounts. Like trying to find a bargain on food at Yankee Stadium. Or the final round of the U.S Open for Kitty Croquet. Premium prices.

I pushed my cart back outside to my Toyota. I pulled on my Dollar Tree eyeglasses and inspected the tape. I gasped. To my horror and indignation, Shoprite had raped me again. I retrieved the eggs and cheese and ran back into the store in a rage. The line had grown longer, as I rushed to return them, clutching the receipt. I snuck around the line and ran through the exit door. Brun Hilda from The Hitler Youth Brigade spotted me, from behind a row of shopping carts in the front. She rushed back in like an agent of the *Gestapo*, hollering at me. I ignored her and ran through the sliding glass doors, shouting like crazy that I *had* to return two items.

"You guys ripped me off," I screamed.

"No returns are allowed," she howled, before accosting me at Customer Service.

"I demand a credit," I bawled, so loud that everyone in the store could hear me.

The store manager arrived. Hilda goosestepped back to her battle watch on the Western Front. I only got twenty-three cents credit for the eggs. The deal on the cheese had expired three days earlier, but I hadn't seen the fine print on the bottom of the sign. What a racket these guys have going. These crooks are legitimized because of Covid-19.

Are these people our hero's? Fuck them. Fine print and exclusions, full of scams. In the old days, *their* mistake would have forced them to give me the overpriced eggs for free. Now a virus empowers Shoprite to emulate a fascist regime.

Almost as corrupt as our government.

I returned home and retired. I felt a frog in my throat and started coughing. I wiped my forehead to check for fever. It felt hot. I wasn't positive that I was negative. But I knew that I was certainly stressed out.

I needed to be tested for Coronavirus. I knew I was at risk and long overdue. But I had no intention of being quarantined. I went to bed and turned off the lights. In the darkness, I remembered what Madame had said about unreliable testing. And the most salient symptom was losing your sense of smell.

I stuck my forefinger up my nose. Then I coughed. By God, I didn't smell a thing.

I rolled over and pulled off my pajamas in a panic as I plunged my left forefinger up my asshole. To my great relief, my nostrils were greeted with the reassuring smell of shit. Coronavirus negative.

Thank you, Governor Cuomo. Thank you, President Trump.

The next morning, I was sitting with Bea in the breakfast nook. Her cellphone went off and she squinted as her face darkened. I heard the muffled voice of Francis. His mother had been awakened by a barrage of coughing fits at five A.M. She was barely able to breathe. Hildy woke up and went to her room in the nick of time to call 911. When Francis didn't answer, she called Demetri in Scarsdale, who showered and dressed. Lucille Alfieri was rushed by ambulance to White Plains Hospital into an intermediate step-down care area designated as Covid unit 4F.

Two days later, she was placed under a respirator.

Francis and Demetri waited in the lobby. They prayed together. The sign read: **Do Not Enter.**

CHAPTER TWENTYFIVE

Sir Gunnar of Youth in Asia was a stout-headed and bleary-eyed lad. Usually inebriated during his waking hours. His hedonism was authentic. He was blessed to be extremely wide of girth.

He finished freshman year on academic probation and 'social probation' in the Spring with a legendary reputation for smashing his former professor— eight months pregnant and a vice dean in The Wharton School who coincidentally flunked him the previous semester— on her forehead with a water balloon, as she had strolled across the red bricks of Locust Walk. Youth swore his innocence, pleading that the balloon had 'escaped from my hand.' He was forced to withdraw his appeal, once vigorously argued on his behalf by The Greek Council, as a plenum of proof confirmed the projectile contained no water at all, as Dean Wormser had sworn under oath, but was inflated by human urine.

*Twas the **blight** before Christmas and all through the frat,*
*Not a creature was stirring, not even a **rat**.*

Sir Gunnar committed this classic couplet to a tiny cluster of his remaining neurons. In less than an hour, while doing his laundry, the stark realization sunk in…. very, very, slowly. It was December. Time was running short. He spread out his clothes to dry atop a rusty radiator that warmed the armadas of filthy germs that proliferated in The Peace House bathrooms. Youth only wore crumpled XXLT, short-sleeved alligator polo shirts, even during cold winter days. He hand-laundered his clothes, including socks and underwear in the sink with a few squirts of *Prell* shampoo.

Suspenders upheld his jeans. He curated a dapper, slightly dangerous, but insolent public image. He never left the house without one of his signature polka-dotted cravats, tied neatly around his beefy, red neck. Sir Gunnar had procrastinated in memorizing the *The Christmas Anthem*. Like he did with everything else, except for chugging yards of ale, playing all-night poker games, smoking three bongfuls of pot at a time, sleeping through all his classes, devouring X- large sausage pizzas in under five minutes, or masturbating to *The Dark Side of the Moon*.

> *The wenches were bare by the fireplace in hordes,*
> *Awaiting the thrusts of Sir Knights mighty swords.*

He realized he had forgotten every unforgettable word of the second couplet. So, he wiped off his belly with tissue, tossed it and rolled over moaning in bed, drifting into a deep, dark, foreboding but eternal beauty sleep.

Sir Jameson of Greenwich was elected *Supreme Bacchus*, designating him as chief overseer of Peace House social life. Neophyte knights were rarely elected to so high an office. Other than the Holiest of the Holies, like the *Grand Whimsey*, *Cosmic Exchequer* or sublime prefecture of the *Sow Rex*, Jay has become a leader in the fraternity pantheon.

Critical to a successful Bacchus, the Holly Jollies culminated with The Christmas Festival. Jay had missed last year's authentic, albeit overtly sadistic, Viking Orgy which splattered buckets of blood, pumice stone, and reindeer-dung over all the trash piles. He was too busy sipping sweet, preppy cocktails, fully committed to joining St. Anthony's Hall.

Unfortunately, Jay had a grandiose vision. As a Greenwich preppie and former St. A's pledge, he wanted to revolutionize the PAX social program. He rose to his feet at a house meeting and announced that all future events, including the ever-popular, co-ed naked quilting bees and all satanic orgies must display 'A Touch of Class.'

His proclamation reverberated like a neutron bomb. The chapter exploded into controversy. Panic and primordial fear prevailed. Many knights questioned their judgements in electing a preppy novitiate like Sir Jameson to so high an office. Brothers frantically whipped hard the lizards beneath their codpieces, like desperate but obedient flagellants during The Black Death. Others screamed agonies of despair, furrowing their brows in anguish, while pondering this insane doctrine. Even Mister E started pooping his piles in the dining room, instead of the backyard.

'A Touch of Class' could imply prohibiting the touching of genitalia. Were these words a code? 'Class' implies imposing strictures on righteous orgies. It could be misinterpreted to force the closure of the Party Ponds or outlaw nudity. Or impose abstinence upon a happy, salacious knighthood. Several elders voiced stentorian opposition. One knight even whispered that Jameson resign. Or subject himself to the sublime agonies of The Supreme Penalty.

A chivalrous order like The Peace House had no desire to emulate the onanistic, monastic culture of the elite but effete St. Anthony's Hall. Especially in light, of a certain recent but incriminating rumor. The esteemed Grand Whimsey, Sir Kofi of Dark Nubian Invader, in counsel with our holiest officers, informed Sir Jameson that each of the two parts of his 'Touch of Class' initiatives must be approved by The Knighthood to be eligible for implementation.

Jay was ordered to clarify his devilish details. Sir Dark Nubian called a meeting and declared that Jay must explain his vague 'Touch of Class' guidelines to enhance the Christmas Festival, as well as for the benefit of future fraternity jollies.

"All permutations and varieties of public copulations are heretofore confined to private rooms."

Jameson said this, as he scanned the room. He heard only a stunned silence. He followed with his second imperative which decreed that each Sir Knight and party guest would receive a special 'Holiday Gift' at every Christmas Festival. A bottle of a California sparkling wine called 'Andre Cold Duck'.

The second imperative was roundly applauded and approved by acclamation.

⚜ ⚜ ⚜

TWAS' THE BLIGHT before Christmas and all through the frat.

For first time in history, these revered words were not recited by Santa. This festival was an execution, a massacre. Nobody in the history of armaments had ever contemplated weaponizing anything as refreshing as Andre Cold Duck. Except for the lethal mind of Krazy Karen who had plotted

Machiavellian revenge upon Eleanor with a cabal of loyal *Knights of the Green Rectangle*. In clandestine meetings held around the fetid, green felt of her beloved Brunswick.

Karen was ready, armed and dangerous. With her corps of trained militia. Dejectedly, she ignominiously pulled on a pair of the simple, plain, green tights traditionally worn by the Second Elf, before hunkering down to over-see the carnage to come. On that fateful night, the gruesome culmination of her despicable, yet virtuoso battle plan.

Poor Eleanor Atwood. She arrived three hours early, wearing a red-se-quined outfit as First Elf. She baked four trayfuls of Christmas cookies: shiny reindeers, little snowflakes, north stars and adorable red and white Santa's. I felt sorry for her, guilty and responsible for her welfare. I was one of only a handful of Sir Knights who never had sex with her. Except for two and a half pacific rim jobs, as requested by my monster, the insatiable Mister Dingle Screw.

I was to blame. I was the knight who had invited Eleanor to join in the jollies of The Peace House.

Little did I realize that an outsider, a foundling like Eleanor, could disrupt the delicate balance of perversions that held our tightly knit, knightly com-munity together. Did I err on purpose? I think not, as I am a 'regular guy'. Did I blunder? Yes— but innocently as I committed an abomination against God or Nature. Whatever. Play Lotto.

Sir Gunnar of Youth in Asia received an unwelcome phone call from his father, a prominent yeoman in veterinary medicine from New Canaan, Ct. earlier in the morning. He had been booted from college, 'dropped from the rolls' of The Wharton School as incompletes from his previous semester had been converted into failing grades. He got the same letter at the PAX house, but had tossed it into the trash, along with three pairs of skid-marked tighty-whities, a wad of sticky- fingered tissues, a bong with a broken kazoo and a warped copy of *The Christmas Anthem*.

Almost sober, he jammed himself into the bright-red Santa Clause suit before opening a bottle of Mad Dog 20/20 for lubricating the evening. I must repeat myself. Before I say another word. I do not wish to exclude myself from any polite company, including my own. Please turn to the next chapter so I can spare you the graphic, shocking, disgusting, horrific, but abbreviated details that allegedly tainted The Christmas Festival.

You have rejected my impassioned plea. Or chose to ignore my admoni-
tion. So be it. I am sick and tired of being bashed, bludgeoned, crucified,
caned and indicted by angry mobs of self-righteous, hypocritical, moralistic
parliamentarians. Take due notice, so I can wax iconoclastic. Or even pornographic. I only tell the Truth, no matter how perverted or deranged it may be.
Life is *not* a bowl of pitted cherries, but I cannot simply throw *veritas* out the
window. Call me puerile. I have confessed to that peccadillo. You can dispar-
age my dirty mind and bad manners and prosecute my indecent morality or
my allegedly low opinion of women. That kind of nonsense.

The only thing you will ever prove is that you are a fool. Play Lotto.

Sir Gunnar forgot *The Christmas Anthem*, so he rushed into the bathroom and passed out on the throne. Puking as he piddled, stinking into oblivion. His sphincter exploded like a Graf Zeppelin, bursting the floodgates of
his bodily dam into a roaring river of diarrhea. He fell off the throne onto the
floor, where they found him the following afternoon.

Six sturdy Sir Knights, supporters of Krazy Karen had lined up execution
style in front of this petrified young cookie chef from Moore College of Art. I
will add, waxing irrelevant, that Eleanor dearly loved the bright watercolors
of the famous local artist, Mary Cassatt, since growing up in her quaint but
ordinary white girlhood in Manyunk.

The squadron grimly shook their bottles of Andre, yanking their lethal
corks in unison— more deadly than the plastic bullets used by Philadelphia
Riot Police. They fired a fusillade into the astonished face of the doomed First
Elf.

Poor Eleanor Atwood did *not* lose an eye. I repeat. She never lost an eye.
The object a knight errant found smushed on the foyer floor was a cherry
cordial. She lost only one of her two front teeth. Jay hit the bullseye. Andre
Cold Duck was literally— a smashing success. Providing piles of broken glass
and an unforgettable evening. 'A Touch of Class.'

On a brighter note, eight Sir Knights, flaunting their utter contempt for
Sir Jameson's ill-fated First Imperative, with wenches fully in tow, executed
a perfect 'Double Octopussy.' Krazy Karen resumed her place of honor after
much too long an abstinence, copulating in her customary left-center-right
position. A nostalgic sight to behold along with a flawless performance of a
carnal configuration, beloved for decades by the Knights of Brotherhood.

Whether or not Eleanor dove into the *Puke* Party Pool or was tossed in by
Karen's vindictive militia remains an open question. What is uncontestable:

Mister E, in solidarity with the righteous mood of our Knighthood, exterminated her memory. He barked thrice after uplifting his left hind leg and despoiled the last trays of her final batch of cookies.

CHAPTER TWENTYSIX

"*April is the Cruelest Month*," wrote T. S. Eliot. The onslaught of coronavirus cases in New York State was the highest in the country, averaging over ten thousand a day. Hospitalizations skyrocketed between the fifth and the eighteenth. The daily death rate spiked to over a thousand. Ten thousand New Yorkers died of Covid-19. There was panic in the streets of New York City except for one inconvenient fact. Most of the streets were deserted.

Cuomo warned us every day. As if he was the only adult in the room, he scolded us like children. New York was running short on respirators and hospital beds, he warned, as if it was our fault. Our ship was sinking. We were doomed to die, unless we followed his mandates and stayed inside our little shells, like hermit crabs.

My fellow Pilgrims, I have been to Hell and back. I saw Lucifer in the flesh. I watched in disbelief as our supreme governor, sitting on his golden throne in Albany, vacillated every day. He'd try to blame President Trump for everything gone wrong on Wednesday. But on Thursday, he'd praise the president for a job well done.

As for me, I blamed them both.

Politicians were making threats. You could see how clueless they were, but someday we would learn the truth. Like the death sentence issued against the sick and the elderly in our state, most vulnerable in our nursing homes.

Thank you, Governor Cuomo.

On the first day of the cruelest of months, one of these deaths was Lucille Laskaris Alfieri.

It took several days for the shock to wear off. The service was held at St. Gregory The Great. Francis scrambled to make the arrangements. The church was filled with flowers and incense but was restricted to four dozen mourners, socially distanced with a dozen in each quarter of the sanctuary. Facemasks were mandatory but singing was prohibited. Father Balaskas, in a flowing, white robe, invoked his greetings from the pulpit with a short message in front of the altar, as he discharged the Holy Funeral Rites of The Catholic Church.

Francis and Demetri followed with readings. The two Alfieri brothers led the processional, accompanied by organ music, past a closed rosewood casket where each mourner dropped a single white orchid. I escorted The Madame ahead of Emily and Peter. Charlotte was forced to remain in Atlanta to avoid the extensive travel risks.

I noticed that Jill and Andy were conspicuously absent at both the service and the reception.

I passed on the dinner myself, catered by Lucy's favorite restaurant. A Greek summer banquet delivered by *Argyros Peloponnesian Grill* in Manhattan, hosted by Demetri and Angela at their Scarsdale home. My mood lightened when I saw Beatrice crying and hugging Francis. And holding his hand, for the first time in years. I returned home hungry for a dinner of a cheeseburger with soup and pot of boiled broccoli. I needed peace and quiet to finish this lugubrious day. At seven, I got an unexpected call from Jameson. He usually worked late, but as usual, he always knew everything about everybody, including the news about Lucy's untimely death.

"I suppose Niko's flowers brightly adorned the festivities?"

"Not a good time to tell bad jokes, Jameson."

"Sorry... Trying to cheer you up. Do they know how Lucille caught the virus?"

"They traced it to Judy Kravitz, one of her close friends. She belonged to that synagogue in New Rochelle where the virus started. She was one of the first victims, practically the Alpha lady. She died two weeks ago."

"Who could have known?"

"Nobody. Until it was too late for Judy or Lucy."

"I have some more bad news for you," Jay said. "Have you been watching Tucker Carlson?"

"Every single night," I lied. "Right after the *Richie Rich* comedy hour."

Jay cleared his throat. "Tucker went to Washington last week to talk to Trump. The Donald is blowing it. The way he's handling the coronavirus. He acts like he doesn't even take it seriously."

"He's been saying he wants to reopen the entire country by Easter. He must be crazy."

"I'm not arguing, Charles. But too many people are dying because there isn't any decent testing. Trump should focus on getting that right first, until we develop a vaccine, or any kind of quick and easy therapeutic."

"Covid has too many symptoms, I replied. "We need something simple. At least, for the testing."

"You're right, Charles. Watch Tucker, anyway. He keeps things simple, just like Baltzell did in our sociology course. You remember Digby, don't you?"

"Well, I should. At least I got an A in his course," I said as I cleared my throat. "We need a medical breakthrough, if we want to Follow the Science. Otherwise, forget it. I refuse to listen to clowns like Fauci or the rest of these phony politicians. The solution is probably right in front of our eyes. But we've missed it in the fog of war. The political war ripping our country apart."

"Okay Charles. But listen to Tucker anyway. *He's one of us.*"

Jameson hung up. I thought long and hard. Covid-19 symptoms included every human frailty except ecstasy: Body aches, headaches, fever, chills, sore throat, nausea, diarrhea, congestion, runny nose, fatigue, shortness of breath.

We'd all been brainwashed. Conditioned to live in a state of panic with acute neurasthenia, as we kept getting got hosed and steamrollered by the political class. Held hostage in perpetual fear of infection by an obscure but fatal contact with Covid-19. As Don Mclean had sung. *'This could be the day that I die.'*

Except for sudden death, finding testing was as unpredictable as it was unreliable. Jameson got it right. I could no longer rely on a medical establishment which has been shanghaied by a corrupt government to monitor my health.

So, I took my life, quite literally, into my own hands.

I recalled the immortal words of Ralph Waldo Emerson from *Self Reliance*: "*Nothing is more simple than greatness; indeed to be simple is to be great.*" I checked my sense of smell— the grungy way, to test for coronavirus in the privacy of my bed, like I had done the previous week. The solution was *simple*.

My day of Truth had arrived. My turn to be great. If necessity is the mother of invention, then simplicity is its willing stepchild. Words that belong to me, *not* Mister Ralph, who said *'One must be an inventor to read well.'*

I had read this problem well. And I had found the solution, lying in bed, literally with my own hands. Specifically, my left forefinger.

Another Billion Dollar Baby was born in America.

The Forefinger Anal Swab Test for Coronavirus. *Covid F.A.S.T.* for short. My third great invention and a 'Beautiful Necessity' in the words of Emerson. An enduring legacy and my own special gift to humanity.

I scoured the attics of memory. I retrieved a concept from Marketing 101, stolen from The Wharton School. The Unique Selling Proposition, or U.S.P. I would market a bourgeoise alternative to the 'naked plunge' to a desperate American populous. Most consumers would refuse to do what I did, even out of desperation. To check their sense of smell utilizing their befouled fingers. As Bertrand Russel inferred, 'They would rather die'.

As altruist and entrepreneur, I wanted to save lives. American lives. 'Le Marechal' did it for America during The Revolutionary War, advising a misguided Washington to attack Virginia. America is a polite society. We put our trust in hygiene. We consume deodorizers, disinfectants and 'green cleaners.' Exterminators kill our bugs and rodents.

To put it simply, like Emerson, we are not easily persuaded to blithely shove our naked forefingers up our assholes. And smell them. Not without special emoluments. Even if it means saving lives. We must be anaesthetized by merchandising campaigns to accept the putrid realities of our animal and organic selfhoods.

I seized the day with marketing genius. Remember the Chia Pet? It might even be possible for me to turn a slight profit along the way, as a just reward for my inspiration and *travail*.

Here is the product description of my latest invention:

CHECKLIST ONE. CONTENTS: Two individual foil packets in each box. Each box includes:

— one lubricated condom (to cover the forefinger)

—one sanitizing hand wipe (to cleanse finger following 'rectal plunge')

— Packaging: 10 boxes per 'Kit'

CHECKLIST TWO. Product benefits listed on each kit.

— Safe and effective on the olfactory organs for humans and pets.

—Utilizes the latest sanitary technologies.

—Disposable, without any specific scientific precautions.

—Easy-to-follow directions in English, Spanish, Aramaic and Swahili.

—Results in less than thirty seconds.

—Natural unisex design.

Each kit contains ten cheap latex Asian condoms and ten generic wipes. The cost of each kit, fully scaled, is under three dollars. *Shark Tank* might do better, but I will not share my invention with anyone. The suggested retail price for the *Covid F.A.S.T Organic Travelers Kit* is $29. 99. As for profitability, pull out your abacus and *do the math*.

Our deluxe version, besides the 'organic' smell edition, adds a zesty 'minty-fresh' scent to every condom. The *Covid F.A.S.T Minty Fresh Kit* is premium priced at $34. 99 per kit. To add a little more 'sizzle' to the U.S.P. I will feature the *Caduceus* on all the kits to flaunt our medical authenticity. This will help us win the battle for shelf space against health care behemoths like Johnson & Johnson. And attract the eyes and wallets of anxious American consumers. I will also establish an eponymic website— MY COVID FAST. Com. No royalties, penalties, or accreditations are needed for my Unique Selling Proposition. I already checked it out. Often confused as an authentic symbol of medicine, especially in America, the *Caduceus* is technically nothing more than a sign of logistics.

The *correct* medical symbol has one snake on the staff, instead of two. I envision MY COVID FAST. Com as an active community where 'Finger Plungers' share 'wellness' experiences. I throw the frisbee righthanded. I am a switch-hitter in baseball. But as a 'Finger Plunger', I learned after only three plunges that I am a natural lefty.

Covid Fast kits might cure Frisbee Finger or other maladies. We will continue to learn more about the clinical side of the product. The MY COVID
FAST.Com community will be crucial to implement my marketing plan.
Whatever. Keep mum about this invention until I build prototypes. And dis-
tribution for the greatest 'Beautiful Necessity' of a lifetime.

Fifteen minutes after eight, I channel surf and hear a laugh. I have alight-
ed on Fox Cable News. The laugh belongs to Tucker Carlson, the purest
falsetto I have ever heard. The laugh of Mozart as depicted by Thomas Hulce
in *Amadeus*.

I wanted more. I was a glutton for his soothing trills. Tucker's blissful,
lilting vocal was a high falsetto giggle. Intoxicating in its purity, truthfulness
and wisdom, like the intricate melodies of *The Magic Flute*.

Tucker wore quaint bowties in his television past, including MSNBC. A
restless, towheaded provocateur against staunch democratic mercenaries like
Begala and Carville. I asked Bea if she watched Tucker on Fox News.

"Yes," she replied, with enthusiasm. "Unless I'm watching The Tennis
Channel. Mr. Carlson is a very polite, young man with a fine sense of humor.
Roxy loves him. In fact, she told me she watches him every evening."

"*Roxy*. You must be kidding. All she cares about is *not* watering the pot-
ted plants."

"Now, she wants to 'Drain the Swamp.'"

"What about his laugh? Doesn't it freak you out?"

"What laugh?"

I dared not mention Tucker again, as April disappeared into May and
the riots commenced in Minneapolis following the murder of George Floyd.
A summer of violence ensued that plagued our cities far worse than The
Coronavirus. I got side-tracked by this discomforting spectacle and I was dis-
tracted by certain personal financial and logistical difficulties that forced me
to postpone the launch of my latest invention. I need not elaborate.

I put the Covid Fast prototypes and website on hold. The shopping
malls remained closed, but death tolls from Covid-19 continued to mount.
The 'Positivity Rate' was high and shipments of P.P.E. were low. There were
hopeful signs from vaccine trials, but no easy therapeutics in sight. Many
Americans were preoccupied with 'Defunding the Police.' I realized that our
country was going straight into The Inferno and Lucifer must be as euphoric
as a bat out of Hell.

I did not wish to return to Hell. I bit my tongue, held my breath and toiled every day. I did my food shopping and took long drives up the Hudson. I commiserated with Ryan or Trey over coffee. I did my best to avoid Jill Paulson, still living on Earth. But I needed a favor from her. To get Mister E into Doggy Heaven. Or at least, promoted to Purgatory.

On several occasions, I considered asking Madame about the time she caught Ryan and Jill in the nude. I chickened out. One ritual I did not forget. Jamming my naked left forefinger up my asshole every night. The naked rectal plunge. I still wanted to live on Earth, as I recalled the musings on death by Walt Whitman in *Song of Myself*:

> "*And as to you death, and you bitter hug*
> *of mortality, it is idle to try to alarm me.*"

I even considered taking Hydroxychloroquine as a precaution.

Trump might be right. What did I have to lose? Jameson was correct about Tucker. So, I decided to start watching him at night and rarely missed his show. Yet, I continued to abhor his right-wing politics, as I do today.

Tucker has a soothing voice. I am a Soldier of Truth and worry about The Deep State. I was beginning to see our mendacious, orange-haired president differently. As an ugly hunchback guarding the Gates of the Heaven.

I called up Jameson later in the week. "Operation Warp Speed is coming. We might even have vaccines by the end of the year," I said. "And I've been watching Tucker every night."

"Good for you. He reminds me of a younger Digby Baltzell," Jay said. "With the common sense of Thomas Paine."

"Frankly, Jay. I mainly enjoy listening to his fluttering falsetto."

"Mozart laughed the exact same way. And Tiny Tim sang falsetto," Jameson replied. "There's a subtle distinction. His warble is different from Frankie Valli and The Four Seasons."

"No argument here. *Tiptoe through the Tulips* was Tim's *magnum opus*," I said. "But Tucker sounds more like Tiny Tim than either Mozart or Frankie Valli. Especially when he burbles choruses at the end of his sentences."

"Tucker makes sensational baby voices whenever he gets really sarcastic."

"Yes, and his falsetto is addictive. Beatrice says she never misses him. Neither does Roxy who started wearing MAGA hats to work until Madame Beatrice chastised her. Roxy's a moron when it comes to politics. But when

Chloe goes into a barking fit, now Roxy screams 'Shut up and obey.' Chloe stops barking immediately. It's a miracle. I tried it on The Chloe Monster myself and it really works."

"Whether it's his elfin ears, brilliant mind or just his gurgle, Tucker is one of us," Jameson said.

A newsflash crawled across my screen: **Anti- Cuomo Riots Erupt in N.Y. Leper Colonies.**

CHAPTER TWENTYSEVEN

As I entered my junior year, the jollies of fraternity life became unprecedented. Krazy Karen, the most prolific nymphomaniac in frat house history racked up her final game of eight ball before graduating in May. She received her Bachelor of Science, *Summa Cum Laude* for her *prima facie* research in *Psychosexual Pathology*.

The pool table was desolate. Now, only shiny billiard balls rolled nakedly over the hard, green felt. Serving as an eerie reminder of Karen's prodigious, yet unforgotten legacy. Sir Koala of New South Wales, re-elected as Sow Rex, organized a ceremony in her honor. The entire chapter attended, along with her parents, the venerable Rabbi Maximillian Merkins of Great Neck and his titillating wife, Mme. Flossie.

On graduation day, Sir Koala had presented Karen with a white rose in recognition of her infallible servitude as a 'Little Sister.' Then we served her an oversized black chocolate donut hole, decorated with a white frosting— a pastry that replicated an eight-ball, upon a white lace paper doily. A single candle was lit. A simple but elegant engagement that provided exactly the requisite 'Touch of Class' that a gala of such magnitude deserved.

In the wake of her retirement, Sir Scuzbag of Brittania addressed the need for new entertainment in the basement. Especially during the fallow winter months, until Sow Rex, spearheading the search for a new house floozie, negotiated the amatory services of 'Sleaze Chick.'

Scuz wasted no time. He arranged for the installation of an electromechanical machine. A glass covered curiosity on stilts, armed with buzzers, bells and flashing lights. Krazy Karen's pool table abode had nary a coin slot, but Pinball was a costly entertainment, requiring a hefty toll of ten farthings per trick. Or three for a shilling.

The lecheries with Krazy Karen had always been provided at no charge. She always concluded our entertainments with multiple orgasms, whereas 'College Queens' did so with drains or tilts. We would clap heartily and shout: 'Tally Ho' to honor performances of talented 'Flipper Men'. Foosball and Pacman elicited similar ejaculations, as I spent many hours with my brothers during study breaks, huddling for refuge and libations inside The Temple of Cannabis.

Sunday mornings, I would awaken hungover from an evening of debaucheries. And inhale the noxious but oddly mentholated aroma of our Chapter Hall. Peering out of a gray, fifty-five gallons trash can, I would observe former maidens descending our staircase. Retired from long Arabian nights of perversions, feasted upon in the hotbeds of lusty Sir Knights, each wench would step into the foyer and flee abashedly to her 'Walk of Shame' across campus.

I needed new stimulations. I walked past Hill Field one afternoon and I noticed a sky ablaze with colorful flying discs. I'd been playing disc golf at Sedgley Woods for three years, using the two-fingered forehand I learned at summer camp and perfected at Taft. I practiced until my fingers bloodied. I developed distance, accuracy and power, but I had never played Ultimate. I owned a couple of 165-gram World Class Frisbees, the official disc. After seeing a notice in *The Daily Pennsylvanian* for Penn Ultimate, I showed up in Superblock, ready for open tryouts.

That's where I met Alan Lockwood.

I turned around and he was staring me in the face. Wearing tortoiseshell glasses and a green and white striped rugby shirt. A second year MBA. Graduate students were authorized to play club sports like Rugby and Ultimate. Suddenly, I had a deja vue. I knew him from somewhere but couldn't remember. We paired off and started throwing. Magic from the start. His style differed from mine. I threw with power, but my motion was rigid. Alan was fluid and smooth. He'd do a double fake and veer off. I developed a knack for hitting him perfectly in stride.

It was uncanny. I could sense his movements and direction, even if I was blindfolded. I realized that if I didn't know him from someplace in my recent memory, then it must have been in a previous life. I kid you not. At lunchtime before the season opener, he invited me to meet him for 'Rice and Veggies' at The Eatery on Locust Walk, along with Mad Dog Merker, the other grad student on the team.

Mad Dog was tall and lanky. A bulldog with a beard, who jumped higher than a kangaroo. He earned his nickname at Tufts because of his reputation for smashing heads. Even the one on top of his shoulders. Now, he was doing penance, majoring in orthopedics at Penn Medical School. Last year, he twisted his left ankle at Princeton. This year, he declared himself ineligible to play in games until further notice. He had a tough class schedule this semester.

Our season commenced on Hill Field. Against the Space Guerillas from Morris County Township of New Jersey. Alan started up front with Flash Smith and I warmed the bench. We fell behind by three scores. Then Stork Krieger, playing in the back, sprained his right hand after an opponent hacked his throw.

I was sent in to make 'The Pull.' A long throw, like a kickoff in football. I hit Alan four times in the second half for mid-range scores and hucked a couple of photons to Flash for two more. We edged them 23 to 21. I was promoted to the starting line-up and hung out with Alan, meeting him daily for practices, games and meals.

My real education commenced with Alan. I met his girlfriend, Barbara and luminaries in the MBA program, like a chess grandmaster from Reykjavik, a Peruvian playwright, a Russian dissident who conducts Shastakovich, scions of international dignitaries and at least two future members of the Forbes Four Hundred.

During the winter, we threw inside Hutchinson Gym, until intramurals intervened. We moved to a hallway and threw past rows of lockers in Biddle Law Library. We suffered injuries that sidelined us during the Spring season.

But my friendship with Alan never waned.

He moved to San Francisco for a career in venture capital. I knew he was working his butt off, but I got a postcard from him in June with his phone number. He wrote me that he loved his job, despite the 'insane hours'. A junior partner was lending him a Ferrari for the summer, so he was planning trips 'Up and down the California coastline.'

Those were the last words I ever heard from Alan Lockwood.

CHAPTER TWENTYEIGHT

"Riots in our finest leper colonies, Charles." Madame Beatrice was alarmed. "All the colonies in the entire state have established impeccable reputations for decades as good neighbors in our local communities."

"Yes, this is true," I agreed. "Except whenever a new polygamy scandal hits the news."

"I haven't heard a word about *that* going on for years."

"Sorry, Bea. What about the child bride in Mt. Pleasant last June? She was barely thirteen. Tribal communities like leper colonies are vocal and riot on issues like freedom of choice. They used to be victims of abominable discrimination, even quarantined on islands. *Leper* was an insult. People used to say, 'He treated me like a leper.' Or 'Growing up leper.' It was almost as deleterious as being branded with a scarlet letter."

"My father insisted on buying our Christmas trees from the colony."

"Sure. They've always had had the lowest prices and remnants of the stigma remains. Now, they're supporting programs outside the gates. The modern colony has evolved into a digital community with critical diversity training and education. They've assimilated the algorithmic architecture of social media. Which is exactly what I despise."

"Charles, I hope you're not telling me you despise lepers?"

"Of course not. I love lepers. I really do. Some of my best friends are lepers, like Brandon…. What'sis name. If he ever needs a favor from me, he gets it, hands down. Our colony has been trying to upgrade our school system for decades. I signed up with Brandon last year. I even volunteered to serve on the executive committee."

"That's wonderful, Charles. I'm glad you're so involved. Why do they have such a problem with our governor? Lepers have always worn facemasks in public, anyway."

"Cuomo is cracking down. For not socially distancing. Lepers love big weddings."

"They have the right to have weddings any way they choose."

"Not to Cuomo. He considers big weddings 'super-spreader' events."

"Then he must be doing it for the sake of public safety."

"No, Beatrice. The weddings are held *inside* colony gates. Cuomo would have whacked them for something else for sure. Bada-bing. Cuomo and De Blasio love lockdowns as much as they love Sharia Law. They want to show everyone they've been raised to the level of Godfather."

"We hardly need more riots, Charles. We have elections to settle these issues."

"Cuomo's election is years from now. Just watch and wait. Lepers have long memories and vote in a bloc. I'm glad somebody's finally standing up to him and rising against our political oppressors. As Plotinus wrote in his *Third Ennead*, 'Bad men rule by the feebleness of the ruled.'"

"But there are so many riots, Charles."

"The wrong kind of riots. And we are feeble. And being ruled by bad men. And bad women. That's the problem in this country. Like Yeats said in *The Second Coming*. 'The best lack all conviction, but the worst are full of passionate intensity.' Some people of color get absolved for looting Macy's for no reason. And all these demonstrations masquerade as excuses for thievery. Law-abiding citizens pay taxes, but they just sit on their butts. Terrified of being branded as racists. Bashed by the media mob and rolled over by hypocritical, power-mad politicians. Public safety, my ass. I'm sorry, Bea. We need to wake up. We must awaken from the perversities that *Wokeness* uses to rule us."

"Tucker said something like that last night on television?"

"Yes. Within the context of 'virtue signaling.' Then he followed his usual diatribe with a cacophony of his finest falsetto's. I was mesmerized. He did a similar segment on the problems in our leper colonies, two days ago. I despise his right-wing politics, but I'm totally addicted to his laugh."

"What laugh? Tucker is a fine, young man. Chloe comes into my bedroom at eight, nestles beside me and we turn on Fox. When Hannity comes on at nine, she immediately trots downstairs into her cage and falls asleep."

"Every night?"

"Every night. One time I turned on CNN by mistake because I had to go to the bathroom. When I returned Chloe was barking furiously at Anderson Cooper and upchucked her entire dinner on my bedspread."

"Could have been worse. Might have been Rachel Maddow. Then, you'd have another shiitake mushroom to clean up." I looked at Beatrice, but she wasn't laughing. Her eyes tightened as her mood seemed to darken.

"What's going on with Jill and Andy?" I asked her. "Where have they been hiding?"

"What do you mean by hiding?" she asked. My question surprised her.

"They never showed up for Lucille's memorial service. Or even to the dinner."

"Yes, it's unfortunate. They should have called me. I would have been able to ask both Ryan and Trey to bring their wives to the memorial service. They would have enjoyed dining on the authentic Greek cuisine."

"Have you ever considered…. that Jill despises Ryan. I don't understand. He's such a great guy."

"Yes, Charles. There is a reason." Madame paused and gathered her breath. "When I was a little girl, I caught Jill trying to seduce Ryan in our backyard. But he had the fortitude to resist her advances."

I was stunned. This was last thing I ever expected to hear from her lips. Divulging this lurid story with utter nonchalance. "How old were they at that time?" I gurgled—although I knew the answer.

"Let's say they were much too young. And Jill was caught demeaning the flowers at Anthony's wake."

I was flabbergasted. I didn't know what to say. "That's unbelievable. Unforgivable," I finally answered.

She removed her glasses and lowered her voice. "Charles, Jill is my big sister. Family I can never shake, like my ancestors. I've lived long enough to learn one lesson, as Shakespeare said, 'To err is human but to forgive is divine'."

"I think that was written by Alexander Pope."

She scratched her brow. "From *The Rape of the Lock.*" Then Madame put her glasses back on and issued a wry grin. "You used to chide me about my corrupt ancestors in Salem."

"They were slave traders who were jurors at the Salem Witch Trials?"

"Yes, Charles. And I've learned I *must* forgive them. There are no real witches, but only bitches in the real world. My sister, Jill simply happens to be one of the bitches. But... I still love her."

The Madame's cellphone rang. "Hello, Francis," she said.

She nodded to me. "That will be wonderful," she answered and hung up. She lowered her voice and smiled. "Francis told me St. Gregory's has returned his deposit. They will not even consider rescheduling any events until further notice. His deposit was also credited back at The Westchester Country Club."

"Does that mean you can have the wedding at St. Mary's?"

"I think so. He wants a meeting with me. In private, before talking it over with Peter and Emily."

"When's the meeting?"

"He'll be here in an hour. Could you please take Chloe out for her walk?"

Franny arrived, as I exited with The Chloe Monster on her leash. Barking herself into oblivion. Walking her was an unruly task, one I tried to avoid. She spun around in circles on her leash, woofing at every imaginary squirrel.

I often asked Roxy to let me water the plants in exchange for performing this debilitating task. We made this trade several times, but she was off today. It took me an hour. I walked Chloe along the annex of Old Sleepy Hollow Road and she relieved herself on Route Nine before we continued to lurch forward, homewards.

I thought Madame's meeting with Franny would be short. I was surprised to see his Ford tank parked in the driveway when we returned. Chloe ran off as soon as I unleashed her inside. I followed her into The Mirror Room.

Francis and Beatrice were standing still, in full embrace. Their arms locked around each other. Their eyes were shut tight, but I could almost feel the warmth of their bodies. I looked above the fireplace and glanced at the portrait.

Anthony Wolcott Alfieri was smiling again.

⚜ ⚜ ⚜

MY FELLOW PILGRIMS. I must confess I lied. I am ready, willing and able to divulge what happened to me after I moved from Philadelphia to California. I lost an entire decade of my life. I had kept up with Sir Mello after he transferred from Penn to UCLA. But he dropped out to join The

Archangels of Golgotha in Santa Monica. I trusted him like a brother. But it was my own dead brother, Jean-Baptiste who saved my life.

I never knew I had a twin who died on the day I was born.

I told Mello about Schuyler Bowden, the girl who had dumped me in Philadelphia. And I needed a new life in faraway place, someplace to help me forget. He promised me The Archangels was the best way to forget every-thing. He had been initiated as a 'Soldier of Christ' to protect 'The Crown of Thorns Procession on Calvary.' Within two years, he received his first halo as an Angel, trumpeting from 'dark clouds' for the 'Ascension of Christ into Heaven.'

I was impressed, but Mello neglected to tell me his father was Grand Seraphim. Who sat on the golden throne upon The Temple Mount. I only learned about it years later after hearing Mello was sent to 'The Paradise in the Clouds.'

I flew into Los Angeles and met him in Santa Monica. Ready to start as a Soldier of Christ, to begin my ascent up The Golden Staircase. On sunny days, I sold flowers on the street. Or bread balls dipped in honey on the beach. We danced naked around wild bonfires. With silver harps and brass trumpets, we sang satanic verses in Pagan orgies.

Then we recited prayers for forgiveness from our Lord, Jesus Christ.

We prayed for Jesus to return, awaiting The Second Coming of Christ. Every year, The Archangels sent forth missionaries into the wilderness. Upon their return, these apostles were raised to Archangels on the altar of the tem-ple. They travelled to heathen villages and jungles of the night. Missions into the Voodoo tribes of Haiti. And dangerous expeditions to convert the zombie population of The Mill Reef Club quarantined on the island of Antigua.

I was promoted to angel. Six years later, raised to cherub before qualify-ing to become an apostle. Mello was one of twelve apostles sent on a mission to Molokai Island in Hawaii. Home of a leper village, once inhabited by Father Damien of the Sacred Heart in France. Deserted by lepers over a century ago, it had served as an island for hunchbacks. Now, it was rumored to be a haven for cannibals. When the mission returned after a year, Mello had disappeared.

The Archangels of Golgotha deemed him a martyr. The Grand Seraphim believed he was roasted alive and eaten by cannibals. I was honored to be chosen as an apostle for our latest mission. The Grand Seraphim blessed me. He had lost his only son but had gained a devout new apostle to proselytize a native tribe, buried deep in the Amazon basin.

Our group was scheduled to fly into Sao Paulo. And resume transport by boat on the Amazon River. I had lost my birth certificate, which I needed to obtain a passport for my flight to Brazil. I called Northern Westchester Hospital in Mt. Kisco and sent their records department a stamped, self-addressed envelope addressed to T. C. Rochambeau in Santa Monica, as they had requested.

Within a week, the birth certificate arrived in California. But the first name was *wrong*, it was the entire lengthy moniker of General Rochambeau, but with my birthdate. My lifelong suspicions were proven correct.

I had a brother, after all. I'd always heard portents from the *Celestial Mana* delivered through the voice of Jean-Baptiste II. My dead twin brother that I had never known.

My correct birth certificate never arrived in time for me to catch the flight to Sao Paulo. The Archangels sent my replacement, or the entourage of twelve would have missed the boat. The boat hit a reef during a squall. It tipped over in the Amazon Basin, two days later. Eleven apostles were eaten alive by a school of ravenous piranha.

Divers recovered eleven human skulls from the riverbed. The skull of the twelfth, my replacement— a bright, young zealot from Indiana had to be cut out from the belly of a gargantuan crocodile. Twelve skulls of doomed Apostles of Christ were sent in a banana crate to Sao Paulo. Then repacked for a voyage to the great altar of The Temple Mount of Golgotha in Santa Monica. If not for Jean-Baptiste, this would have been my fate. Play Lotto.

CHAPTER TWENTYNINE

I got sidetracked over the summer. Jameson pulled a fast one on me, reneging on his offer to share the 'senior suite' in the chapter house. He had found another roommate, Cody Melnick, his girlfriend from Kappa Kappa Gamma. Her parents finally stopped throwing shitfits about her 'living in sin with a goy boy.'

Not exactly 'the worst of times' for me, either. Jameson claimed the genius who discovered electricity, Ben Franklin, among his lesser achievements, had insisted that Americans must: 'Fart proudly.' Jay deserved a Medal of Honor. He won every farting contest at Taft, except one—but only after some asshole told Tony Grotto, the hulking center on the varsity football team, that 'Beans are good for your heart.'

Tony devoured a gallon of firehouse chili at dinner. Then at midnight in The Tabernacle, following a 'Flick of his Bic,' he imploded into a raging fireball, which set off the fire alarm and sprinklers in the Horace Dutton Taft dormitory. I had roomed with Jay without the civilian protections of the E.P.A. but assumed I would die from methane poisoning.

I left Taft in the nick of time. Now, I scrambled to renew my lease on Pine Street. I switched out of poly sci into Finance 303, taking Alan's advice. He spoke four languages, including Japanese and every computer language, but if he ever suspected the truth about me, he kept it to himself. Our friendship started with a Frisbee. But it persisted for other reasons. If he had suspicions, I would have confessed my story to him. As I am doing now, but only for you.

I called him in mid-August, the day after Hurricane Betty clobbered the East. His phone was 'temporarily out of service,' so I just assumed that he had moved to a new address. The semester started after Labor Day. The big news in *The Daily Pennsylvanian* was swirling around campus. Dr. Snowden Lawrence— an alumnus of the college and dental school was arrested on drug charges at his luxurious home in suburban Devon.

I hadn't seen the good doctor in years. I figured after dental school he moved far away. Not only was he dealing drugs but was masterminding one of the largest cocaine distributorships in the East from Main Line Philadelphia.

I thanked God for my blessed 'good timing.'

I was lounging on the sofa, enjoying the infectious minty-fresh bouquet. Along with the purple majesty of the trash mountains. I gazed up at the great antlered head of a water buffalo, protruding from hard-rock maple panels over the fireplace. Mister E trotted over to slobber deliriously. I fed him a Slim Jim and picked up a copy of the September issue of *The Pennsylvania Gazette*. I glanced at a story on Penn football and thumbed over to 'Obituaries'.

Alan Reichelm Lockwood, San Francisco. July 4th An associate at Hambrecht and Quist. In a car accident. A founder and The Godfather of Penn Ultimate Frisbee. 'The Ancient One' played four undergraduate years and two as a Wharton MBA. His mother is Barbara Reichelm Lockwood CW 55'. His father is William Herndon Lockwood D 57.'

⚜ ⚜ ⚜

JAMESON, UNREPENTANT FOR HIS MANY TURPITUDES,

exhibited customary *chutzpah*, as he dared to ask another favor. Penn Law School deemed his admission 'Most likely.' He added a course to his schedule and begged me to join him.

'Social Stratification' was taught by Professor E. Digby Baltzell. Eminent sociologist, Penn alumnus and Old Philadelphian who had prepped at St. Paul's and belonged to St. Anthony Hall, long before it was overrun by catamite proclivities. He became famous for proliferating the term: WASP— White Anglo Saxon Protestant.

Jameson considered himself a preppy expert. He practically had a doctorate, but I was focused on Finance. My coffers had become exhausted over the years, forcing me to prioritize business. I needed to find myself a decent paying job. Or revert to the drug trade after college and risk getting busted and arrested like Dr. Lawrence.

Jay got it right. Digby cracked my soft-boiled egg of a mind, three days a week. One knight in our fraternity compared his course to *The Preppie Handbook*, which was *bullshit*. Baltzell focused on Alexis de Tocqueville. How the monarchy and aristocracy of the *Ancien Regime* failed to govern France, which became ripe for a revolution as the proletarians took over. They ruined The Roman Empire and will eventually do so in America.

The aristocracy was guillotined by the *Sans Culottes*, as Grandpa Rochambeau ranted. Like the mobs in our streets, today. History repeats itself. I should have read the leather tome atop his *Playboys* as a teenager. Tocqueville infers The French Revolution would not happen in America. Now we have the burgeoning power of Wall Street and Big Tech. I fear Tocqueville may be wrong. Things are going in the opposite direction nowadays. Play Lotto.

I ran onto the turf to start the season in Ultimate Frisbee. It didn't feel right without Alan. Following an invocation by Danny Gold, our squad of forty plus, joined hands and formed a circle in the center of Hill Field, representing a Frisbee in his memory. 'The Ancient One' was absent for the first time ever. But we felt his presence and spirit, even as he had wafted away like a disc in our unholy universe. The strongest link in our chain, lost forever.

I also felt dead on our temporal field without him. But I know I will see Alan Lockwood again.

I spent time hanging out with Mad Dog, who plays like a lunatic but jives like a comedian and insists Ultimate should transmogrify itself into a contact sport like Hockey. If it ever wants to make it into the Olympics.

He resumed competition and sprained his right ankle against Columbia. He refused to leave the field. A budding orthopedist should have known better, but he wasn't called Mad Dog for nothing. Ankle broken in two places. He'd crutch over to meet me at The Eatery for Sicilian whole wheat pizza and iced teas. He knew Alan two years longer than I and helped give me a sense of closure. Then he got a call from Alan's fiancée, Barbara, who had Alan's ashes pressed by Wham-O into the #10 mold of a 119 g Super Pro. She asked him to give me one of these discs and another to Jim Powers, the founder of Sedgley Woods and The Philadelphia Frisbee Club.

I gave up Ultimate in December. It depressed me to play without Alan, so I settled for a few double rounds at Sedgley. Baltzell assigned his text, *The*

Protestant Establishment along with *Democracy in America,* my grandfather's preferred reading, except for *Playboy.* I wondered if Grandma ever knew about his hidden magazines. I always felt weird whenever I saw her in her bra or looked down at Grandpa's yellow toenails, as he sat in his boxer shorts.

They slept in separate beds. I realized I could have read Tocqueville during my summers in Westport, but I only exposed myself to the Playmates of the Month. So, I am hilarious, but to my main point, Digby connected because he linked subject matter, centering on Tocqueville to the contemporary moral, political and economic issues.

If he was alive today, he could explain our current malaise. Better than the charlatans railing on television. Sociological explanations of Obama and Trump and our dastardly politics, with his voice booming over a crowded lecture hall infused with the immediacy of a small classroom. Garbed in slightly untattered tweed sportscoats reminding us of the civility of the ineluctable Mister Chips. Goodbye, Dr. E. Digby Baltzell. We will miss you.

I never dozed off or cut a single class. I decided to turn in my final for a grade. Problematical as it was for me, I wanted to validate one course in the Ivy League. Jameson and I, as usual, sat together for the final lecture. After wishing his goodbyes, Dr. Baltzell shouted, "Charley Dodgson. Please see either me or Marilyn after class."

Charley Dodgson. I guess I wrote it on my blue book. Nobody *ever* calls me Charley.

I walked with Jameson to pick up my exam. Then I chickened out. College would be finished after next semester. Why press my luck and risk getting unmasked a semester early? I turned on my heels and walked out.

Jay met me later at the frat. He had tried finagling my exam back from Marilyn using a makeshift story. She was a bitch, Jay reported. He even tried to talk to Digby, but Baltzell was mobbed by his fans. He did catch a glimpse of my grade, he said, as Marilyn, one the teaching assistants, was rustling through the alphabetized N through Z bluebooks as she handed them out. I got a B Plus on my exam, Jay said, which I knew translated to a B for my final grade.

"Are you sure," I questioned him. "I thought I aced it."

"Positive." Jay answered, with celerity. His own bluebook had an A minus scrawled on the cover, circled in red. He would receive an A for his final grade.

"Sorry, Jay," I said. "But I must respectfully call *bullshit.* Were you wearing your glasses?"

He gave me an incredulous look, imbued with a phony expression of pain in his lying eyes.

Sorry, my fellow Pilgrims. Jameson never did see my grade. He was *lying.*

Excuse me, as I wax periphrastic. Despite his amazing grace, unfailing modesty, brilliance in the legal profession as senior partner of Ropes & Gray and despite how much I love him and his wife, Sarah Winslow and their three amazing grown-up children and how I have relied on his counsel since Time Immemorial and should be eternally grateful to lick his boots with impunity and admit I owe him my life, scarred, meagre, pathetic and mediocre as it is.

Jameson Bigelow Twombly is a *bastard.* I got an A on my final. Most likely, an A plus. I swear to God.

⚜ ⚜ ⚜

FROM THE GHOST of Charles Lutwidge Dodgson—not Lewis Carroll, the prurient author, but me, an imposter and former drug runner, I finished *extracting* my unaccredited college education at The University of Pennsylvania as Sir Charlemagne of Frisbee, noble Sir Knight and duly initiated into The Peace House.

Oscar Wilde observed, "*The first duty in life is to assume a pose. What the second is, no one has yet discovered.* I was eager to begin my discovery and transition into a new life. I felt like Julius Caesar after crossing the Rubicon. The proverbial New Adam had now been born again as Toulouse Charles Rochambeau.

In the words of F. Scott Fitzgerald, like Gatsby, I realized the 'platonic conception' of myself. Armed for battle like a Rochambeau, I began my victorious march with 'the best minds of my generation.' I never allowed mine to be 'destroyed by madness.' I would obliterate the frauds and mendacities of the past by building a bridge from today into the 'orgiastic future.' But I knew crossing the pontoon into this exciting new domicile required a fake resume.

God bless, Jameson Twombly. He drafted one in minutes with bullet points sprinkled with legalize. He showed me his draft of my cover letter. I dropped off the resume at the printers on Ludlow and ordered fifty copies. And matching envelopes on the finest white cloth bond. Before he left for his summer job at Sullivan & Cromwell in New York, he wrote down a name and phone number. The name was Walter Peck. A Sigma Chi from Wharton who graduated two years ago and worked in center city. Jay met his sister, Carrie at the Kappa Kappa Gamma formal last Spring. Peck also served as a liaison officer for his firm responsible for recruiting new talent from the college ranks.

I called and asked for Mr. Peck. I wasn't familiar with names of investment houses, like I used to be. He took my call, slightly out of breath and I asked him if I could please—at the very least— just *please* let me send my resume.

"Bring it in with you next Tuesday. Okay? Seven A.M. Sharp."

"Okay," is all I said. Keeping it as short and simple, like he did. I wrote down his address on Walnut Street, along with the name of the firm: Drexel, Burnham, Lambert.

The interview lasted twenty minutes. He never read it, but might have glanced at it for a wink, while chain-smoking Parliaments and flashing smiles, focusing mainly on the green blips dancing across his Compaq.

I had graduated from Wharton with a B.S. in Economics, Magna Cum Laude, majoring in Finance. I interned at Goldman Sachs in New York the previous summer. Also endearing was my volunteer work. 60 hours a month for the Children's Program at the Philadelphia Zoo. My cover letter touched upon global pollution. And the loss of tribal Identity among indigenous Choctaw Indian tribes and the hopes and dreams of my autistic sister, Indigo Rochambeau. Born with Down Syndrome and living at home in Oklahoma with my widowed mother. A Twombly masterpiece.

"Don't worry about money," he said, with a wink. My starting date was in two weeks. He apologized for my 'measly starting salary'. "You'll get paid, Charles," he coughed. "Everyone does. Stick it out. Everyone eats what they kill."

Walter spoke the truth. Within six months I learned everything I needed to know about eating money. I ate it so fast I choked on it and became a fat cat. He never deigned to check my resume or verify my brilliant college career. But I had sat in six Wharton business and finance classes, including Speculative Markets and Management Accounting.

Thanks to Alan Lockwood. Destiny ordained we met playing Ultimate. I never got the chance to thank him which haunts me to this day. I cry buckets when I remember him. He helped me master the jargon I learned in class as I collated business, finance, philosophy, politics and *Le Monde*. He was my guru. Except for a few exceptions that proved the rule, without him, my education at Penn would have been 'basically useless'. I will see him again. In Heaven, or in another life. The passage of time cannot diminish perfection.

As far as my job, I did it on my own. Bothering everybody for extra help. And more. I brought in croissants and jams, donuts, gourmet tea and coffee. Making friends with co-workers at every level. It always helps to make friends. I kept everybody loose with naughty jokes. Careful and strategic. We were passengers on an open boat. Prisoners with an existential problem. Surviving fourteen-hour workdays. Under the tar heels of Michael Milken, far away in Beverly Hills. Yet so close. Stomping hard on us, like *The Invisible Man*.

We found our little oases of escape. From the daily grind and onslaught of stress. Some guys settled for peep shows at Kingdom Come Shots. Or massage parlors with quickie hand jobs for lunch. Or salons where you get your cock rings fitted, two or three times a day, by young Asian girls. Secret rooms in bars where you blew weed, while getting blown. Or snorting white lines in private, loaded to the gills. Making big bucks. Spending it bigger. Then burning it all up.

Traders went to City Tavern on Friday nights or La Truffe. Or Olde Original Bookbinders, if they brought wives or girlfriends. Otherwise into clandestine dive bars with hookers. Cutting cards to decide who picks up the checks like mafioso chieftains. Somebody told me about a less grungy new place on Front Street called The Monk's Inn.

That's where I met Skye. Elizabeth Schuyler Bowden would have been inscribed on our Tiffany wedding invitations— until she gave me the pink slip. I was sitting alone at the bar, after ordering a rum drink called a 'Balzac.' I took a sip and she swiveled over on her stool and smiled in my face. She asked me how 'good' it tasted.

"Not as tasty as your pussy."

My first instinct was to blurt this out, but I *never* said it. Maybe, I should have, as she dumped me, anyways.

CHAPTER THIRTY

I wouldn't have blamed Jay or Sarah for cancelling my invitation to Wellesley. I love my annual summer weekend in July, but they invited me long before the arrival of Covid-19. They didn't cancel, if I was willing to comply with all the absurd restrictions and travel mandates. My first road trip out of state, since the start of the pandemic.

Traffic was light on The Mass Pike on Friday as I arrived half an hour early. A hot and humid night. After beers and chef salads, we called it an early night. Saturday afternoon, we drove north to the Essex County Club in Manchester. Sarah's family, the Winslow's have belonged there, since raptors roamed the sandy beaches of the North Shore.

Heat. Hottest day of the year. Everyone sweating buckets behind their masks, but Jay and I marched onto the grass tennis courts, parched with brown patches. They would shut them down on Sunday—a day too late for me. Within minutes, I was burning on a hot plate of grass. An hour later, I waved to Jay and staggered off the court. The score was tied, four to four but my face felt like a chunk of burning charcoal.

Jay trotted over, seemingly bewildered by my lack of stamina, even though his face was redder than a plum tomato. He was more drenched in sweat than I, yet he insisted I finish the match, two out of three sets. Otherwise, I had to ignominiously concede. I sneered at him and swilled down half a pitcher of ginger ale and grape juice. When I resumed play, I double-faulted, twice in a row, dropped my racquet on the court and shouted 'uncle.'

We showered and dressed. After passing a checkpoint, where they took our temperatures, the three of us relaxed with cocktails outside on the patio. It was hot and humid, especially for us in our masks. We chatted with several other parties, while shuttling the masks on and off during conversations, wedged between sips and bites.

When our table was ready, we sat down inside for dinner. Sarah mentioned that her sister, Margie, who had played squash at Vassar with Beatrice, had heard a report from Xinhua Media Agency that Gaucho Burrito was being investigated by the Chinese FDA. Accused of serving taco shells made from cow corn. I wasn't surprised.

"Doesn't Bea's brother-in-law work for them?" Sarah asked me.

"Not anymore. Chip used to be the vice-president of quality control at Tummy Tum. He retired three years ago. Not that he ever really needed the job. He inherited zillions from his father." I didn't bother to mention Jill.

"His father was a genius," Jameson blurted out, before taking a sip of red cabernet.

"Why do you say that? "I asked. "Because he made tons of money?"

"Not in the least. Plenty of morons make billions but Andy pioneered the export of American obesity to China. Morbid obesity. American obesity. He was way ahead of the curve. I saw an article on Tummy Tum on the internet, gone viral on social media. Winky's has double the amount of unsaturated fats, dextroglucose, cholesterol, heavy metals and fecal vacuoles than any variety of Kentucky Fried Chicken. Some of the other Tummy Tum restaurants are even worse. Deadlier than bioweapons. Loaded with fats and calories. Ever eaten a hotdog at Fido's?"

"Are you kidding. I heard the food is greasy at the Doghouse in Waltham," Sarah answered.

"Not just greasy. The dogs and fries are *double* deep fried in canola oil. Like planting time bombs in your stomach that destroy your arteries and ruin your health. Forget about cake— let them eat Tummy Tum and they'll die of malnutrition. America will rule the world. Paulson realized obesity can be used as a strategic weapon against our enemies. It's been our only retaliation against China for plaguing us with their latest exported batshit virosphere."

"Covid-19 might be *their* retaliation against *us* for giving *them* morbid obesity?" I suggested.

"Possibly. Big Junk Food could be our secret weapon for bioterrorism. Obesity and Bariatric care are major topics on cable T.V. Diabetes incapacitates the poverty-stricken in America. In both urban and rural areas. Look at the facts. Mostly fat people die of covid. The prevalence of morbid obesity makes us more vulnerable to assault."

"Karl Marx said 'Religion is the opiate of the people'," I said. "Do Tummy Tum restaurants subjugate the Chinese populous even better than religion or Marxism?"

"Absolutely. Look at it this way. Tummy Tum is only the *opiate*—not the *religion*. Big Junk Food is loaded with calories, fats and sweeteners. More addictive than any drug. We can still defeat the Chi Coms for world domination. Our secret weapon is by inflicting obesity. Paulson infiltrated our junk food into China, a stroke of genius. We may never be able to conquer the *Red* Chinese. But we can incapacitate the *Fat* Chinese, if they ever invade us."

"Jameson," Sarah answered, shaking her head. "Have you been watching Tucker again?"

On our drive back to Wellesley, I realized Sarah and Jay had spent a small fortune entertaining me. Probably to reciprocate for many gifts I have sent them over the years. I have never revealed my identity as The Bargain Shopper until now. Please keep mum. As you can see, Jameson's competitive pathology has nothing to do with money. He has three older brothers, who probably beat him into bloody submission, ever since he was a little boy.

Back home, Jay and I went out on the patio with two bottles of wine. Sarah retired to bed. After finishing a glass of red burgundy, Jay sprung out of his chair. Then it hit me— I had a major attack of the natty dreads. I felt it coming. The mahogany backgammon board, a game that was a very big thing at Taft. Jay had taught it to enough unwitting Rho Alpha Chi stooges to rake in enough winnings to finance his entire college career of boozing and wenching.

"Know why Tummy Tum restaurants are popular in China?" Jay spread out the board on the glass table.

"Tired of eating Chinese?"

"No. They don't even eat the same kind of chink food we eat, Charles, like wonton soup," Jay said, as we set up the board with the counters. Backgammon is the perfect venue for sitting around for palaver and booze. Jameson is a demon that refuses to lose, as I wax poetic, utilizing adjacent musical sentences. Whatever.

"What kind of food? Do they eat crap like horse meat in China?"

"Try the Wuhan Happy Family Pu-Pu Platter. Favorite combo in the wet market. Crispy Horseshoe Bat Wings, Moo Shu Rat and Kung Po Kitten. With Chinese vegetables, snow peas and fried rice."

'What about eggrolls? You forgot the eggrolls."

Jay took a sip of wine. "For a few more Yuan, you get eggroll. Fortune cookies are free."

We were playing for only a dime a point. After an hour, I had built a slim lead. I decided to divert his concentration from the game, so I asked him, "Remember Tony Grotto?"

His jaw dropped. "Of course. I think about Tony all the time," Jay replied. "I keep a jelly jar full of his ashes in my medicine cabinet. He was my room-mate in lower-middler year before you came to Taft. I miss him like a brother." Jay rolled the dice out of his hand instead of the dice cup.

"How could a catastrophe like that happen?" I asked. "How was it even scientifically possible?"

"Shit happens. Every sport has risks. Frog Bowling, Bullfighting, and Fart Lighting. The medical examiner blamed this tragedy due to a rare bodily methane gas inversion. Unfortunately, Tony was born with a congenitally dis-tended anal canal. He became a statistic because some asshole convinced him that beans are good for your heart, without mentioning any of the *caveats*. At least, Taft mitigated the tragedy by omitting the details in his obituary."

"I can't even remember. What did it say?"

"Tony died *suddenly*. His family might not have appreciated hearing the specifics of his death during his memorial service. It might have created the wrong kind of mood in the chapel. Quite the understatement, if you were in the bathroom like we were. *Suddenly* was exactly the right euphemism for a self-inflicted incineration. Especially following such a lively and competitive evening of Fart Lighting."

"I totally agree. But Tony reminded me of an exploding *pinata*."

"A bit too bloody for a *pinata*, Charles. Did you realize Tony went to Taft on a full scholarship? At least, his family was spared the expense of paying for a wake or a casket. Or splurging on a funeral home. Funerals are expensive."

"So are professional cremations," I added. "I heard Tony came from West Virginia. He was always listening to blue grass music, and I remember him telling me that his father played the banjo."

"Sure. His dad was a coal miner. Tony was the first member of his family to graduate from elementary school. We kind of looked upon him as a dumb jock— but he was considered the *Einstein* of his family."

"I'm sure Fart Lighting was frowned upon in the coal mines," I observed.

"Not only frowned upon but it's been raised from a misdemeanor to a felony."

"So, what do they do for fun nowadays? Frog Bowling is just as dangerous."

"Not with the proper footwear, Charles. It's destined to become an Olympic sport."

I maintained my lead for two more hours. Then three more, until it was well past midnight. Jay became obsessed with the score, twitching his cramped fingers but he refused to call it a night.

"Tony won that contest fair and square," I piped in. "Sorry, Jay, but Tony beat you handily, butt to butt. Nobody ever mentioned Tony's big win, even in his eulogy. I was extremely disappointed."

"So was I. Everybody only talked about football. They were afraid of making Tony into a martyr."

"I never thought anyone could beat you farting, Jay. But it might have been of some comfort to the Grotto family, especially to his little brother, Edgar, if our headmaster had praised Tony for his big upset win."

"I guess he came to bury Tony. Not to praise him."

At three in the morning, I was falling asleep. Jameson said, "I used to be anal compulsive. I haven't done any competitive farting since college. Sarah and I love participating in the twilight mixed doubles at Essex. Socializing with other couples on warm summer nights, before dinner. Nothing too intense or demanding on our assholes."

"And very *chic* prior to cocktails."

"It works even better after wine and cheese."

"What kind of wine and cheese?"

"Muscatel and Limburger."

"The perfect pairing for Fart Lighting."

"Definitely. We never should have outlawed it at The Somerset Club."

"Muscatel and Limburger?"

"Of course not, you idiot, I mean Fart Lighting?"

"Why, too dangerous?"

"No. Tony's death was a fluke. Or Bic would put warnings on their lighters. Somerset assholes hate farting."

"Everybody still farts in the Billiards room at The Racquet Club, following the Court Tennis matches."

"Charles, that's *recreational* farting, like we do at Essex. Totally clandestine. You don't get it. You're trying to compare a workhorse to a racehorse. They keep it on the schedule because Billiards or Court Tennis will never become Olympic sports. The Racquet Club is full of wannabes. They wannabe a Mecca for Fart Lighting."

"Maybe they simply enjoy the smell. Sir Drekstain loved the minty scent of the Peace House."

"It's all about *cachet*, Charles. The international appeal of the Olympics."

"What about Frog Bowling?" I asked him.

Jameson simpered as he gammoned me in the final game. A score multiplied by an astonishing eight turns of the doubling cube. Smiling like a foolish, yet moronic idiot, he had finally taken the lead.

I yanked out my wallet and handed him a five-spot. Desperate for sleep, I waived my thirty cents in change, slogged up the staircase and retired to the guest room.

Sarah had quaintly left a mint on my pillow. A minty mint, I learned, as I chomped on it, undressed and fell into bed. I pulled off my boxer shorts and administered the protocols of Covid F.A.S.T Organic— without the kit. The naked forefinger plunge, which stunk to high heaven. Praise the Lord. Thank you, Governor Cuomo. Yet, I was much too tired to go into the bathroom and wash the stench off my sticky left forefinger.

I fell asleep in peace. Covid-19 negative. Thanks again, President Trump.

CHAPTER THIRTYONE

Schuyler Bowden worked at Tiffany's in center city. Her job didn't pay as well as you might think. She commuted from her parent's home in Rosemont. She was a few years younger than I and a recent graduate of Harcum Junior College. Penn guys always loved to say 'Harcum Park'em and Fark'em.'

Her auburn hair was streaked blonde. She had light blue eyes and skin, tan and smooth as a baby. Her body was small and tight with the supple breasts of a Geisha girl.

I never bothered to ask Skye what she studied in college, but it must have been either mainline gossip or pot, since she never got enough of either one. She never even knew that Balzac was a prolific French novelist before becoming transmogrified into a specialty cocktail at Monks Inn, with a splash of white Vermouth.

Skye knew everybody. At least, she pretended she did. Like she did with everything she didn't know anything about, except for clothing. She considered herself a *fashionista* and owned racks of dresses by Lacroix and Albert Nipon. She kept mental notes on everyone, even people she despised or pretended she did, fearful of forgetting critical tidbits. Her conversations originated with chatter on the latest fashion trends but concluded with a barrage of invasive questions. Mainly about somebody's personal, social, cultural or financial background.

Her father was president of the local credit union in Bryn Mawr. Their home in Rosemont was a tiny English Cotswold, with three bedrooms. A flagstone patio with a gas grill reposed in the backyard, next to a small garden. Her mother pretentiously referred to it as 'La Terrasse.' But the best times I spent with Skye were at her family barbecues.

Too bad everything with Skye and me went downhill.

I was making amazing money at Drexel. But I got tired of living in the student ghetto. Time to move on. I relocated to a rehab on the 300 block of Fitzwater, in the heart of Queen Village. An up-and-coming neighborhood that adjoined Olde City and Society Hill. You could find street parking back then and walk or jog to an amazing array of *avante garde* shops and restaurants in the *Montparnasse* of South Street within minutes.

Skye wanted to escape. Mostly from her parental nest. She *thought* she did, but she really didn't, as I later learned. Not in the least. My mistake. Signs were showing from the beginning. Bad signs. We'd only been going out for a month when Skye asked me to double date with her college roommate, Daphne Duckworth. 'Ducky' would have been the maid of honor at our wedding. Until Schuyler decided to dump me for good.

Ducky's boyfriend, Roland Messerschmidt, a bulging bellied Villanova grad at Penn Mutual was looking to do something 'urban cool' on a Saturday night, near my apartment. I pictured going to a campy event, slightly artsy, but naughty enough to push the envelope. The T.L.A. was playing a John Waters Film Festival. Enough to tweak the moral limits of a few local bumpkins trying to escape the outer provinces.

We met at my place on Fitzwater. Then toked up and walked over to the theater. *Polyester* started at 4. I was the only one who had seen it. Rollie recited some lame Catholic joke that he had probably concocted as a dull young altar boy, followed by a fusillade of clichés, as we waited in line.

Something about a 'Cum Union'. I never got the punch line. I still don't, but the rest of them laughed like hyenas. I took this as a positive sign. They were stoned into oblivion or lost in space. I figured they might be ready to venture out and take 'a walk on the wild side.' They laughed like hyenas again and again, until *Polyester* ended. We sauntered to an Italian eatery on South Street. I spouted movie jargon, like 'parallel editing' and 'montage' I had learned in film class.

I advised them to look for satires and metaphors Waters employs in the next film. And social issues, like the failure of geriatric care, cultural biases towards crimes against nature and the decline of the American bourgeoise.

We discussed 'Cinema' pretentiously over dinner. Stoned as hell. We were all psyched for the next film, which started at seven. I warned them all but took Skye aside first. Although classic John Waters, the next movie wasn't mainstream but loaded with graphic sex and violence. She ignored me like the rest of them, but I was happy to see her blotto and feeling so risqué. But it was crickets. I was the only one laughing during *Pink Flamingoes*. I reminded myself to screw them all as I had warned them in advance, with flashing yellow lights.

I kept belly-laughing. Louder, during my favorite scene, 'The Asshole Dance.' Even louder when it ended with Divine gobbling a pile of dogshit. Somehow, I was certain I heard Ducky trying to restrain her muffled giggles. Wrong again. We walked out of the T.L.A with the girls hiding their faces, watery-eyed and sniffling in silence, like a pack of phonies. This reminded me of a redux of a scene in *Taxi Driver* when De Niro took Cybil Shepherd to a porno flick.

Unlike Travis Bickle, I had warned them. Yet, they were all in agreement. Only I was to blame for this unconscionable lapse of judgement and taste. They summarily convicted me of violating all three of them. Daffy the Duckling refused to look me in the eye. Roly Poly Messershits was even worse. His cheeks puffed out like a pig bladder, his face beet red. He frowned at Skye, before tilting his swollen head right over to me and brandishing it in my face. As condescending as the Eunuch Pontiff Maximus of Cybele, who had been miraculously violated, sexually.

I walked home alone. And considered the distinct possibility that Skye might be done with me. To my great surprise and relief, she called me up early the next morning.

I must confess. To something strange and unnatural. The 'Farkum' part with Schuyler *came* much later, no pun intended, long after I expected. We never had oral sex until we got engaged. She preferred letting me lock myself into her loins and dry hump her on the bed, fully clothed in her pink kimono. Feel free to call me pathetic.

It was mechanical; a crab canon, like irrigating a ditch. I felt like a trespasser. Or a necrophiliac. Skye was careful, clinical, precise. I ignored the remonstrations from my monster, Mister Dingle Screw. I wasn't pissed off,

since I Follow the Science and assumed our fairer sex was born with hor-
mones to protect the maidenhoods of our species.

I was making incredible money at Drexel. Like hitting the lottery every
day. I bragged to Skye about my gelt and showed it off by buying dozens of
new shirts, three suits, five pairs of Gucci loafers and a brand-new white
BMW 325 convertible. We drove around the Mainline on weekends, checking
new listings on the local housing market.

I must have been hallucinating. I envisioned myself with a wife, three
kids, a white picket fence and sheepdog in suburbia. One Saturday, sitting in
my BMW, I waited for Skye to get coffees from a Wawa, before inspecting a
fixit-upper in Wayne. I flicked on the radio. News flash: Fugitive drug kingpin, Snowden Lawrence sentenced to forty-two years in prison at a Virginia
courthouse. He had changed his name to Jack Dorsey, but the FBI tracked him
down. The radio started playing *Uncle John's Band* with Jerry singing, "When
life seems like easy street, there's danger at your door."

I heard Garcia sing it over and over. Just this line. Again and again, like
I was living in an episode of *The Twilight Zone*. It sounds crazy, but I kid
you not. It really happened and set me off with an attack of the natty dreads.
Then Skye returned to her seat and passed me my coffee, along with *The
Philadelphia Inquirer*.

Dr. Lawrence was simpering at me again on the front page.

Somehow, I forgot this insidious line. Completely. I swear to God. I forgot this fateful warning from The Grateful Dead: "*When life seems like easy
street, there's danger at your door*".

How could I forget? Maybe it's my imagination, but things happen for a
reason. Everything isn't serendipity. This was divine intervention, a warning
of clear and present danger. Sent to me from the *Celestial Mana*.

Skye was bragging to her parents. About my big bucks. Next thing you
know, she's telling me her father can get us a great deal on a thirty-year jumbo
mortgage. But only if we buy a house together.

Skye was the one who popped the question to me.

Unfortunately, I said yes. Nobody expected mighty Drexel, Burnham,
Lambert would be banned from the securities industry three months later.
After Drexel shut down, Skye freaked out. I told her not to worry, but to
keep looking for houses. I arranged an interview with Janney Montgomery
Scott. I was hired within a week, at a lower base salary, but with decent

bonus potential. I breathed a sigh of relief. JMS was no boiler shop, but a venerable old-line firm.

My new boss turned out to be an old-line bastard, with aquiline features. Rogers Emlen came from an ancient Quaker dynasty and wore tailored three-piece Brooks Brothers suits. I give him full credit. For his complete and utter *assholism*, to use the term coined by Divine in *Pink Flamingoes*. He set me up. I was the perfect stooge.

I should have known better. Everybody hated Drexel. We were dining on steak and lobster while our competition chomped on hotdogs and beans. I'm sure he had an axe to grind. After checking my resume with the University and verifying it was fake, he hired me and set his trap. He was fully hedged. JMS and I bore the risk. We might even become rich. But the downside for me, not Emlen, was that my career was finished. It turned out to be the *latter*.

Within three weeks, Rogers coerced me into making risky trades. Three derivatives in Japanese yen and two in European currencies. All my bets were covered. Big payoffs for everyone if I made the right call. But Emlen never bought any hedges like he had promised. I called up Tokyo on Thursday night.

All three of my carry-trade positions denominated in Yen had blown up.

I raced into work Friday morning. Rogers had called in sick— but only I was sick as a dog. I had made a point of never discussing business with Skye. In this case, I assumed I was hedged and at long last, my monster was euphoric. We were enjoying peak experiences in our sex lives, including an exciting variety of *novelle fellatios*.

I admit that I was *surprised*, but not exactly *shocked* to learn that my favorite leg, the one in the middle, Mister Dingle Screw, was *not* exactly the first clapper to make music in *her* bell.

The next morning, the buzzer went off at Fitzwater. The mailman arrived with a certified letter, requiring the signature of Toulouse Charles Rochambeau. Skye jumped off the sofa and ripped it out my hands. As if she had been secretly waiting for it to arrive. I had been terminated by JMP for a falsified resume. University records confirmed that I had never been a student— much less an alumnus. JMP reserved their legal rights to prosecute me for outright fraud. And significant financial damages. Signed J. Rogers Emlen.

Skye went berserk. Screaming and bawling like a sick cow for almost an hour. "I knew this was coming," she ranted. As if my catastrophe was hers alone. Like Gregor Samsa in Kafka's *Metamorphosis* and in her Philistine blue eyes, I had been transmogrified into a giant cockroach. Yet, I could still jack-off thinking about her, until I moved to Santa Monica for a decade and committed my grief to the recognizance of The Archangels of Golgotha.

I donated all my money and earthly goods to the order. Desperate to forget Schuyler at any cost. I replaced her memory with a decade of barking at the moon, running naked around wild bonfires at midnight and being pleasured by the pagan trinity of Sex, Drugs, and Rock and Roll. As you already know, I am lucky to be alive. Play Lotto.

When I recovered from my grief and moved back East, Jay Twombly, who knows everything about everybody, told me that Schuyler had married a 'draggletailed Temple Law grad' and an assistant district attorney in Bucks County, PA.

Strangely, I felt happy for her.

I no longer think about Schuyler. Nor do I hold an ounce of resentment against her as she remains the only incidence I ever made towards normality in my life. Perhaps, the closest I ever came to achieving The American Dream. Now I wonder if we ever loved each other at all. Or was it only The Dream that both of us loved?

The Dream, like *Maya*, might have been an illusion. But it might have been all for the best because this dream, like our love, for a brief, shining moment seemed tangible and real to me. But it was only a dream.

My American Dream, which was doomed to burn in Hell.

CHAPTER THIRTYTWO

The guest list for Emily's wedding had to be pared down to forty, as required by Governor Cuomo. But the ceremony was as beautiful as Madame Beatrice had envisioned. Peter and Emily received 'the church's protestant blessings' at St. Mary's Episcopal Church on a perfect Saturday morning in September.

Charlotte recited The Lord's Prayer. Demetri Alfieri followed with a reading from *Divina Commedia*, a poem by Henry Wadsworth Longfellow, which concluded with a line of verse that caught everyone by surprise:

> *I lift mine eyes, and all the windows blaze*
> *With forms of saints and holy men who died,*
> *Here martyred and hereafter glorified;*
> *And the great Rose upon its leaves displays*
> *Christ's Triumph, and the angelic roundelays,*
> *With splendor upon splendor multiplied;*
> *And Beatrice again at Dante's side.*

Francis escorted Emily down the aisle in a strapless, white embroidered Carolina Herrera, as sunlight burst through the stain glass windows. But instead of turning left, Franny took a sharp right over to the seat next to Madame Beatrice, just as the poem foretold. Christ and Longfellow were very much *alive* at the wedding —not dead, as was implied in the E.E. Cummings poem that Bea had recited to me in her parlor, almost a year ago.

A luncheon followed the ceremony next door at Sleepy Hollow Country Club. All the flowers in the church and banquet tables were done by Niko's Flowers, as Beatrice had insisted. Including a special arrangement designed by Nancy to honor the spirit of Joseph and Lucille Alfieri— very much alive.

Everybody raved about the flowers. And I must heartily concur.

⚜ ⚜ ⚜

RESIDENT
GREEN MOUNTAIN VIEW TERRACE
MRS. SABINA ROCHE

OCTOBER ARRIVED in a cloak of blazing red and gold. I was hearing optimistic reports about vaccines, on the horizon, but the news was dominated by the upcoming elections. Trump had caught Covid-19 and recovered to hold more rallies. Biden mostly hung out in his basement. The best news was that Charlotte announced her engagement to Michael J. Cutter of Atlanta—a fine young man, the day before I left for Vermont.

Halloween was near and the leaves were falling along the Taconic. Molly called me on my cell, as I turned onto the route to Southern Vermont. She had already picked up our mother at her retirement community for her ninetieth birthday party— originally planned as a surprise with 140 guests in the ballroom at The Equinox. Now, all my nephews and their families had to cancel their original plans to attend. The party was limited to the four of us.

Molly warned me on the phone. Strict new house protocols had been imposed by Governor Scott, requiring quarantines, testing and facemasks. Rules that applied to guests and residents at every hospice in the state. Fortunately, our mother was allowed to be released for a few hours to celebrate her landmark event.

Molly asked me how recently I had been tested.

"Uhhh...just last night," I answered, sparing her the grisly details. I told her that I had recently located a reliable new testing facility, practically at my fingertips, thanks to Governor Cuomo and President Trump.

Chef Pierre was baking the birthday cake from scratch, using the freshest, local, organic ingredients. I parked my car, walked inside and peered into the living room, which had a ceiling higher than The Mirror Room. Mom was lounging in an easy chair, sitting across from Dr. Goldstein. Nobody was wearing masks.

Molly waved to me, and I sat down on a sofa. Jeff's hair was mussed up, crazy as usual, with dark brown eyes shining like polished stones. Dressed for business in a dark gray suit, a red rose pinned to a lapel. I had a sinking feeling of an upcoming pedantic lecture. "Charles, let me start here. The brain is a complex and mysterious organ," he said, in his phoniest bedside manner. I had been shanghaied once again. "Paranoid Schizophrenia is not a transient condition. And it cannot be monitored by an MRI. Psychiatry relies on clinical judgement interactive with the *patient*."

Psychiatrists thrill to their abstractions to discuss the human brain. Only other people's brains— never their own.

"We hope this will be a recovery year, despite the Coronavirus," said my mother.

So, do I. Last Christmas, she acted crazier than a loon.

"Beatrice said you helped do her Christmas shopping again," Molly said.

"I broke all previous records for quantity, I replied. "My net discount totaled 89 percent. Even better when brick and mortar reopened in June. Everything went into ultra-clearance. Even Macy's dropped their drawers. I got over 90% off on clearance at both Kohl's and Macy's."

"Beatrice says you're *Mister Cheapskate*," chuckled Dr. Epstein. "Ever feel constrained by your budget?"

"Beatrice never calls me Mister Cheapskate."

"No matter. The important thing is that you're working. You need structure with regular exercise, meditation or Yoga. You've never had to work, Charles. Except for that gopher job at Drexel that Jameson got you, many decades ago."

"Bullshit. What about Macy's"

"Macy's only lasted for a month during the holidays. You've been *helping* Beatrice…. for what… a dozen years?"

"Thirteen. I was promoted to *major domo* after nine," I reminded him.

"Bea told Molly that she received dozens of thank you notes last January from all the hospitals and homes in the Hudson Valley you sent the gifts. You should be very proud of your charitable work," he said.

"Charles does all the wrapping by himself," my mother added.

Molly shuffled some papers on her lap. "I have a few messages for you, Charles. From some of the people on your list. We're supposed to do this at least once a year. It's part of your outpatient requirement."

"What list are you taking about?"

"Your Assertive Community Treatment support group. The good people that support your Cognitive Behavioral Therapy, like Beatrice, Jameson and Dr. Fledderjohannes."

"Dr. Fledderwho?"

"You know who. Jon, your college friend," Mom piped in. "The son of Dr. Zebulon Fledderjohannes. Try to remember. Dr. Zeb treated you for severe depression after your second suicide attempt in Philadelphia."

"I only remember the Archangels of Golgotha."

"All the anti-depressants had failed. Without the Electroconvulsive Therapy you received at The Fled you probably have killed yourself. You were in and out of the Institute for over nine years following your first ECT. I know it's difficult but *try to remember.*"

"I'm sorry, Sabina," Jeffrey said. "Charles has excised this period out of his memory."

"Your ACT group is just as important as your medications," Molly said. "You need to remember your past traumas so you can confront them head-on and eliminate them."

"Your meds also prevent relapses," Jeff said." I need to be totally positive before I cancel them."

"I don't remember," I reiterated. "Mello was eaten alive by cannibals."

"Don't blame Dr. Jon for your treatments," said Dr. Goldstein. "Your subconscious blocks your past disorientations. Then it replaces them with phantasmagoria. Crazy images of Heaven and Hell. Devils, Serpents, Angels, Zodiac and so on. To tailor these fantasies and cancel out the bad memories of your past psychological landscape," said Dr. Goldstein.

"Try to remember, Charles, said Molly. "You and Jon were classmates at Penn when Jeff studied under Dr. Zeb at UCLA. Jon transferred to UCLA after his father was diagnosed with stage four throat cancer, and eventually assumed the reins at The Fledderjohannes Institute. They both helped to save your life, Charles, especially Dr. Jon," Molly said, as she stared at Jeffrey. "Explain to Charles how his O.C.D metamorphized into Paranoid Schizophrenia."

"The dysfunctions are similar. Hallucinations. Thought disorders. Loss of Function. Psychosis. Our thoughts, feelings, behaviors and dreams are mediated by the dopamine in our brain circuits. When the neurotransmitters become unbalanced, the mind gravitates to the theatre of its most comfortable beliefs. Or psychotic delusions," Dr. Goldstein stated, "which is exactly what happened to Charles in college."

I can imagine Jeffrey in a white coat, with dark horns and an evil grin prior to my lobotomy. Brandishing a rubber mallet before bashing all four of my brain lobes into oblivion. Whatever.

"You've harbored an unnatural hatred towards your father since adolescence," Mother reminded me.

Molly added, "We need to continue this conversation, Charles. Daddy has been dead for decades, but Dr. Jon can help manage your ACT group with us, along with Beatrice and Jameson."

"Madame Beatrice gets phone calls from Santa Monica," I told her. "Are they about me?"

"Yes and no," Molly said. "You need to reconnect to your past to flush out your delusions. Your traumas remain repressed, like your hatred of Daddy. And several others. You need to face them and communicate. Especially with the people who were involved during the times of your most acute psychosis—even if you hate them."

Molly pulled out a picture postcard of Christ on the Cross at Calvary.

"What kind of *people?*" I asked her.

"Like Sister Karen," Molly answered as she started reading: 'Still in Ossining but transferred from Maryknoll to the Dominican Sisters. Sorry about what happened in college, but I *never* came on to Charles. Or thought my roommate would call the campus police. Just got a card from Eleanor in Hawaii. I am still a volunteer giving guitar lessons to fifth and sixth graders. Would love to see Charles again when he is ready. I only live around the corner. Tell him I forgive him. And I still pray for him every Sunday at Mass. Love, Sister Karen."

"*Krazy Karen.* Like the song by Simple Simon says, *Still Crazy After All These Years.*"

Molly dropped the card and pulled out a note. "Eleanor says you weren't her type, but she's still grateful to you for introducing her to the party scene at Penn, since she met her husband at St. Anthony's Hall." Molly paused and smiled. "An art history major, as I remember. She told me that she had a major crush on 'Jon Whatsis Name'. Maybe, I should tell Eleanor that his real name is Fledderjohannes?"

"From St. A's. Just what the world needs. Another Boston Marriage," I replied in disgust.

"Charles, stop this nonsense. Jameson said you were blackballed by The Hall because you urinated in their yard during a rush smoker. He only joined that Peace House *shithole* because of you."

"The flowers in their garden were dying of thirst."

Mom countered, "Molly...Stop being such a snob. I went to some wonderful orgies at The Peace House before I met your father at Alpha Sig. I always remember them fondly whenever I take a sip of a mint julep." Mom turned to me. "Eleanor sent us a new batch of cookies in January. All the way from Honolulu this year."

Molly ran her fingers gently over her brow. "Eleanor also wrote that Cadwallader sold their art gallery on 18nth and Walnut. They've retired to their country home in Valley Forge and their son recently moved to Villanova."

"Delicious," mother said, nodding. "Christmas cookies with macadamia nuts."

"Schuyler E-mailed her regards and regrets," Molly said. "She declined to join our group for personal reasons. She just lost her appeal on the divorce settlement and the bank foreclosed on her clothing boutique in Yardley, *The Pink Kimono*. She doesn't hate you but needs to forget you. Your suicide attempt on the trolley tracks still freaks her out."

"Her pink kimono still freaks me out. Why doesn't she hate me? C.S. Lewis said it best: 'The opposite of hate is not love, but indifference.' What the hell does she expect?"

"You need to feel better about yourself," Jeffery said. "You repress bitter feelings. CBT is the way. I'm sending my observations for peer review to The Westchester Behavioral Health Center. And copy them to Dr. Jon at The Fled."

Kippy Bilado, the sous chef entered and announced, 'Luncheon will commence at one.' In the meantime, he offered to fulfill any requests for drinks or snacks. Mom gestured *no* with her right hand.

For all four of us, as if she was the boss.

Molly stared at me. "Karen never charged you with rape. If you were a student today, you'd get all the psychiatric help you need. Forty years ago, the chancellor was forced to expel you. She deferred it until your senior year because of Daddy, but he still quit The Wharton Board of Overseers. Mental illness used to be considered a character flaw. Nowadays, they utilize peer-to peer counseling and mental health monitoring. It wasn't your fault, Charles."

"Psychodynamic Therapy brings the unconscious into the conscious," Mom added. You need to revisit these terrible memories lest they become imbedded. We can help you rebuild your self-esteem."

"Don't you remember why you left Taft?" Molly asked me.

"Of course. Daddy couldn't afford to pay the tuition."

"Charles, it's quite simple," Dr. Epstein intervened. "You moved into the bathroom and started skipping all your meals, classes and activities. Until they carried you away in a strait jacket."

"I needed a vacation from Jameson."

"No Charles. You were washing your clothes with mouthwash in the toilet. The beginning of your lifelong obsession with excrement, another one of your psychoses. You don't even realize how disgusting you can be."

"Wrong again, Jeff, I washed them in the sink with shampoo. Only my socks and underwear. Jameson had turned into a vampire, so I was obviously afraid to sleep in the same room with him."

"Point of order, Jeff," Mom intervened. "Charles developed these obsessions because of his father. He was never toilet trained until he was ten, but Daddy insisted on trying some Pavlovian method to speed things up. He regretted it until the day he died, but Daddy had a Bipolar Disorder. Although he never took Lithium, like your uncle Frank."

"Mother. Please don't say that you blame Daddy," Molly pleaded.

"Of course not. But he went into a depression. His accident occurred two days after your last suicide attempt in Philly. Daddy blamed himself. He never should have gone out on his hog on the Sawmill during a thunderstorm."

Jeffery nodded. "Manic depression is partly genetic. The vampire fantasy Charles experienced at Taft was a classic panic attack," he said, scratching his brow. "A manifestation of what Molly says you call 'an attack of the dreads.'"

"The natty dreads. Worse than a heart attack."

"Your underlying condition was also Bipolar," said Dr. Goldstein. "It probably started long before you showed any signs of obsessive-compulsive disorder or Schizophrenia."

"So, they put you on Lithium. Depakote wasn't available back then, Molly said."

"You made an amazing recovery at Dobbs Ferry High, Charles. National Honor Society and you were accepted to Wharton early decision, just like your father," Mom said, beaming with pride.

"You showed no more signs of disorder until college," Jeffrey said. "Everyone thought you were cured. But Schizophrenia often appears in people in their twenties. Or even earlier."

"Dad was so proud of you, Charles," Molly said. He called up Warren in Omaha. They were both Class of 1951 at Wharton. Fraternity brothers at Alpha Sigma Phi. And they……

Mom interrupted. "God how I hate snobs. My first year at Bryn Mawr, I went to my first party at Zeta Psi, full of preppy bores. Then I met Richard at a party at Omicron on 38th and Spruce. First, I went out on a date with Warren. He was a geek—but a nice geek. His father was a Democratic congressman from Nebraska. Which didn't stop him from joining the Young Republicans. He was elected president when Daddy joined him in the group."

"I'm surprised Buffet would join the Republicans," Jeffrey said.

"He never liked Philadelphia," Mom said. "He transferred to Nebraska after rooming with Daddy sophomore year, but they had already cemented a lifelong friendship before their political affiliations diverged."

"Daddy loved talking business, politics and economics with Mr. Buffet for hours," Molly said. "Along with Charley. They both flew in from Omaha and attended Daddy's funeral service at St. Thomas in Manhattan."

⚜ ⚜ ⚜

PROMPTLY AT ONE, Chef Pierre rang the dinner bell and we retired to the dining room. A sumptuous buffet of 'Philly Favorites' was set out. Pork scrapple, scrambled eggs with cheese, German potato salad, coleslaw and hoagie rolls for making ribeye cheesesteaks.

Mom looked me in the eye. "When you were being treated at the institute, Daddy finally wrested control of the trusts from Uncle Frank. IBM was our largest holding back then," she said, before nibbling at her cheesesteak.

"Daddy sold every single share of the IBM and traded it into Apple," Molly said.

"Warren and Charley thought he was crazy," Mom added. "Daddy always preached technology is the future. Your Uncle Frank was lazy and greedy. He invested all his proceeds from the trusts in B movies, marinas, luxury truck stops and a chain of discount whorehouses in Nevada. He left your Aunt Amanda, flat-broke, before he died."

"We sent another check to her nursing home. Also, to pay for your cousin's bills," Molly added.

"I haven't talked to Clarence in years. What's he been doing, recently?" I asked.

"Crystal Meth. We hope he can get out of rehab this summer," Molly answered.

"We *should* always help people in need," Mom said. I read in *Forbes* that billionaires have gained half a trillion in wealth since the pandemic started. What's our increase been so far, this year, Molly?" Mom asked.

Dr Epstein chimed in, "Including the charitable trust, roughly four and a half billion." Jeff was smiling like a Cheshire cat. "Your mom finally broke into the top thirty in *The Forbes 400* this year."

My mother scrunched her face. "The only thing I care about is my Philanthropy Score. *Forbes* finally raised it from four to five hearts this year. Billionaires need to step up to the plate. I've been doing regular zoom calls with Melinda on charitable giving, and she's been up to date with Warren. Mckenzie Scott is such a doll. There are way too many billionaires rich enough to own major-league sports teams that are major league *cheapskates* in philanthropy."

Dr. Epstein chomped on a pickle and nodded. "Charles, a billion dollars was considered big money when I married Molly. Thanks to your father's wise investments we are blessed. To put it bluntly— we are filthy rich."

"I save money every day. I am The Bargain Shopper. I never pay full price."

"Your father founded our family office," Jeffery said, sipping from a cold mug of foaming lager. He wiped his mouth off with a napkin. "Two Wharton MBA's and an undergrad intern. We are overweight equities in all three portfolios, including Roche Charitable. Our Apple stock, including accrued dividends, has doubled since the pandemic started."

"You shortened the name of the foundation to Roche," I said.

"Ask Molly," Jeff replied.

"You should move into the big house in Dobbs Ferry," Molly blurted.

"Too long a commute. Don't change the subject, Molly. Why did you shorten our name?"

"We have three people on the household payroll in Dobbs. Don't you miss the Hudson?"

"Not at all, it only gives me the dreads." I said, realizing Molly had punt-ed. I bit into my cheesesteak and scooped macaroni salad on plate. I noticed Mom's badge: Sabina Roche. "You did it too, Mom. Your maiden name is Ingersoll."

"I'm also known as Mrs. Richard Roche."

"But your married name is Rochambeau."

"Forgetting your name happens to people in your condition," Molly said. "It's a problem we need to resolve."

"Don't tell lies. Everything you say is a lie. I can prove it."

She wiped a bit of egg off her mouth. "I'll have to remind you again, Charles. Your great-grandfather's name was *Rothstein*— not Rothschild. He changed it to Roche, not Rochambeau. Fredrick Rothstein studied to become a rabbi, but he became a successful furrier and decided to move to Westchester. He was blackballed by every realtor in Bronxville, so he purchased his first home in Dobbs Ferry."

"He changed his name because of antisemitism?"

"He loved the Adirondacks, but he was never allowed into The Lake Placid Club, even as a guest. But he only changed his name because his broth-er was an infamous gambler. 'The Fixer' of the 1919 World Series."

"Remember The Black Sox Scandal," Mom said, sipping cider from a crys-tal glass.

Molly stared at me. "Arnold was murdered by the mob during Prohibition. Fredrick changed his name to *Roach*, married a Methodist, started a family and covered his tracks for a fresh start in life."

"I beg to differ," I replied. General Rochambeau met Washington in Dobbs Ferry and they followed a trail of glory to the surrender at Yorktown. Facts are facts, and truth is truth," I said firmly. "Our great-grandfather really moved there in honor of *Le Marechal*. As a Rochambeau, I am proud to be a Soldier of Truth."

"Your family has a great legacy," Mom answered. "But one of furriers— not soldiers. And no more criminals. They made their fortunes legally, in peace, not war. But you still have delusions of grandeur. About Charlemagne, Rochambeau and your latest fantasy, The Goldstein Army."

"Facts are facts, and truth is truth," I retorted.

"The more you understand the treatments, the better your chances for recovery. We hope and pray. We will do anything, however long it takes. And give up everything we own to cure you. It's not your fault. If it takes a miracle, we will wait for it," Molly cried, wiping away tears. "You're my little brother and we will always *love* you, Charles."

Molly has a great difficulty in admitting the obvious flaws in her arguments. "I noticed how you and Jeff managed to swill every last drop of my vintage Rothschild wine."

"Charles. Let's set things straight, once and for all. We always end up back on square one. Grandpa hated the name *Roach*, so he changed it to *Roche*, before entering Columbia. That's our family name. He majored in chemistry and invented the highest-quality imitation fur ever produced. Our name is Roche."

"He went into business with your grandfather, Fred, the furrier," added Dr. Epstein.

"Only at first," Mom added. "Then he trademarked *Faux Fur* and sold it through department stores as *The Roche Collection*. He was revered as 'The furrier with a conscience.' He became an icon for the activists of the animal cruelty movement and expanded an industry under assault. In the process, he built a franchise. Sadly, he died of a stroke, only three days after he sold *Roche Furriers* to an international conglomerate."

"I remember that day very well, Mother. October 19. A terrible shock," I replied.

"Face the facts, Charles," Molly said. We are not descended from warrior kings or nobility. Grandpa patented a process for *Faux Fur*, a simple invention that made us rich."

"The nobility barely knew the difference with his minks. They were *beautiful*," Mom said.

"The Gabor sisters considered his Siberian sable coats a *necessity*," Jeff added.

"I guess I'm as Jewish as the Rothschilds. What about our French ancestry?" I asked.

"You and I are Christian. Molly converted to Judaism when she married Jeff. All three of my grandsons had their bar mitzvahs. Dylan married a Presbyterian and converted. But there's no French connection on our family tree. Not a drop of French blood in your veins."

The dining room speakers blared *Happy Birthday*. Chef Pierre carried in a silver tray with a cake, followed by Kippy and the entire staff. Everyone joined in singing, as Mom blew out nine wax candles with one monstrous breath.

The cake was a masterpiece. Pumpkin cheesecake double-tiered, topped with whipped cream and cherries. Surrounded with flakes of almond. Glass dishes of apricot and raspberry compotes on the side.

Chef Pierre cut the cake. Mom invited everyone to share in the eating.

When dessert was finished, they cleared the table and Kippy returned to the dining room with four Irish coffees. Jeff turned to me and asked, "Charles, are taking your medications every day?"

"Yes. Santa Monica talks to Madame every month. Bea orders my refills."

"Which ones?"

"Lorazepam and Zyprexa. Vitamin C and dark red kidney beans."

"Why do you order beans?" Jeff asked, oblivious to my humor."

"Because they're rich in omega three fatty acids. Beans are good for your heart."

"Any side effects with any of these drugs?

"Like blood in my stool?"

"More like an abnormal dopamine signaling. Dry mouth or irregular heart palpitations."

"Just blood in my stool. And methane gas. Blasting out of my ass."

"Charles, those are improbable side effects for these medications."

"When I'm constipated, I always have an epiphany. I fart proudly, like Ben Franklin."

"Stop being funny," Dr. Goldstein replied, forcing a smile. "I'd like you to progress into self-management now and I'll continue as your case manager along with Dr. Jon. We prefer to keep things in the family. What about your diary? It's an integral part of your outpatient program. Have you even thought about it, since we talked last Christmas?"

"I've been writing like a madman since Fourth of July. Over 65,000 words."

"Really." Dr Goldstein's eyes widened. He shifted on his seat and stared at Molly.

"I'm proud of you, Charles," she exclaimed.

"It' s more of a journal. My *Confessions*. I'm ready to write the final chapter."

"Will it read like the *Confessions* of St. Augustine?" my mother inquired.

"Exactly. A paragon of *Caritas* and my pilgrimage as Soldier of Truth through the wilderness and chaos of a daemonic pandemic. I don't trust the Pharisee's who control the book trade. I will publish it myself, like Walt Waltman did in 1855 with his first edition of *Leaves of Grass*."

"What a wonderful inspiration, Charles. You can explain, step-by-step, the trials you endured to triumph in your lifelong battle against Paranoid Schizophrenia," Mom suggested.

"My goal is to tell the Truth. About the destruction of The American Dream."

Mom turned and looked me straight in the eye. "It is not your fault, Charles. Schizophrenia has a genetic component and there is a history of mental illness in our family. Uterus infections are another factor. I caught a viral infection in Hong Kong while on vacation with your father when I was two months pregnant. You were the baby in my womb."

"You obviously mean both me and Jean- Baptiste?"

"Jean-Baptiste who?"

"My brother, Jean- Baptiste. He died the same day I was born."

"Charles, what in the world ...." Molly blurted out. "Are you hallucinating again? Has Charles been overdosing on his antipsychotics?" she asked, turning to Jeff as her face turned beet-red.

"So, my older brother was killed by another Chinese virus?" I shouted.

Molly slapped at me in the air. "Charles, enough nonsense. I thought we were making ..."

Mom interrupted, "Charles, how in the world did you ever think...?"

"... I needed a copy of my birth certificate for a new passport. Mt. Kisco Hospital sent me one for Jean-Baptiste. So, I learned about my dead twin brother. He's buried in Kensico only ten minutes away from me."

"Charles.... You were born in Tarrytown. Our mausoleum is in Sleepy Hollow Cemetery. You never had a brother."

Mother started to cry. "Sonographs were primitive back then," she whimpered. "Nobody knew I was carrying twins. Not even me. There was only one heartbeat. Even the doctor and nurses were caught by surprise in the delivery room." She stared at Molly. "So, my poor little baby died before I could even give him his name."

"Is this true mother? Or is Charles going crazy again," Molly shouted.

Mom shook her head. "Charles is telling the truth. I don't know how he could ever know. Neither your father nor I ever said a word about this to anybody."

"Mom... What was the *name* you would have given him?" I asked.

"There was only one heartbeat, Charles," she repeated, sobbing, as she wiped away her tears. "But I was planning on naming him John," she said. "In honor of John the Baptist."

EPILOGUE

My fellow Pilgrims, our long journey is over. Along with my final passage to Hell and back. I can set my compass to The Gates of Heaven. I beseech you to join me in prayer for my family as they cling to their Grand Illusion. I am a Soldier of Truth. I conclude my *Confessions* as a man of Faith and Science, born into the wrong century, but transmogrified into The Bargain Shopper. I am a regular guy on a dying planet, but I've learned that it always helps to make friends. Except for my *Covid Fast* technology, no quick or reliable tests or therapeutics exist. Or any authorized vaccines. Play Lotto.

I am waiting for The Second Coming of Jesus Christ.

Thomas Wolfe wrote in *The Story of a Novel*: "*One writes a book not in order to remember it, but to forget it.*" I heartily concur and intend to forget my own confessions. Allow me to add a caveat of my own: '*The only thing critics know about fiction is that they don't know how to write it.*'

Emerson teaches us simplicity makes us great. Truth and Falsehood are not opposites, but counterparts on a continuum, like Time and Space. In my opening, I placed myself 'somewhere in the middle'. I was wrong.

I conjoin the quotes from Holden Caufield and Nick Carraway by a conjunction:

> "*I am the biggest liar that you ever saw in your life,* **but *I***
> *am one of the few honest people that I have ever known.*"

Behold these phrases are not *contradictory*, but *complementary. Knowledge* is communicable. Passed from father to son. Generation to generation. *Wisdom* must be earned and is only learned from experience.

I have lived long. I am a pensioner and one of these sages, although born from half a zygote. Like General Rochambeau, I have my own legacy to attain before joining my brother in eternity. Where sinners become Brahmins again. *Samsara* describes the cycle of birth and death. And rebirth. And the primal urge that drives our destinies. Do you think I'm crazy?

I confess to *Govinda*, my friend and confidant. Jean-Baptiste divulged my fate in his service as messenger. From whom Pierre Teilhard de Chardin described as 'The Omega point of the Universe', the *Celestial Mana*, The Kosmic Soul. Whatever. My brother was an Angel of God. He was sent to assist me to faithfully perform my duties on Earth.

The Roman Empire was founded by Julius Caesar, murdered by Brutus in 44 B.C. Rome was sacked by the Visigoths in 42O A.D. I lie down in darkness, at two in the morning on election night. I have quelled my monster, Mister Dingle Screw with limpid white shoots of hope from the headland. I stare at Alan Lockwood, interred inside a Frisbee, hanging on my wall. I pray for Mister E in Hell, as I look down upon the cheerless landscape of my naked belly.

Thank you, Doctors Lo Mein and Ravioli. I am taking a vacation day to monitor this election. I turn on my television. Except for Arizona, the election was looking good for Trump. Clueless Joe Biden has always worried me. I worry even more about Xi Jinping. China sent us an airborne virus to retaliate against 'Big Junk Food.' We had inflicted obesity upon their proletariat. Beijing wants to rule us and prefers the guise of Joe Biden ruling from the White House. 'The Laptop from Hell' proves that Hunter was paid off by the Chicoms. Need I say anything more about the Dauphin, a monster of The Deep State lagoon?

I'm neither Democrat nor Republican, but a confirmed Royalist. I believe in the Divine Right of Kings. Democracy would fail in ancient Greece. So would the Roman Republic. As a descendant of Rochambeau and Charlemagne, I was ordained to bestow a golden crown upon a brilliant orange head. Donald J. Trump must be crowned King to drain the swamp.

Redemption is an ideal of Christianity, as The Madame has learned. Tocqueville observed that 'Families are always rising or falling in America.' The Wolcott family will rise again. Now, I must say goodnight.

⚜ ⚜ ⚜

IT IS ELEVEN IN THE MORNING as I awaken in the light. I turn on Fox. Democrats, the new Visigoths are exhausted. From looting and burning cities, spreading mayhem and violence. Now, they are stealing the election. As Yeats observed, '*Mere anarchy is loosed upon the world.*' Now, Biden, like Robespierre is ready to storm the gates of The Bastille.

To paraphrase Yeats again in *The Second Coming*, 'His hour come round at last', Joe Biden 'slouches towards' Washington from a 'stony sleep' in his basement. Ready to be sworn in as the new American president.

As a Soldier of Truth, I would learn of the veracity of *The Big Lie*.

Mark Twain observed, "A lie can get halfway around the world while the truth is getting its boots on." Fortunately, I was born a Rochambeau with a military mind. I will never allow the royal blood of President Trump, like that of King Louis XVI, to collect in the wooden troughs beneath the guillotine.

And cruelly dipped with the handkerchiefs of *Les Sans Culottes. Vive L'Ancien Regime!*

The Roman Empire is ripe for a comeback. Jean-Baptiste II informs me that I am the reincarnation of Julius Caesar. Ready to defeat Vercingetorix as I had previously done in The Gallic Wars. Cato, the elder has been reborn. Into the body and soul of Tucker Carlson. *Carthago delenda est.*

I forgot to tell you. I remain apolitical, so I never even registered to vote. Yet, I am ready to spearhead the resistance. I will proclaim Tucker as the voice of the revolution, the Voltaire for a new Enlightenment, fully armed with a virtuoso falsetto. He is one of us. Shut up and obey. Drain the swamp. Do the math. Play Lotto. Now, I will wax metaphysical.

Whitman wrote "*There will never be any more perfection than there is now, nor any more heaven or hell than there is now.*" I will lead the revolution and crown our first American monarch, King Donald the Great. In Heaven or Hell. The Age of Pandemic is a tragedy. Our politics are a farce. So why do you think I'm crazy?

I am The Bargain Shopper. *Caveat Emptor.* My grandfather taught me an ancient French maxim, adopted at Chateau Rochambeau. Simple as the words of Emerson. Madame Beatrice learned it well. Wisdom that applies to everybody. Even to her sister Jill, the wicked *bitch* from Hell. Which requires patience and experience. Read it for yourself and ponder it once more. I must heartily concur. An *ethos* so simple, that it must be God's *honest* Truth:

"Tout comprendre c'est pardonner."
"To understand all is to forgive all."

ACKNOWLEGEMENTS

This novel was inspired by the exuberant Master Francois Rabelais of Torraine (1495-1553) Benedictine monk and Doctor of Medicine, 'the sanest of all the great writers.' 'Perhaps the only sane one,' as John Cowper Powys said of him. Religious iconoclast, but no atheist. A pioneer of the modern novel who plowed an original path for comedy, using humor, parody and satire which influenced Renaissance literature in Europe. A father of the French idiom that continued in the works of Moliere and Ionesco. I confess I have borrowed many ideas, metaphors and the language of *Gargantua* and *Pantagruel*. I hope to reinvigorate his legacy in my own humble attempt at satiric literature.

I am also indebted to Lloyd I. Sederer M.D and his book, *The Family Guide to Mental Health Care*, Carol Saline for Dr. *Snow* and the *Harvard Medical School Family Health Guide*.

Many thanks to the great John Barth, Henry Miller and Kurt Vonnegut. I thank our modern master, John Irving whose own brilliant fiction and advice on the art of the novel provided great insight. I also thank my late cousin Ted Allen, Walt Bratic, Glen Butler, Reid Longley, Monica Hill, Bill Wulsin, Lili Robins and Jim Zorn for their helpful comments. And special thanks to the lovely ladies of *Gretchen Scott*, a women's clothing company (www.gretchenscottdesigns.com) in Pelham NY for their generous hospitality during the Covid panic, as I wrote this novel.

PHOTO CREDIT: ETHAN LATOUR